Sugar Spinelli's Little Instruction Book

Is this Lost Springs bachelor auction a hoot or what? All that beefcake, as we used to call good-looking guys. Today, they call 'em hunks, not that it matters. A rose is a rose, as someone said—Shakespeare, maybe?

Take that Shane Daniels, for instance. He was a scrawny little kid who wasn't afraid of the devil himself, and today he's a world champion and cute as a bug's ear. Call him hunk or call him beefcake, he's a rose who's gonna give the woman who gets him a run for her money. I sure would like to be a fly on *that* wall, honey....

Dear Reader,

We just knew you wouldn't want to miss the news event that has all of Wyoming abuzz! There's a herd of eligible bachelors on their way to Lightning Creek—and they're all for sale!

Cowboy, park ranger, rancher, P.I.—they all grew up at Lost Springs Ranch, and every one of these mavericks has his price, so long as the money's going to help keep Lost Springs afloat.

The auction is about to begin! Young and old, every woman in the state wants in on the action, so pony up some cash and join the fun. The man of your dreams might just be up for grabs!

Marsha Zinberg
Editorial Coordinator, HEART OF THE WEST

Shane's
Last Stand
Ruth Jean
Dale

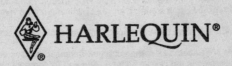

HARLEQUIN®

TORONTO • NEW YORK • LONDON
AMSTERDAM • PARIS • SYDNEY • HAMBURG
STOCKHOLM • ATHENS • TOKYO • MILAN • MADRID
PRAGUE • WARSAW • BUDAPEST • AUCKLAND

Ruth Jean Dale is acknowledged as the author of this work.

ISBN 0-373-82592-7

SHANE'S LAST STAND

Visit us at www.romance.net

Printed in U.S.A.

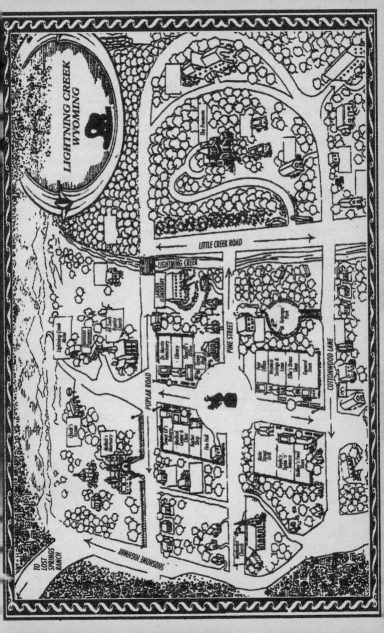

A Note from the Author

Let me tell you about books: Some are easy to write and some are hard, and until I start putting words into the computer, I can't be sure which is which. But now it can be told—*Shane's Last Stand* is one of the easiest books I ever wrote, because I just loved the whole project from day one.

When I first heard about the HEART OF THE WEST series, a story leapt into my head, with every jot and comma already in place. I knew Shane and Dinah from day one; the process was not one of revelation but of joy. Of course, the proof of the book is in the reading.

Here's hoping—!

Ruth Jean Dale

For my cousins, Deanna and Claudia, who can get lost before they even get out of town, but are an inspiration to me nonetheless. I love you both! Wanna do tea?

PROLOGUE

"No, no, a thousand times no!"

Even with her back against the wall, Dinah Hoyt Anderson figured there were some things she simply couldn't do. Surrounded by friends and neighbors equally determined to overcome her objections, she tried to edge toward the open front door of the chamber of commerce office to make her escape.

Instead, she bumped into Keith Woodruff, portly mayor of Bushwhack, Colorado. Keith must have weighed more than two hundred and fifty pounds, blocking all hope of a quick exit.

He gave her a "good ol' girl" thump on the shoulder. "C'mon, Dinah, it's for the good of the entire community. We wouldn't send you out on a manhunt if it wasn't absolutely one hundred percent necessary." He spoiled the sincerity of his appeal with a guffaw.

The distinguished white-haired owner and namesake of Hardy Guthrie's Haberdashery, who also happened to be president of the Bushwhack Chamber of Commerce, looked exasperated. "Let the poor girl catch her breath," he scolded the mayor, launching into a "good cop, bad cop" routine. "It's crystal clear to everyone on the Old Pioneer Days Committee that if we're to lure Shane Daniels back here for any reason whatsoever, Dinah's the only one with a snowball's chance in you-know-where to pull it off. If you keep pressuring her this way—"

"Now, Hardy, I ain't pressuring anybody."

"Keith, if you don't call that pressure, I don't know what it is."

"Land's sakes!" Georgia Anderson, Dinah's mother-in-law, pushed through the committee members to station herself beside their quarry. "Dinah, you come set yourself down over here and we'll explain exactly what it is we need you to do, hon."

Dinah moved obediently to a chair, but her stubborn streak had already kicked in. Whatever they had in mind, she wasn't about to go along with it. The minute they mentioned Shane Daniels, they lost her.

Hardy thrust a colorful brochure into her hands. She frowned. "What's this?"

"A brochure for a bachelor auction to be held day after tomorrow at Lost Springs Ranch for Boys in Wyoming," Georgia said. "Shane's one of the bachelors. He's going to be auctioned off like a side of beef, along with a bunch of other guys who grew up there." She laughed and shook her gray head, her expression mischievous. "Did you ever? I can't believe he'd go for something like this, but apparently he did."

"Yuck," Dinah said in a superior tone, but she couldn't help glancing down at the glossy publication. It looked like a Chippendales convention, all that beefcake on display.

Including one professional bull rider stripped to the waist and staring off the page with challenging blue eyes that said, "Bid on *me?* I dare you!"

Shivering, she covered the offending photograph with her hand. "I still don't get it," she said. "Why on earth do you people want to buy Shane, anyway?"

"It's simple and brilliant." The mayor preened, patting the belly extending over the straining leather of his belt. "Old Pioneer Days hasn't been doin' all that well lately and our fine merchants are suffering.'' He glanced around at the little crowd of head-nodders. ''We've known for a long time we needed to do something about it, but what?''

Hardy took up the recitation like a well-rehearsed member of a comedy team. ''Then this brochure turned up. It's for a fund-raiser for that foster-care ranch up in Wyoming where Shane grew up. They're bringing back a dozen or so of their boys who've made good and auctioning them off to the highest bidder. We've already taken up a collection so you can go buy Shane Daniels for us.''

''Simple,'' Mayor Woodruff said again, his jowls quivering.

''If it's so simple, somebody else can do it.'' Dinah started to rise, but numerous hands darted forth to forestall her.

''Now, now,'' the mayor said with pompous sincerity, ''don't be hasty. You know that when Shane left there were some…hard feelings.''

''A few,'' she agreed dryly.

''So buyin' him is just the first step. Then the buy-*ee* has to talk him into doin' what we want done.''

''Which is?''

''Let *me* explain,'' Hardy intervened, obviously afraid the mayor was going to antagonize her, not entrap her. ''We want Shane to use his celebrity to salvage Old Pioneer Days. We want him to be grand marshal of the parade and then put on a big exhibition bull ride to draw the crowds.''

Dinah rolled her eyes. ''Is that all?''

''Actually, no.'' Hardy reached beneath the table and withdrew a large piece of cardboard attached to a small wooden stake. ''We also want him to acknowledge Bushwhack as his hometown so we can put up these promotional signs all over town and print some up for new city limits signs.''

With a flourish, he whirled the stake around so she could read: Bushwhack, Colorado, Home of World Champion Bull Rider Shane Daniels. Elevation 7,462 Feet.

Georgia patted Dinah's arm. ''You can do it, hon,'' she said encouragingly. ''After all, Shane's first job after high school was at your daddy's Flying H Ranch—shoot, he learned his fancy moves on Flying H stock. He owes you.''

''Furthermore,'' Keith said, ''everybody knows Big Tom Hoyt was like a daddy to the boy, even if he was a wild young fool. Now that Big Tom's gone, we gotta count on you.''

Murmurs of agreement seemed to contain a degree of fondness for Shane, even pride, that hadn't been apparent ten years ago.

The mayor nodded emphatically. ''Doesn't Shane Daniels owe this town something—hell, for simply putting up with his escapades? Sure, he left under a bit of a cloud because of that elk incident, but now he can make amends by comin' to our aid in Bushwhack's hour of need.''

Dinah felt the noose tighten. She'd never expected to see Shane except in a rodeo arena. To deliberately seek him out…to satisfy the curiosity that had built for nearly a decade…

''Hon,'' Georgia said, ''it's your civic duty to do this for your hometown. How hard can it be?''

Dinah nearly groaned. If Georgia only knew…

CHAPTER ONE

SHANE KNEW HE WAS RUNNING late, but he wasn't going to worry about a little thing like that. It was bad enough coming back to Lost Springs Ranch under these circumstances. They could take him when they got him or not at all.

Damn, he felt stupid climbing out of the Dickersons' big old station wagon in front of the arena where Rex Trowbridge, the director of Lost Springs for Lost Boys, as Shane privately thought of it, had told him the auction would be held. Not that he'd have had much trouble figuring that out. The wooden bleachers overflowed with people—women, mostly.

Shane liked women and a goodly number of them liked him, but he couldn't see any advantage to being ogled by the multitudes. Ah, well, anything for good old LSLB.

He grinned at the elderly couple beaming back from inside the rattletrap automobile. Ben Dickerson had ranched in Wyoming for decades, his beloved Mabel at his side through good times and bad. Shane had done a little work at their Bar D when he was a kid and they'd treated him fair and square.

They'd also seemed downright pleased to give him a ride to Lost Springs after he'd made his way by plane to Casper and by bus the rest of the way to Lightning Creek. They hadn't asked any embarrassing questions about why a rodeo champion was coming into town afoot. He appreciated that. He didn't want to admit he was just trying to save some money.

Now he said, "Much obliged for the ride, folks."

"Glad to help." Ben waved the thanks away. "Me 'n' Mama here enjoyed hearin' about the glamorous life of a big rodeo star." He winked. "Hope you bring in a lotta money because this place sure does need it. From what we been hearin', it's on the verge of closin' down. Any way we can help, we're glad to." With a final wave, he drove off to find a parking spot in the crowded field designated for that purpose.

Shane knew what Ben Dickerson was talking about because he dropped by Lost Springs every chance he got. In his line of business, that was usually several times a year, since he and his road partner, Josh Kilmer, crisscrossed the country traveling from rodeo to rodeo. With every winning ride, Shane tried to donate at least a little bit of the take to his alma mater.

Without the intervention of Lost Springs, he'd probably be in jail today—or dead. Shane Daniels liked to repay his debts.

He heard a roar of applause and laughter from the arena and turned with the same fatalistic determination he occasionally had to call on to convince himself he really *did* intend to climb aboard a ton of heaving, snorting killer bull. He hadn't wanted to come back for this fund-raiser, but as Rex had pointed out with unrelenting patience, neither had a lot of the other bachelor alums of this foster-care facility in south-central Wyoming.

It wasn't necessary to convince Shane the old place was worth saving. He might only be a bull rider, but he knew guys who'd gone on to become doctors, lawyers, cops—even politicians, but you couldn't expect a hundred percent success rate. That jab had earned a wry grin from Rex, who was proud to number a senator among the graduates of Lost Springs.

And no, the senator wasn't coming back to make a fool of himself for good old Lost Springs. He was married.

Shane wasn't.

Just get it over with, Shane counseled himself. What was it gonna amount to, anyway? A date with a stranger, a personal appearance at somebody's party, a speech on rodeo to some civic group, a seminar on how to ride rank bulls, endorsement of some honky-tonk or restaurant…

He could do all that standing on his head. He could—

Groan. A whole herd of buckle bunnies charged, their sights obviously set on him. Worse, he knew the one in the lead, and she made his blood run cold.

Wynona Sweet, early twenties, was a rodeo groupie who'd hit on every cowboy Shane knew under the age of forty. Wynona was from Texas, had no visible means of support and had been on Shane's trail for a couple of years now. She wore big hair and tight clothes, and subtle she wasn't.

A horrible thought struck him just about then: if *she* bought him, he was in for one helluva ride.

"Shane! Shane! Shane!" A bevy of giggling females, all dressed in rodeo flash with spangles and beads and fringe and lots of cleavage, surrounded him. Hands touched, stroked. Voices chided, "You're late! Where you been, you sweet thing? We took up a collection and came all the way to this middle-of-nowhere place to buy you."

Wynona reached for him, her curved fingers reminding him of talons. He skittered back, bumping into the woman behind him. "Sorry, ma'am." He raised his hat in apology. Although accustomed to being surrounded by admiring fans, he was still uncomfortable with the buckle bunnies, so called because a cowboy's belt buckle was their favorite souvenir. He'd heard it said that Wynona had a whole saddlebag full of the damned things.

Even before he finally won the world champion bull rider title for the first time last year after a half dozen near misses, he'd enjoyed his share of attention from the fair sex. But that was nothing at all compared to what it got to be like afterward.

When he was younger and just starting out, he'd probably have enjoyed the thought of being a notch on some woman's bedpost; that's what the rodeo cowboys were to these women, just like rock stars were to the groupies who followed them around. But now that he was older and presumably wiser at twenty-nine, he'd discovered that he really didn't care much for women in bunches. Mob scenes were not his thing.

You're gettin' old, Daniels. Maybe it's time to start thinkin' about—the hell it is!

Behind the gushing women, small boys began to gather. The current inhabitants of Lost Springs stared up at one of the ranch's success stories with huge, awe-filled eyes. He was living their dream and he felt that responsibility acutely. He'd been in their shoes not so very long ago.

"So?" Wynona challenged, drumming her fingertips on his red plaid shirt. "Say something, honey. What're you doin', hopin' I'm the one who buys you?"

A redhead he'd seen only at a distance at his last couple of rodeos gave him a slow, sexy smile. "Not you, Wynona—*us*!" Her expression turned kittenish. "There're five of us put in on this," she explained. "We've been saving our pennies ever since we heard about this auction. Think you can handle all five, Shane?"

Jeez, he didn't even want to think about trying. "No, ma'am," he said, edging away, knowing that the more polite he got, the less they'd like it. "I sincerely doubt I can."

"Honey," the redhead said, "if you can ride a bull, you can ride anything."

"Anything on four legs," he modified, careful to keep that unadorned expression of sincerity on his face. "If you'll excuse me now, I see some friends I gotta say hello to."

"But they're waitin' for you at the auction," Wynona complained, gesturing toward the stands. "You've already screwed up the order."

"Damn," he said with exaggerated regret. "Maybe it'll all be over before I get there. I'd sure hate that, but I still gotta say hello to some friends."

Breaking through the ring of women, he was instantly surrounded by an admiring flock of boys of every age and size, most of whom he knew by name. All of them chattered away at once, eyed his big world-champion belt buckle, begged for autographs, reached out tentatively to touch him.

He saw the boy he'd been in each face turned hopefully toward him. His success, such as it was, gave hope to every one of them. All they saw was the glamour and excitement of a rodeo champion, not the danger or the punishment or the frequent disappointments.

He'd seen the same things as these boys in the beginning, when he was casting around for a reason to get—and stay—out of trouble. If they found out the truth, he wouldn't be the one to tell them. Rodeo wasn't the life they thought it was, but he could honestly say he was doing the thing he most wanted to do, crazy though that might seem to those who made their living wearing suits.

That thought made him feel considerably better, since he didn't even own a suit, had never owned a suit and didn't want to own a suit. Digging into his shirt pocket, he hauled out a ballpoint pen he kept handy for just this purpose. And as he signed the scraps of paper they thrust at him, he talked. "How's it goin', Eddie? Bring that history grade up, did you? That's great. I knew you could. And, Alan, I see you got that cast off your arm. I guess you'll think twice before you try to wrestle any more a these tough Lost Springs calves."

"Aw, Shane." The boy named Alan stuck his hands in his pockets and hunched his shoulders defensively. "I coulda done all right if Sam hadn't caught me. I was surprised, that's all."

"Well, partner, I've been surprised a time or two myself. Just be sure you don't make the same mistake twice."

Shane kept signing and talking, wondering as he did so if there was some black market for his autograph that he knew nothing about. He must have signed six or seven times for some of these boys and still they kept coming back and asking for more.

A movement toward the back of the crowd caught his attention even in the midst of the small talk. A boy of perhaps eight stood next to a much larger kid, although he didn't look to be that much older. Suddenly the big boy gave the smaller one a shove that sent him to his knees. The big boy said something Shane couldn't hear, but the curl of his lip indicated it wasn't a compliment.

The hair on the nape of Shane's neck prickled. He didn't know the big boy, but he knew the small one. Eli Dodge was a wiry little kid who'd been at Lost Springs slightly less than a year. He'd become a particular favorite even before Shane had asked Sam Duncan about the boy. The former coach and counselor at Lost Springs had sighed.

"Not a bad kid," Sam had said, which wasn't too meaningful because he would have said the same thing about

Jesse James as a child. Sam didn't think there was any such thing as a bad boy. "That kid was pretty beat-up when he come to us through the welfare system. Seems he was gettin' old enough to interfere with his ma's…profession…and she just turned him in like an overdue library book. You know what he said the first time I talked to him? He wants to be a cowboy. Kid had no idea which side of a horse to crawl up, but he wants to be a cowboy."

Sam gritted his teeth and shoved his battered cowboy hat to the back of his head, revealing receding white hair. Eli's story obviously hurt him, but this wouldn't be the first boy Sam would set upon the path to responsible adulthood.

He had worked at Lost Springs for a good forty years and was now using his pension to remain on the ranch, still nurturing and guiding boys to manhood. As he had nurtured and guided Shane.

Eli now came up off the ground like a catamount to fling himself at his much larger tormenter, his small face screwed up into a mask of fury and his fists flailing away.

God, the little runt reminded Shane of himself at that age. He would have done the same—had done the same, in fact. Yeah, Shane's last stand!

"Here, now!" Shane waded through the suddenly silent boys and hauled the two combatants apart by the scruff of their necks. He glowered from one to the other, his stern gaze eventually settling on Eli. The kid's left eye was already reddening; he was going to have a real shiner tomorrow, but it would be a badge of honor.

"You," Shane said. "I've been lookin' for you."

Eli's dark eyes narrowed and that stubborn lower lip thrust out. "What for?" He leaned away, putting more pressure on his neck. A multitude of expressions crossed his face, suspicion eventually predominating.

This kid had been hurt. Shane felt something tighten in his chest until he could barely breathe. He could be looking at himself, a small boy determined to face down a world that had never done a damn thing for him up to that point.

"I got something for you," the man said to the boy. Releasing both kids, Shane unbuckled his belt and dragged the heavy tooled leather strip from the loops on his jeans. He'd made up his mind, but he had to do this fast or he wouldn't do it at all.

He handed the belt to Eli by the buckle, the leather trailing to the ground as he knelt. "Here," he said. "From what Sam tells me, you'll win one of these yourself some day. In the meantime, maybe you'd like to hang on to mine for good luck."

The boy stared at him with mouth agape, as if he couldn't believe what was happening. Shane couldn't believe it, either—that he would so calmly hand over the only material possession in the world that meant anything to him. Hell was going to freeze over before he won another world champion buckle.

"You mean—" the boy gulped "—for keeps?"

"Yeah," Shane growled. "For keeps!" At that moment, he was convinced he'd lost his mind.

Then Eli's face lit up like a Christmas tree and Shane felt the tightness in his chest ease. *What the hell? It's only leather and metal and my jeans are tight enough they won't fall down.*

The boy stretched out a trembling arm and Shane laid the buckle on his open palm.

It was bigger than the small hand.

Shane stood up abruptly, pleased when the other boys

fell back around Eli in awe. The kid's social status had just skyrocketed.

"Well, fellas," he said, "I guess I'd better be movin' on now." He gave them a conspiratorial wink. "They're about to auction me off like a danged cow—" He raised his brows. "Like a danged *bull*. The things I do for Lost Springs!"

Turning away while Eli basked in the envy of his peers, Shane stopped short. Sam Duncan stood a few paces back, his smile bittersweet.

"They sent me to hurry you along," the older man said.

"Yeah, sorry to be so late." Shane said it automatically; he'd often apologized for his many infractions when he was an inmate here. "The guys—" He glanced back at the circle of boys reaching out to touch Eli's prize with reverence.

"Yeah, I saw." Sam's gaze softened, as did his voice. "Shane Daniels, you do Lost Springs proud. Welcome back, son."

DINAH HOYT ANDERSON drifted toward the bleachers, puzzling over the scene she'd just witnessed. The Shane Daniels she knew would never have given away the symbol of his success. *That* Shane Daniels never gave anything away, including what he thought or felt. Just remembering the boy he'd been made her stomach tighten and her palms grow damp.

She'd never been a match for him and wasn't now. Why, oh why, had she let the good citizens of Bushwhack, Colorado, bully her into coming here? Even before she'd seen Shane, she'd known she was making a big mistake. In fact, she'd been hoping he wouldn't even show up. They'd called his name earlier, only belatedly realizing he wasn't there with the other bachelors seated self-consciously on folding chairs around the auctioneer's podium. His failure to appear had been both a relief and a disappointment to her.

If he wasn't here, she could hardly be blamed for not "buying" him, she reasoned. Although in actual fact, buying him would be the easy part. She had three thousand of the town's dollars in the pocket of her jeans. That would surely be more than enough. No, the hard part would come next: talking him into doing what the town wanted done.

Shane felt no loyalty toward Bushwhack, she knew that with certainty. He'd never heard of it before he was eighteen years old and had only lived there something less than two years. He'd never gone to school there, never had family there. The closest to family had been his boss: her father, Big Tom Hoyt. She'd thought Shane had felt *something* for the rancher; certainly Tom had felt something for the rebellious boy.

The way Shane left, though…

She sighed. Shane had left *her,* not her father or the town.

Now here she was, the person he was least likely to be glad to see, charged with the task of talking him into returning to Bushwhack. Once there, he would have to do for free what he was paid handsomely to do in his real life, plus claim as his beloved hometown the community he'd left behind without so much as a fare-thee-well.

Sometimes, Dinah thought, life just wasn't fair.

Finding a spot to wedge into near the end of the bleachers, she settled down to wait. The sun beat down relentlessly, making her long for the cool pine forests of home. She didn't belong at a bachelor auction in the first place. She had no desire to join in the catcalls and whistles of the raucous crowd, although the auctioneer was calling up some really good-looking, sexy men. All she wanted was to get this over with, make the necessary arrangements with Shane in an entirely businesslike manner, pick up the few things she'd stashed at the Starlite Motel in Lightning Creek and head for home, a good ten-hour drive. Then she could get back to—

"You biddin' or lookin'?"

Dinah returned the smile of a big blond woman cramming herself into a tiny space at the end of the row in front of her.

"Biddin', I guess." Although she hated to admit it.

"Good luck, then." The woman's grin grew wider. "I'm just lookin' myself, and there's plenty to see." She laughed. "Hope you get the one you want, honey." She winked a big blue eye. "And if you luck out, I hope you know what to do with him!"

Dinah didn't consider that a laughing matter, but everyone else within earshot seemed to.

SHANE SCOOTED INTO a folding chair next to a guy wearing expensive designer labels, a high-priced haircut and an only half-concealed grin. Good old Flynn Morgan, still looking over the competition and figuring the angles.

Shane stuck out his hand and said in a low voice, "Good to see you, Flynn. Run any good cons lately?"

Flynn looked the cowboy over before putting out his own hand. He even managed to crack that smile. "If it's not little Shane Daniels," he said. "What is it you say to a cowboy—howdy?"

Shane stifled laughter. He'd always liked Flynn Morgan, though God only knew why. You never could tell what he was thinking or what he'd do next, and if he had any friends at Lost Springs, Shane didn't know about it. Of course, Flynn was several years older than Shane, who felt kind of flattered the guy even remembered his name.

"Howdy'll just about do it." Shane kept his voice low. "Am I late?"

"Yes, but who's counting?"

Shane looked around at all the people in the arena, feeling like a fish in a glass barrel. "Figure Lost Springs will make any money on this shindig?" he inquired.

Flynn shrugged, looking completely disinterested. "Some."

"Sold!"

The auctioneer's hammer slammed down and Shane snapped to attention. He strained to catch the amount of the winning bid but failed to do so in the general hullabaloo. Whatever. He tried to calm down, tried not to look at Wynona up there in the stands with her friends, tried not to think about what might conceivably lie ahead. All he wanted was to do his best and get out of here so he could meet Josh and the outfit for the next rodeo, which happened to be in Tall Timber, Colorado. Not a whole lot of money to be made there, but every little bit helped. He needed—

"Shane? You coming on up here or do you just plan to sit there like a bump on a log while I holler your name?"

Shane sat bolt upright, caught completely off guard. Even Flynn Morgan laughed and started a rhythmic clapping. As one, the other bachelors broke into a chant to match Flynn's cadence: *Shane! Shane! Shane's last stand!*

Embarrassed but trying not to show it, Shane rose to his feet and held up his hands modestly. It was an "in" joke with former residents of the ranch and he tried to take it with good grace. But he couldn't help thinking that although there were probably worse things than people who knew all your secrets, none came to him at the moment.

"Let's see…" The auctioneer shuffled papers. "What we've got here— Finally! Better late than never—is a gen-u-wine world champion bull rider. And, ladies, that's no bull!"

Shane rolled his eyes and grimaced. He felt like a danged fool, standing here with everybody gawking at him. He was gonna feel even worse if he went for a buck-ninety-five, but what the hell. He could always say he'd tried. Hooking his thumbs in his belt loops, he rocked back on the heels of his cowboy boots and gave them his cock-iest grin.

They were paying for it. He'd try not to disappoint any-body.

"Says here," the auctioneer continued, reading off that blasted brochure, "that in five words, this boy is kind, gentle, unselfish, friendly and sensitive."

From the stands, Wynona hollered, "Who wrote that?" Shane grinned back at the laughter. "A committee of my closest friends," he said into the microphone. Which was the truth. He, Josh and a bunch of the guys got sloshed at a honky-tonk bar just after Shane got the bachelor auction questionnaire. They'd had a high old time coming up with words they thought would draw generous bids.

Gentle had been Josh's contribution. He'd nearly col-lapsed laughing when he put it forward, seeing as how Shane had spent a good hour earlier in the day glaring at a big black bull and promising in raucous tones to ride the bejeezus out of him.

Which he'd done, not too gently, winning that day's go-around.

"Most embarrassing moment for this young man is—"

"Shane's last stand!" one of the bachelors hollered.

"Hey!" Wynona yelled, waving her white cowgirl hat

in the air, "we know all about his many fine qualities. Why don't you just start the biddin'?"

Things were getting out of hand and the auctioneer apparently realized it. Tossing down the script, he opened the bidding, which quickly rose to one thousand nine hundred and fifty dollars. Okay, so the high bid came from Wynona and her friends, who participated gleefully. At least Shane wasn't going to end up standing here in the blazing sun with egg on his face.

"One thousand nine hundred and fifty dollars," the auctioneer intoned. "Going once...going twice..."

"Two thousand dollars."

Shane squinted, trying to see who'd upped the ante. The voice had come from the far end of the stands, but he couldn't spot who it belonged to.

No matter, she was probably preferable to Wynona and company.

Who now shouted, "Twenty-three hundred!"

The crowd was growing more and more interested, stirring, murmuring.

"Twenty-four hundred," the strangely disembodied voice called from some hidden location.

"Twenty-five hundred!"

Wynona was getting mad and it showed. It had taken a hurried consultation with her cohorts before that last bid was entered.

"Twenty-six hundred."

"Dammit!" Wynona was on her feet now, not even sitting down between bids. "Twenty-seven hundred."

"Twenty-eight hundred."

"Twenty-nine hundred!"

The crowd seemed to hold its collective breath. The other bidder said...nothing.

"Twenty-nine hundred," the auctioneer said cautiously. "Going once…going twice…"

"Three thousand dollars." The unknown woman said it on a sigh, as if she really didn't want to go that high but had started something she had to finish.

Shane felt a prickle of concern. Who *was* that mystery bidder?

"Oooh!" Wynona turned to huddle with her friends. All five of them dug around in jeans pockets, which wasn't easy considering how tight those jeans were, pulling out bills, even coins.

"Ladies, we don't have all day," the auctioneer cautioned. "We have three thousand dollars. Going once—"

"Three thousand one hundred and twenty-two dollars and fifty-seven cents!"

Shane didn't know whether to breathe a sigh of relief or desperation. It would help him decide if he could see this mystery bidder, but she was totally beyond his field of vision.

"Anybody else?" the auctioneer encouraged the crowd. "If not—"

"Three thousand one hundred and fifty dollars—and no cents."

A soft "Aaah…" drifted from the crowd, turning as one to see Wynona's reaction. Which came with a clearly audible "Aw, damn!" as she plunked herself back down on the bleacher.

So Shane was not falling into the hands of that coterie of buckle bunnies, after all. Instead, his services had been purchased by some unknown woman who apparently had more money than good sense.

Would this, he wondered as he acknowledged the applause of the crowd with a friendly salute, be a case of "out of the frying pan and into the fire"?

CHAPTER TWO

"SO NOW WHAT HAPPENS?" Shane asked, interrupting Lindsay Duncan's determined march toward the arena exit.

Lindsay, who was Sam's niece, had inherited Lost Springs Ranch for Boys from her parents and had a lot at stake here today. She gripped her clipboard all the tighter but managed a smile. "Whoever bought you—your services, I mean—pays up and then tracks you down to tell you what you'll have to do to earn those big bucks."

Shane grimaced. "Did you see who it was?"

"Yes, but it's no one from around here. I have no idea who she is or what she's got in mind." Lindsay patted his arm. "I know this auction isn't most guys' idea of a good time, but just remember, you're doing a great and wonderful thing for our boys. Be brave, cowboy."

"Yeah, sure, I'll do that." He watched her walk quickly away, feeling the weight of responsibility grow even heavier. He'd have to be a good sport about this, whatever it turned out to be, for the sake of all the boys who needed Lost Springs just as much as he had.

No point in hollering before he was hurt, he decided. Hell, he could have been bought for something real simple and real easy. If not, there was no point worrying until he had reason. Shrugging, he went in search of the source of all the tantalizing smells wafting through the arena. He'd done his part; now his fate was in somebody else's hands.

BALANCING A PAPER PLATE of ribs and a beer cup, Shane looked around the food pavilion for someplace to set either one of those things down. "Hey, Shane!" a voice called, and he turned automatically toward the summons.

A skinny guy with a ponytail motioned toward an empty picnic table and Shane trotted over. News guy, obviously; he had a photographer with him, a woman toting the usual assortment of cameras and gear suspended from straps around her neck. As Shane approached, she fired off several shots, then turned with a wave and headed toward the arena.

By then, Shane had placed the guy. "Yo, Stan." He deposited the cup and plate on the splintery tabletop. "How's it goin'?"

"Not bad." Stanley Fish raised his brows, looking pleased with himself. "I'm here on assignment, actually. For *Clue Magazine*?" When Shane didn't react, Stan frowned. "*Clue*—you know? You *have* heard of it, of course."

"Afraid not. Unless it's got a horse or cow on the cover, I'm not likely to pick it up."

Stan didn't take this news flash with good grace. "Well, hell," he said, "it's only a national newsmagazine. Guess if you're not a fan, there's no point putting your picture in it, now, is there."

If he thought that was going to alarm Shane, he had another think coming. "None whatsoever," he agreed. He looked at his plate, overflowing with food. "Want a rib? They look real tasty."

"No, I do *not* want a rib. See you around, cowboy."

Shane stifled a grin as the reporter stalked away. Stan always had been kind of a prick. Even so, it might not have been such a good idea to deliberately—

"Shane?"

That single hesitant word cut through him like a laser, causing the hair on the nape of his neck to rise and his breath to knot up somewhere between his belly and his throat. He didn't recognize the husky tone, and yet it froze him to the spot with its haunting familiarity.

When he neither answered nor turned, the woman who'd spoken moved around in front of him and then he really *did* think he was losing it. He hadn't seen Dinah Hoyt in almost a decade. Her voice had matured; it was lower and sexier than it had been before. Even so, he should have recognized it instantly.

She'd changed, too. New curves softened her slender body, which was now clad in dark western-cut slacks and shirt. She seemed womanly instead of girlish, as he remembered her so clearly.

The same glossy dark brown hair was pulled back in a single braid, visible beneath her white Stetson. Behind those oversize sunglasses, he knew her eyes were a clear green with golden flecks of light. And when she smiled, which she wasn't doing at the moment, she'd have a dimple in her right cheek.

He'd kissed that dimple.

She swallowed hard, as if she might be privy to his thoughts. "Aren't you going to say anything?"

He blinked; he was still there and so was she. "Yeah," he more or less croaked. "Hi, Dinah. Long time, no see."

She laughed and it broke at least part of the tension. "That's the truth." She glanced at the table, where he still sat with a sauce-covered rib in one hand and a beer in the other. "Mind if I join you?"

"Feel free." He put the rib down belatedly and licked his fingers. "Did you just happen to be in the neighborhood or...?"

She sat down. "You know why I came," she said.

"I sure as hell don't." He figured if she had murder on her mind, she'd have tracked him down years ago.

She spoke bluntly, the way her old man would have. "I came to buy you—your services, that is."

He felt as if he'd been blindsided by a runaway train. "That was *you* bidding against the buckle bunnies?"

She frowned. "You didn't know?"

"Not till this very minute." He shook his head to clear it. "Your voice…it's different."

"Not that different." Her lower lip jutted out.

That lovely, full, delectable lower lip. Shane swallowed hard, took another deep breath and pulled himself together. "So what is it you want from me…exactly? After all these years, I gotta say I'm surprised as hell."

Now it was her turn to brace herself, and he saw her visibly straighten her shoulders and draw a quick breath. "Personally, I don't want anything, not a damned thing. I'm here representing Bushwhack."

He laughed incredulously. "What the hell does Bushwhack want me for? What do I have to do to earn that three thousand bucks for dear old Lost Springs?"

"No big thing. Just spend a weekend in Bushwhack doing your rodeo star act for Old Pioneer Days, that's all." She looked down at the rough-hewn table, picking at a crumb with one blunt fingernail. "Plus…a little bit of exhibition bull riding."

His brows shot up. "That's *all?*"

"Well…" She looked up again. "They—we also want you to claim Bushwhack as your hometown."

"Are you kidding?" He shot up from the bench, both hands braced on the table, then sat back down hard. "You folks are out of your ever-lovin' minds."

"I told them you'd say that—in so many words, of course."

"Old Pioneer Days is over the Fourth of July, if I remember correctly."

"That's right."

"That's one of the biggest rodeo weekends of the year."

"I'm not surprised to hear that."

"Besides, why should I give away a bull ride for free? That's how I make my living."

She nodded. Her mouth had thinned out to a tight line.

"As for claiming Bushwhack as my hometown—not in this lifetime. I don't have a hometown and if I wanted to claim one, it sure as hell wouldn't be that dinky little burg. Jeez, Dinah, what kind of sucker do they think I am?"

For a moment she just sat there looking at him. He wanted to reach across and rip those dark glasses from her face so he could see her expression, but didn't figure he had any right to anymore. So he repeated, "What kind of sucker?"

"The kind who honors his obligations." She finished on an up note, as if it were a question. "The whole town took up a collection and that's what I used to bid on you. Old Pioneer Days is in trouble, Shane. We need a draw and you're it."

"The hell I am." He shook his head decisively. "The folks in that town never liked me. What makes them think I'd risk my hide for their lousy hometown party, anyway?"

"I don't know. Blind, stupid hope? Desperation? Honesty and fair play? Three thousand-plus dollars?" She was getting real mad; she'd always had a temper. "You did agree to be auctioned off, am I right?"

"Yeah, but under duress."

"Still, you went along with it. What did you think someone would plunk down thousands of dollars for? Your autograph?" Suddenly she swayed back and her mouth opened in a soft *O*. "I get it. I'll bet you wanted that woman with the high hair to buy you. I'll bet you were in cahoots. You probably gave her the money for the bid."

"No way!" He shuddered at the thought of what Wynona had in mind. Still…

"If you hadn't been so cheap, your plan would probably have worked. A big rodeo champion could certainly have given her more than three thousand dollars to bid with." Her lip curled down derisively.

"Now, just a damned minute—"

"Hi, Shane, can I have your autograph? I saw you ride in Cheyenne and you're the greatest!"

Automatically Shane whipped around to find a gangly teenage kid standing there with a goofy grin on his face. Not a resident of Lost Springs—he wore cowboy boots that none of the boys here could afford. Hell, they were better than Shane's.

"Sure, kid." He accepted the piece of paper. "What's your name?"

"Tyler. I live in Denver, but we're visiting in Casper so we came over for the day."

Shane wrote, "To Tyler, who knows his rodeo. From his old pal, Shane Daniels." Not too smart or original, but he had other stuff on his mind. He gave the kid his autograph, said a quick "Thanks for asking," then turned back to Dinah, who was waiting patiently.

"Where were we?" he asked.

"You were just about to tell me to go get my money back, I think."

If he did, that would mean three thousand less for Lost Springs Ranch. He could make it up himself, but that would leave a hole in his Someday Fund.

And dammit, it just wouldn't be fair.

"Okay," he growled, "you got me. It'll screw everything up but I'll come."

She drew in a breath with such obvious relief that he felt like a jerk for being so surly.

"And you'll ride?" she pressed.

He glowered at her and finally said, "Maybe."

She frowned. "What do you mean, 'maybe'?"

"Well," he drawled, annoyed by her persistence, "I can't very well do a demonstration ride at the Bushwhack Amateur Rodeo if I'm hurt, can I?"

She looked surprised. "*Are* you hurt?"

"Not yet, but you never know what's around the next bend in the road. I could get stomped by a bull. I could get hit by a car crossing the street. I could—"

"I get it." She gritted her teeth and clenched her hands into fists on the picnic table. "The fate of an entire town is at stake and you're acting like—like a prima donna."

"Naw, I'm being straight with you." Damned if he'd make this easy for her. "If you're worried, there's one way you can make sure I stay healthy."

"And that is?" Her tone brimmed with suspicion.

"You can travel the rodeo circuit with me until I'm due in Bushwhack, make sure I'm safe and secure and see to my every need."

"In your dreams!" She laughed and he saw that dimple.

"In that case, you and Bushwhack will just have to take your chances that nothing bad happens to me." Not that he expected anything to happen. It had been a couple of years since he'd been hurt badly enough to take time off, but you never knew.

"Gladly." She raised one brow. "And the third thing?"

"What third thing? Haven't I agreed to everything? What do you want, blood?"

"I want you to claim Bushwhack as your hometown."

He leaned forward ominously. "Dinah Hoyt, there's no way in hell I'll ever call that wide spot in a Colorado road home. I don't have a real home. I've never had a real home and I probably never will."

For a long moment they stared straight at each other, although he still couldn't see her eyes as he longed to do. Then she smiled, and the impact of that faint curving of her lips took his breath away all over again.

"Gee, Shane, why don't you tell me how you *really* feel?" The smile widened. "Of course, you *did* agree to be auctioned off like a head of beef...." She cocked her head, her expression impish. "Okay, I'm putting you on. I'll tell them the hometown's negotiable."

"Dammit, Dinah—"

Wynona appeared out of nowhere, without her pals this time. "There you are, Shane." She gave an exaggerated wave and sashayed over to the picnic table. "Honey, I am *so* sorry I lost out in the bidding." She squinted at Dinah. "Are you the lucky winner?"

"That's me—lucky," Dinah agreed, deadpan.

"You treat him right, you hear?" Wynona laughed; she was a good sport, anyway. "Shane baby, I'll be seeing you in Cheyenne or Las Vegas, for sure." She blew him a kiss, adding to Dinah, "You be good to him, okay? But not *too* good."

"Absolutely."

Dinah sat there until Wynona was lost in the crowd. Then she said, "I guess we've taken care of business. I'll tell the mayor to expect you in Bushwhack July 3."

"Who is the mayor these days?"

"Keith Woodruff."

Shane laughed incredulously. "You're kiddin'. That big bag of wind?"

She looked offended. Drawing herself up, she gave him

a cool glance. "Keith tries very hard to do everything he can for the good of the community."

"I'll just bet."

She rose. "Just report to Mayor Woodruff on July 3, okay? He'll have a place to put you up while you're in town."

"Uh-uh."

She looked startled. "What do you mean, uh-uh? I thought we had everything all worked out."

"I mean uh-uh, I won't report to Keith Woodruff. I'll report to *you*. You bought me and you're responsible for me."

"Oh, for heaven's—" Again with the tight lips, again with the glare. "Are you going to be a pain about this, Shane?"

"Probably." He also rose. "I'm always like this when people are using me. If I'm gonna be the star attraction at Old Pioneer Days, the least you can do is treat me good. Besides, you promised Wynona you would."

"That's her name, Wynona?"

"If it was Reba, I wouldn't call her Wynona. What do you care?"

He thought he saw a slight reddening of her cheeks and was pleased.

"I don't." For a moment it looked as if she was going to stick out her hand for a formal farewell, but instead rubbed her palm down the side of her jeans. "Goodbye, then."

"Where you headed now?"

"Why—" She looked startled, as if she wasn't prepared for that obvious question. "Back to the motel in Lightning Creek. I'll start for home bright and early tomorrow."

"You drove?"

"It's only ten hours or so."

"Then you can give me a lift back into town." *And tomorrow you can give me a lift to Tall Timber, Colorado, so I can hook up with Josh,* he thought, but knew it was too soon to say. He'd have to work on her to get her to go out of her way for him, but he was confident he could pull it off.

Fairly confident, anyway. "You want to ride back to town with me?"

"Hey, it's no big deal."

"You don't have wheels?" she countered.

"I flew into Casper, took the bus to Lightning Creek and bummed a ride out here."

He knew what she was thinking: rodeo champion bumming rides? But her manners were too good to allow her to say it out loud.

"Okay." Her reluctance was a mile deep. "I suppose it'll be all right."

He supposed it would be, too, just as soon as he had a chance to charm her into driving a hundred miles or so out of her way for him.

DINAH STEERED THE PICKUP truck out of the parking lot and pointed it southeast toward Lightning Creek. The day was hot and bone dry, the sun radiant in a cloudless sky. Her skin felt all tight and tender, her eyes gravelly and parched behind the dark glasses.

Inside, she felt even worse.

Darting a glance at the lean and wiry man lounging next to her on the bench seat, she tried to be calm about her situation. Unfortunately, age had only improved him. Too-long black hair curled over his collar, and his blue eyes still tended to frost over. But those eyes could also flash with all kinds of happier emotions.

As a kid he'd been cocky; as a man he was still cocky,

but there was a self-assurance about him that reminded her of something she'd heard one of the old ranch hands say a hundred times: "It ain't brag if you can back it up."

Shane could back it up—and had.

He shifted toward her. "I was real sorry to hear about your dad passing on," he said abruptly.

She darted him a quick glance, wondering why it had taken him so long to bring it up. "Thank you. I was surprised you didn't come back for the funeral."

"I didn't actually hear about it until a couple of weeks after the fact." He hesitated, then added, "I wouldn't have come, anyway. I wasn't sure I'd have been welcome."

"Of course you'd have been welcome." But that wasn't true and she knew it even as she spoke the lie. If he'd shown up, both of them would have had a hell of a lot of explaining to do. Better he'd stayed away.

After a few more miles of green pastureland and winding road, he said almost reluctantly, "Has Bushwhack changed much since I left?"

"Some. I'm surprised you'd care."

"I don't *care*. I'm just mildly curious, is all."

"Well, we've got more new drive-in restaurants than you can shake a stick at. The lumberyard has changed hands, and Jim Potter's son has taken over the plant nursery."

He grinned, his teeth brilliantly white against the dark tan of his face. "Not many changes, huh."

"Not many."

"You're running the Flying H, I suppose."

Her heart skipped a beat. "I'm trying to." She added quickly, to change the subject, "So what about you? Is being a big rodeo star as great as you thought it would be?"

"Not much in life is as great as you thought it would

be.'' His mouth twisted in an almost smile. ''But yeah, I'm enjoyin' myself. Rodeo's a license to be irresponsible, which is fine with me. It's a lot tougher for the married guys, though. Always traveling, entry fees to pay whether you're winnin' or losin'...''

She nodded, turning onto Shoshone Highway, which skirted the western edge of Lightning Creek. ''Where would you like me to drop you?'' she asked politely, slowing the pickup.

''I don't think I'm quite ready to be dropped,'' he said. ''I haven't had a chance to look the old town over. Do you mind?''

''Why—'' Startled, she scrambled for a way to refuse but found none. ''I suppose not.''

''Just keep driving, then. Take a left on Cottonwood Lane and another left on Main Street.''

Slowing still more, she did as he directed. She'd seen a lot of small towns and had found most of them charming, as she did this one. To think of Shane growing up here was strange, though. To her, Bushwhack *was* his hometown, whether he acknowledged it or not.

She didn't meet much traffic, probably because everyone was still at Lost Springs Ranch. She was acutely aware of his interest as he switched his attention from one side of the street to the other.

''Reilly's Feed Store—I had a fight with Sean Reilly that the whole town talked about for months.''

''Was that Shane's last stand?'' she asked innocently.

He shot her a quick, startled glance. ''*He* thought so, at least at the beginning.''

''I see. Any experience with Twyla's Tease 'n' Tweeze?'' she asked, reading the name on the window of the next building. ''What a plethora of pink!''

''I don't do pink,'' he said. ''Besides, that's new since

I was here.'' He pointed to the restaurant next door. ''I know the good old Main Street Grill, though. Locals call it the Roadkill Grill.''

''Ugh.'' The street widened ahead to accommodate the statue of a cowboy on a bucking horse, which Dinah steered carefully around. ''Colorado Springs has a statue of a man on a horse in the middle of one of the streets downtown,'' she offered. ''It's kind of goofy, but most people seem happy about it.''

''General Palmer,'' he said. At her look of surprise, he explained. ''I usually make the Pikes Peak or Bust Rodeo there.''

On the next block they moved slowly past the town hall, the fire station and sheriff's office, plus several businesses. At Poplar Road, she hesitated.

''Which way now?''

''Well…'' He gave her a hooded glance. ''Straight ahead is the Starlite Motel.''

Her heart leaped as if he'd made an indecent suggestion, even though she realized she'd already told him she was staying there. ''That works for me,'' she said, ''but I repeat, what about you? Do you have a room at the motel or is there somewhere else I can drop you?''

He grimaced. ''You sure don't catch on very fast,'' he complained. ''I'm not staying anywhere. Maybe you'd like to invite me back for a—''

''Not a chance.'' Crossing Poplar Road, she parked in front of the All Souls Baptist Church but kept the motor running.

''You don't know what I was going to say.''

''Don't I?''

He considered for a moment. ''Okay, maybe you do, but I don't have anyplace to bed down and that's a fact.''

''You're a big boy. You'll think of something.''

"Yeah, all I need is a little time and a decent meal. When's the last time you ate?"

"I had coffee and a stale doughnut before I left the motel this morning."

"That settles it, then. I'll buy you dinner at the Roadkill Grill."

"You don't have to do that."

"Hey, you graciously gave me a ride into town, didn't you?"

"Yes, but—"

"Keep arguing and I'll let *you* buy *me* dinner. I'm not proud."

He crossed his arms over his chest and grinned at her, the same cheeky grin she'd fallen for a hundred times. Meek as a lamb, she pulled a U-turn and headed back down Main Street.

Anything was better than taking him to a motel.

THE MAIN STREET GRILL was nearly empty. A waitress waved them in, indicating they were to sit anywhere.

Shane promptly led Dinah to a seat near a window in back. Grinning, he waited until she'd slid in the booth before sitting down across from her.

"I brought my first girlfriend here," he said, reaching for a plastic-coated menu. "We'd eat French fries and drink Cokes and moon over each other."

She felt a little twinge, although she knew she hadn't been his first girlfriend. He was, after all, a high school graduate of eighteen when she met him. "What was her name?" She pulled out a menu stuck behind the napkin dispenser.

"Rose…Rose…"

"You're not sure of her name?" Dinah demanded sharply, offended for that other girl. Maybe he hadn't remembered Dinah's name, either. Maybe when asked, he'd have said, *Diane...Diane...*

"Hey," he defended himself, "I remember *her,* but her name was weird. Everybody called her Rose, but it was really something like...Roselle? Roslin..."

"I take it you didn't keep in touch," she suggested dryly.

He grinned. "Perceptive of you."

She put down her menu. "What do you recommend?"

"What's the subject?"

"Food!" She felt her cheeks warm. Everything he said to her seemed to lead into dangerous territory.

"Can't beat the hamburgers."

"Then that's what I'll have."

"Are you always so agreeable?"

"You know I'm not."

"No, Dinah, I don't. Not anymore."

Into the suddenly serious atmosphere, the plump and middle-aged waitress appeared to plunk down two glasses of water and a page from her order pad.

"Shane Daniels, you won't remember me but—"

"Sure, I do—Dotty, right? You used to work at the bakery."

Dotty's smile was brilliant. "That's me, all right."

"I used to have money for one cookie but you'd give me two and say they were day-old."

She nodded, obviously surprised by his insight. "You were just about the cutest little dickens I ever saw. I could always see the devil in those blue eyes."

"You still can," Dinah suggested sweetly. What did you say about a man who couldn't remember his first girl-friend's name but instantly recalled the woman who gave him two cookies for the price of one?

Dotty laughed. "That's the truth. What I'm wonderin'

is if I could trouble you for an autograph? I've got this ten-year-old grandson who saw you ride in Cheyenne last year and he thinks you walk on water.''

"Dotty, it's no trouble at all. What's his name?''

"Davey—make it David.''

"To David.'' Shane said the words as he wrote on the page from the order pad. "Mind your mother and grandmother and maybe someday you'll grow up to be a champion, too.'' He signed with a flourish: "Shane Daniels, Professional Cowboys Rodeo Association Bull Riding Champion.'' He offered the sheet to Dotty with a grin. "Hate to brag but kids usually like that.''

"It's not brag if you can back it up,'' Dinah said softly.

Shane looked startled but it was Dotty who spoke.

"Ain't it the truth. Thanks, Shane. That kid's gonna be thrilled to death.'' Dotty tucked the slip of paper into her pocket and pulled out her pad at the same time. "So what can I bring you and your lucky lady friend?''

That was the second time in one day Dinah had been called "lucky'' to be associating with Shane Daniels. At the moment, she felt anything but.

CHAPTER THREE

SHANE FINISHED the last bite of his hamburger and eyed his companion warily. Dinah seemed to be loosening up, at least a little, but she was obviously growing impatient to finish the meal and escape.

She glanced at her watch for the third time in five minutes and he figured it was now or never. With a controlled flourish, he rested his right wrist in his left hand and probed the bones and sinews carefully.

She rose to the bait. "Is something wrong?"

"Well, I wouldn't want to worry you but..." He gave her his most charming grin. "I think I'm beginning to feel a real bad sprain about to happen."

"What!" She caught on right away and glared at him. "Are you trying to blackmail me?"

"Yep, that's about it."

She settled back, crossing her arms over her breasts. "Okay, why don't you save some time and just say it. What is it you're trying to get me to do—not that it's going to work."

"Nothin' all that much. I just want you to go to the rodeo in Tall Timber with me."

She did a double take. "Tall Timber, *Colorado?*"

He laughed, delighted. "That's what caught your attention? I want to sweep you away with me, or vice versa, and all you pick up on is Colorado?"

She looked embarrassed. "You surprised me, that's all.

Naturally, I have no intention of going to a rodeo with you in Tall Timber, or anywhere else for that matter.''

"Why not?''

"Because…because it would be stupid,'' she said, floundering.

"I don't see anything stupid about it. You like rodeo, don't you?''

"You know I do, but—''

"You've never seen me compete, have you?''

She hesitated just a hair too long.

Amused, he said, "Dinah Hoyt, don't you lie to me, now.''

"I'm not.'' But she was obviously flustered.

"When? Where did you see me ride?''

She sighed and hung her head. "Three years ago at the National Western in Denver.''

"Three years ago…'' Then he remembered with a grimace. "I got banged around a little bit on the second go-around, as I recall.''

She shivered. "You could say that. It was more like gored, actually.''

"Yeah, but I got up and walked out of the arena.'' He'd been proud of that, considering how that damned Red Devil bull had scooped him up on those ugly twisted horns and tossed him against the gate like a sack of corn. Even at that, he'd got off better with that particular bull than a lot of cowboys he could name.

"Actually, it was more like you limped out of the arena.'' She didn't seem impressed. "Look, I'm heading back to my motel to get a decent night's sleep. I'll be leaving early in the morning so—''

"Tall Timber isn't that far out of your way, is it?''

"I don't know—a couple of hours, maybe?'' Her eyes narrowed. "Why do you ask?''

"Because…" How to phrase it?

She drew an exasperated breath. "Shane Daniels, are you asking for a ride to Tall Timber?"

He looked at her sheepishly. "Actually, I'm trying *not* to ask. I was hopin' you'd offer. Will you?"

"Not hardly." She pursed her lips. "I don't get it. Do you always count on the kindness of strangers to get where you're going?"

"You're no stranger, Dinah."

The air thickened, became hot and static between them. She licked her lips and shifted in her seat. "I guess we're not," she said faintly, "but you know what I mean."

"Yeah, I know what you mean." He was fighting his own battle with memories. "Look, here's the deal. My travel partner went ahead with our outfit—that's a pickup and a little old trailer. I figured on coming here, selling my soul for good old Lost Springs, then wrangling a ride back to Casper—or all the way to Tall Timber, if I got lucky." He smiled ingratiatingly. "Did I get lucky?"

She gave an uncomfortable little laugh. "Honestly, Shane, why didn't you just come right out and ask in the first place?"

"What fun would that be?" He was really grinning now, enjoying himself again. She was gonna tumble, he knew it.

"Okay," she said with obvious reluctance, "I can't think of a good reason not to, since I've already imposed on you on Bushwhack's behalf. I guess you talked me into it. We'll meet—how about here at six for breakfast, and then we can take off right after."

"No dice."

"What do you mean, no dice? Don't you get up that early? Really, Shane, if you want to ride with me, the least you can do is—"

"Six isn't too early," he explained patiently, "it's too late."

"Well, if you think I'm—" She stopped talking to regard him with those clear gold-flecked eyes.

He reached out very deliberately and covered her hand with his. She stiffened and caught her breath and he nearly did the same, the impact was so stunning. "We've got to leave tonight," he said in his most reasonable tone. "I'm riding tomorrow."

"That's...impossible."

"Why?"

"Because—because I'm tired and I'll have to pay for a night in the motel whether I'm there or not. I've got to pack, I've got to—"

"Grab a nap, then. We can leave as late as midnight and still make Tall Timber in time."

"But I hate traveling at night." She sounded really annoyed. "It's hard to stay awake."

"Not when you've got a good travel buddy. We'll keep each other awake. Besides, I'll drive. I'll even help you pack."

"Darn it, Shane..."

She was weakening. "C'mon, Dinah. Help me out here for old times' sake."

She slid her hand from beneath his. Judging by her chilly expression, he'd made a mistake with that "old times' sake" plea.

Then she sighed. "All right," she agreed. "We'll leave at midnight—but I still think this is a lousy idea!"

AT 12:05 THEY WERE in Dinah's pickup truck heading south on Shoshone Highway toward Interstate 25, Shane behind the wheel. Dinah had objected, of course, but he'd pointed out quite rightly that he knew the area better than she did.

If he knew it at *all,* he knew it better than she did. She'd never been this far into Wyoming before; previous visits had been limited to a couple of trips to the big Cheyenne Days rodeo. Now that she thought of it, she was quite a homebody compared to Shane with his roving ways.

Stifling a yawn, she stared blankly out the window into the darkness. Not a star was visible in an inky sky, and once they cleared the edge of town, there were no lights, either. For all she could see, they were alone in the middle of the universe.

He spoke into the intimacy of darkness, illuminated only by the pale glow from the dashboard. "Take a nap if you want to. I'm wide-awake, so you don't need to try to stay awake to keep me company."

"I'm not. I'm just having a hard time waking up." Which was true. Rattled and pursued by memories, she'd only fallen asleep about an hour before he came banging on her door. No wonder she was groggy.

He slowed the pickup, then turned onto a small farm road.

"I sure hope you know where you're going," she said. "I'd hate to get lost out here in the middle of nowhere."

"I always know where I'm going." He flashed her a devilish grin. "At least I do once I get there."

Into the warm closeness of the truck cab, she said softly, "You haven't really changed at all, have you, Shane."

"Did you think I would, Dinah?"

The silence stretched out to a taut line, and then she said, "I can dream, can't I?"

SHANE DIDN'T KNOW what the hell she meant by that so he shut up and concentrated on his driving. Not that he needed to. He knew this part of Wyoming like the palm of his hand. He'd ridden these roads on horseback and by car and bus. He knew the men who ranched and farmed this land, the men who drilled for oil and gas, the men who mined the trona—soda ash to out-of-staters—used in glass and detergent and paper.

Wary by nature and nurture, he'd grown up intensely aware of his surroundings. In Wyoming, that meant *land* more than *people*. He'd been delighted to discover, through the unceasing efforts of a social studies teacher, that his adopted state was the most sparsely populated in the union.

But his interest in the state had been more intellectual than emotional. Although he had long since realized and acknowledged how much he owed Lost Springs Ranch for Boys, it had never been home. More like a college, he'd decided, although he'd never gone to college himself. But that's how Lost Springs was: you went there, you stayed until you learned enough to get by on your own, and then you left.

As Shane had done after he'd graduated from high school.

He'd always known he'd be a cowboy when he grew up. According to Sam Duncan, he'd announced that as a foregone conclusion within six weeks of meeting his first cow. He'd reveled in work with the ranch herds, loved the ranch horses more than the people.

It was Sam who'd put Shane in touch with Big Tom Hoyt a few weeks before high school graduation. Big Tom was a Colorado rancher who'd hired other Lost Springs boys before Shane. "He's a hard man but a fair one," Sam had warned. "No Lost Springs boy has ever let him down."

Less than two years later, one had.

Shane belatedly realized he'd gripped the wheel so tight his hands hurt. Relaxing his hold, he glanced at Dinah to see if she'd noticed. She was staring out the side window as if she didn't even realize anyone else was in the cab.

Thinking back now, he didn't know why Big Tom had hired the mouthy hotshot Shane had been then. He'd felt loyalty to nothing and no one. He belonged nowhere in particular and doubted he ever would.

But he was a helluva cowboy and he knew it, even though he hadn't started dreaming of rodeo stardom yet. Watching the lights of Glenrock grow closer, he thought about the wild young kid who took chances and did things—

"What town is that?" Dinah asked suddenly.

"Glenrock."

"That's where we pick up I-25, right?"

"Yeah."

"Then I know where we are. I can drive from here."

"What's your hurry?"

"It's my truck," she reminded him, "which means I get my way without having to justify myself."

She looked as if she expected an argument out of him. Not likely.

When he'd gone to work on the Flying H, he'd been confident he could handle any critter on the ranch. He soon found out that the only exception was the rancher's daughter.

DINAH PULLED OUT of the truck stop, careful not to slosh steaming coffee on her hand. "Cheyenne, here we come!" she announced.

"Yeah."

She glanced at him, already slumped in the corner against the door. "You going to sleep?"

"Maybe. Not right away."

"Want to talk?"

"Depends."

She could feel him watching her from beneath the brim of his hat. "Nothing sinister." She finished her coffee and tossed the empty cup onto the floor. "I was just wondering about Lost Springs Ranch for Boys."

"I always called it Lost Springs for Lost Boys."

She heard a kind of melancholy in his tone and was glad she'd brought the subject up. She'd known where he came from, of course, but he'd never talked about it much. "How old were you when you went there?" she ventured.

The silence was so long she didn't think he was going to answer. Then he said, "Nine."

It felt like a major accomplishment, getting that much out of him. "It seems like a nice place, Shane. The people there really seem to care about the boys."

"Yeah, I guess they do." Again the long silence. "It's not a home, though."

"It must be the next best thing. It certainly is well-known. How long has it been around?"

"Fifty years, give or take."

"I saw cattle driving in, and a few horses. Is that just for show or—"

"It's real," he said quickly. "Lost Springs was a working cattle ranch before taking in the first maverick kid. The ranching operation has been kinda…unwinding of late, what with the antibeef faction yellin' their fool heads off and all. Then when Mr. and Mrs. Duncan died, Lindsay—"

"Lindsay?"

"Their daughter. Lindsay's having a tough go of it. Maybe this auction will raise enough to help out some, but in the long run—" He shrugged.

"Did you have enough time to renew old friendships

while you were there?'' She changed lanes to pass a twelve-wheeler.

"I didn't leave any friends behind when I left.'' He sounded amused she'd think so.

"What about…what about teachers, counselors, people like that? Surely—''

"Dinah, I've been back before. This isn't my first visit in twelve years. I get back every once in a while.''

"Oh.'' Deflated, she thought about all he'd said. If he had no friends and didn't consider the place home, why did he keep going back?

What was he looking for that he had been unable to find?

THE HIGHWAY CONTINUED its gentle curve south while Shane dozed in his corner. Not even a radio broke the silence inside the cab of the pickup truck. Unable to resist any longer, Dinah finally gave up and let her thoughts drift back to events that had changed her life.…

She remembered the first time she'd seen Shane as if it were yesterday.

Her father had gone into Bushwhack to pick up the new hand he'd hired, sight unseen, on the recommendation of an old friend at the Lost Springs Ranch for Boys. She'd known other cowboys who'd come that route, and without exception, they'd been quiet, polite, hardworking young men.

Then her father's pickup pulled into the ranch yard and *he* jumped out. Shane stood next to the truck, fists on his hips, head thrown back, breathing great gulps of fresh pine-scented Rocky Mountain air.

He was slender, just a boy still, but his shoulders were broad and his carriage arrogant as he walked toward the house beside the much taller man. Even considering the physical differences, he somehow had never seemed to be in Big Tom's six-foot-three shadow. This boy obviously didn't just consider himself equal, he considered himself *more* than equal.

His name was Shane Daniels, which she already knew, and she detested him at first sight. He was a smart-ass; he was too full of himself; he thought he was far superior to the sixteen-year-old daughter of his employer.

"Yeah, hi," he said impatiently when they were introduced. He ignored her outstretched hand, and those chilly blue eyes never warmed for her, not even a little. "Okay if I get on over to the bunkhouse, Mr. Hoyt? I'd like to get settled in and go to work."

"Sure thing, Shane, but call me Tom or Big Tom. All the hands do."

"Whatever." Judging by Shane's frosty expression, the man was taking liberties.

Big Tom smothered a smile. "You saw the bunkhouse on our way in. Go on over and grab any bunk that's empty."

Shane nodded. "Then what do you want me to do? You said something about some cows you want moved?"

"Slow down, boy!" Big Tom clapped a friendly hand on Shane's back, nearly staggering him. "No need to jump in before you been here fifteen minutes. Tell you what—" The man gave the boy a considering look. "Put your stuff away, then go pick yourself a horse outta that far corral. You'll find gear in the tack room. Saddle up and take a look around."

Suddenly the ice was gone from Shane's eyes. Dinah remembered blinking in astonishment. He was really a good-looking boy when he wasn't frowning and glowering at everybody.

"Thanks." Shane turned away. "Thanks a lot, Mr. Hoyt."

"Big Tom!"

Shane, on his way back to the pickup to grab his duffel, didn't turn around, but his voice floated back to them. "Thanks a lot, Big Tom...."

Dinah had turned and stomped inside the house, her father following. "I don't like him," she exploded. "He thinks he's really hot stuff and I just don't like people like that."

"Give him a chance, girl," her father suggested mildly. "That boy's had the kind of life you can't even imagine. Why don't we both just give him a break, here?"

That annoyed Dinah, too. What could be worse than losing your mother when you were just seven years old? "He's stuck on himself," she said. "He's not such a much."

Annoyed without understanding why, she set about getting her father's dinner on the table, never once wondering if Ruben Hicks, the old ranch hand who cooked for the crew, would have anything saved for the new boy.

Well, maybe she thought about it in passing. A couple of hours later she heard hoofbeats and looked out the window to see Shane loping past on a good bay quarter horse. Stepping quickly onto the porch, she hailed him.

He approached with obvious reluctance, scowling. On horseback, he took her breath away; bay and boy were *perfect*.

"Uh..." She licked her lips, suddenly intimidated. "Did you get something to eat? I didn't know if Ruben, I mean, if you didn't, I—"

He just sat in the saddle looking down at her with a superior smirk on his face. "Do you always stammer like that?" he asked.

"I don't stammer!" She clenched her hands into fists and stood taller. "Maybe only when I'm talking to rude—to rude—"

"Rude what?" he challenged.

"Rude...rude *boys!*"

He laughed. He actually laughed at her. "Look, little girl," he drawled, "I've been hired to do a man's work and I'll be drawing a man's wages, so don't think you can get a rise out of me that way. Go play with your dolls and don't bother me."

"Ohh!" She actually stamped one booted foot like the brat he obviously took her for. "Just hold your breath until I try to do something nice for you again. I hope you starve to death!"

He lifted the reins in a casually competent hand. "No, you don't," he said. "Someday you'll grow up and realize how stupid you're acting."

Touching heels lightly to the horse's ribs, he rode away, leaving one very angry, very offended, very...young girl behind him. Hate at first sight, she comforted herself that night while she prepared for bed. If there was such a thing as love at first sight—and she firmly, romantically believed there was—then there had to be the opposite.

For almost two years, she believed what she told herself that night. And then one day she realized that her first gut reaction to him had been so new and so scary to her innocent heart that she had completely misunderstood what was going on....

THEY CHANGED DRIVERS again in Cheyenne some three hours after they left Lightning Creek. They met in front of the pickup, stopping just short of bumping into each other. Shane stepped aside to let her pass, which she did, and he thought she was unnecessarily careful not to touch him. "Want any more coffee?" he asked.

She shook her head. "We've got bottled water. That's all I want at the moment."

"Must be nice to be so easily satisfied." He climbed into the pickup and she did likewise, both making a production out of snapping seat belts and checking mirrors.

"You've been awful quiet since I woke up," he said, starting the engine. "Got something on your mind?" If she regretted bringing him along, he might as well jolly her out of it right away.

"Not really." She sank back in the seat. "Well, sort of. I was thinking about my father."

She turned her head to look at him. In the reflection of the neon lights, she looked pensive and very, very appealing. It took considerable willpower to refocus his attention on the road.

"Big Tom was a good man," he said gruffly, not wanting to encourage further conversation. For the truth was, he'd been intensely jealous of Dinah's relationship with her father.

BIG TOM WAS EVERYTHING a father was supposed to be.

He could handle cattle and horses with the best of them, which was real important to Shane; he could see through excuses and lies with ease; and he was fair and honest with all his dealings.

He was also willing to take a fatherless boy under his wing and make a man of him. Before too much time had passed, Shane found himself judging his responses and reactions by a single yardstick: What would Big Tom think?

Then, as often as not, Shane would do the opposite. Because no matter what he'd said to Dinah that first night on the Flying H, he wasn't quite a man yet, even if he thought he was. The first time Shane got into a fight in town, Big Tom sat him down and had a serious talk with him about the duties and obligations of manhood.

"I don't mind my men fighting just for the hell of it," he explained, "so long as it's a fair fight with an equal opponent. Larry Woodruff is *not* an equal opponent."

Shane saw red. "What'dya mean, he's not equal? He's two years older and forty pounds heavier!"

"But he's not equal up *here*." Big Tom tapped his forehead lightly. "Be fair, boy. You got more sense in your little finger than that big galoot's got in his whole body."

Somewhat mollified, Shane muttered, "Then what the hell am I supposed to do the next time some guy calls some woman a slut—and worse?"

For a moment, Big Tom was silent. Then he said, "You're supposed to do exactly what you did, and give him one for me, too. Okay?" He stood up, then hesitated. "Mind tellin' me who he was talking about?"

"Okay, but I don't want it goin' any further." Shane glowered at Big Tom until the man nodded. "It was…Heather Curtis." He barely whispered the name.

Big Tom looked stunned. "But, boy, she *is* a…"

Shane grinned. "Yeah, I know, but I figure that just makes her need protection more instead of less. Hell, she thanked me afterward."

"I don't doubt it." Tom banged a big hand on Shane's back. "Forget everything I said. You done good."

But Shane hadn't forgotten anything Big Tom ever said to him. Soon he found himself resenting the time his mentor spent with anyone else, even with the daughter he obviously adored. That daughter, unfortunately, was a pain in the butt for Shane.

She was, he'd decided straight away, an ungrateful brat. She had her father wrapped around her little finger and she knew it. Even if Big Tom and Shane had plans, she thought nothing of busting in and demanding to go here or there, do this or do that. Jealousy grew in him, sparked by one resentment after the other.

By the time Dinah was a senior in high school, the two were barely able to be in the same room without striking angry sparks. But by then, a horrible truth was beginning to dawn on Shane: these were sparks of a different kind.

She'd changed, grown. She was no longer a bratty kid, she was a bratty young woman...gorgeous, though, with long slender legs...a narrow waist above shapely hips...breasts that had blossomed with soft new curves. Her face had changed, too, cheekbones more pronounced and mouth fuller.

Now he fought with her for another reason—because he didn't dare do otherwise. She was the daughter of a man he idolized...and she was also a virgin. He knew this because he'd made it his business to watch over her. The word was out: trifle with Dinah Hoyt and you'd have Shane Daniels to deal with.

Shane knew that nobody wanted to face up to "that crazy Daniels kid," even though at twenty he no longer felt like a kid. He couldn't hold half the male population of Bushwhack County off forever, though.

Something had to give, and it did...the night of Dinah's senior prom.

CHAPTER FOUR

As THEY DROVE THROUGH the quiet of the early morning, Dinah relived that same fateful night ten years ago. She'd worn a black dress to her senior prom, a strapless dress with tight bodice and flouncy skirt. She'd made a point of showing the dress to her father while Shane was at the house going over stock lists with the boss.

Holding the dress up against her the way all girls do, she whirled around the room ecstatically. "Isn't it beautiful?" she demanded.

"Yeah, it's real nice." Her father barely glanced up. "Now, about this heifer, Shane..."

She studied Shane through half-lowered lashes, pleased that he was looking at her and not at her father. "Do *you* like my dress?"

He shrugged and his mouth curved down sarcastically. "What's to like? It's a dress—whoopty-do." And he, too, concentrated on the numbers on the page before him.

But she knew. He didn't like it, and he didn't like Greg Wells, her date, any better. Of course, she wasn't all that crazy about Greg, either. But he'd asked her and nobody else had. She wasn't going to sit home on prom night the way she'd been doing so much lately. You'd think she was Typhoid Mary when it came to dates.

So she wore her black strapless dress to the party and tried to pretend she was having a great time in the gymnasium, which was decorated in a "South Seas Idyll" theme. But it really wasn't that much fun, especially as the evening wore on and Greg grew bolder and more insistent, finally almost dragging her outside the back door.

She wasn't worried, though. She knew how to take care of herself. She figured she could probably mop the sidewalk with Greg, given the edge of being a girl; if she felt it necessary to slap his face, he couldn't very well slap her back, could he?

When he hauled her into his arms, she rolled her eyes and tried not to mash her dress when he kissed her. One kiss couldn't hurt, could it?

Big mistake. One just seemed to make him want another.

"Greg!" she commanded, pushing him away. "Get hold of yourself, for heaven's sake."

"C'mon," he panted, "give. You know you want it. Let's get out of here, okay?"

"No! All I want is to go back to the dance." She batted at his reaching hands, thoroughly annoyed.

"Not so fast." He wrestled her into his arms again and he was breathing hard. "I'm already in deep enough so I might as well get something for my trouble," he muttered.

She turned her head away and his mouth landed on her jaw. "What's that supposed to mean?" She couldn't believe how strong he was, holding her crushed against the chest of his rented tuxedo.

"Like you don't know," he sneered. "Your watchdog's gonna be on me like a duck on a June bug, anyway, so I might as well get something out of this."

"Stop it, Greg! I don't know what you're talking about. All you're going to get here is trouble."

"Yeah, from Shane Daniels, but I'm not afraid of him. The rest of the guys might let that smart-ass cowboy run 'em off, but I figure just because he's got his eye on you himself is no reason I should back off. Who the hell does he think he is, putting out the word that anybody who lays a finger on you will answer—'' As he said that, Greg laid more than a finger squarely on her right breast.

She gasped, as shocked by his accusations against Shane as she was by his groping. ''I don't believe you.'' She knocked his hand aside. ''Shane wouldn't—''

''*Shane would!*''

She had just a glimpse of Greg's shocked face before he was jerked away and hurled headfirst into a lilac bush by a furious cowboy. Shane grabbed her hand and hauled her toward the curb, looking mad enough to kick a cow dog.

''Wait!'' She tried to pull her hand out of his iron grip. ''Stop! What do you think you're—'' She braced the heels of her fragile black pumps and tried to resist the inexorable pull on her arm.

Shane's face was a thundercloud. ''Your father's across the street. He saw the whole thing and sent me to bail you out.''

''What? Daddy—'' All the fight went out of her at the thought of her father and Shane witnessing her inability to control teenage lust.

Humiliated, she forced herself to follow Shane meekly across the street and into the meeting hall where members of the local Cattleman's Association had gathered. Her father was waiting for her in the lobby, his face like granite.

''Dammit, girl—''

''Don't you start on me!'' She covered her face with her hands, trying not to tremble so violently. ''I didn't know Greg was going to try anything like that.''

''You know it now. Did you thank Shane for coming to your rescue?''

''Thank him!'' She jerked her hands away from her face

so she could glare at her "rescuer." "I didn't need him butting in. I didn't need either one of you butting in. I could handle Greg."

"Little girl, you don't know half as much as you think you do—about men, anyway." He grimaced. "Or boys, either, for that matter."

"Daddy, I swear to you—"

"Don't bother." He cocked his head. "You want to go home now?"

"I sure don't want to face Greg after all that." She wasn't sure if she meant after he'd manhandled her or after her father's hired hand had galloped into the fray.

Big Tom gazed at the tight-lipped and silent Shane. "In that case, take Dinah home for me, will you? We got some real important details to hash out here and I'd hate to leave now. Although," he added to Dinah, "I will if you want me to. You're sure as hell more important to me than any meeting."

She started to tell him yes, she wanted her father to take her home. But then she glanced at Shane and suddenly she knew how she was going to make him pay for this embarrassment. If what Greg had implied was true, Shane himself was vulnerable. She'd lead him on and then...

Without finishing the thought, she lifted her chin. "You go back inside, Daddy. I'm sorry I upset you. I'll...go home with Shane."

She heard Shane's sharp intake of breath but didn't think her father had.

SHANE REMEMBERED RIDING toward the Flying H that night, Dinah saying into the chilly silence, "All I had to do if worse came to worse was scream." Her voice sounded strangely husky but no longer angry. "Greg wouldn't have knocked me down and had his evil way with me, you know—at least not right outside the high school gym.''

''Probably not. He'd just have groped you and slobbered on you a little more. Maybe that would have been okay with you.'' Shane gave her a quick, slanting glance, trying to hide his fury beneath an icy surface. He'd hated seeing that idiot paw her, but she sure as hell didn't seem all that broken up by her little misadventure.

''Sore loser,'' she said softly.

His scalp prickled. ''What's that supposed to mean?''

''You heard what Greg said. Is it true?''

''Which part? The part where he said you wanted it?''

She sucked in her breath. ''No, the part where he said you had your eye on me.''

''That's only obvious, since I was there when you needed me.''

''I didn't need you...at least, not to fight my battles. Shane...''

She laid one small hand on his thigh and he nearly jumped out of his skin. Her fingers curved over the rigid muscle; his heart slammed against his ribs and he forgot to breathe for a moment.

He gulped. ''Jeez, Dinah, what the hell do you think you're doing?'' He barely had breath to say it.

She slid her fingers around until they wedged between his thighs. ''Finding out for myself, Shane.''

''Don't—God, don't start something you can't finish.''

''I can finish it. I'm eighteen, an adult. I *want* to finish it...with you, Shane, not with Greg.''

He slammed on the brakes and the pickup swayed to a halt in the ranch yard before the front door. There were no lights inside, nor any in the ranch compound. Everyone had gone into town for one reason or another.

They were alone.

He reached for her without a word and slammed his mouth down on hers. The kiss was long and hot and hungry, not to mention way overdue. He was first delighted, then dismayed by her enthusiasm.

He hadn't been guarding her for himself—had he? When had jealousy and animosity turned into this searing hunger? He didn't know, yet here it was, bursting like a ball of flame in his gut. Nuzzling her ear, he touched the swell of her breast above the stupid black dress. She made no objection, none at all.

"Come inside," she whispered, her voice ragged and her breathing loud. "Shane, come inside with me."

He groaned. "I can't do that. Your father—"

"Isn't here. After the meeting, he'll get into a poker game and be gone all night. He'll never know. No one will ever know except us. Shane, I mean it!" Pulling back, she cupped his cheeks with her hands. "I swear to God, if you don't I'll—I'll find someone who will." Her voice rose. "Because I'm tired of being a wallflower, tired of being a tomboy. I must be the last virgin in the senior class at Bushwhack High School and it's humiliating."

He groaned. "Dinah, we'll regret it if we—"

"Are you getting tired yet?"

Shane jerked behind the wheel of Dinah's pickup and tried to get a grip on the present: hurtling toward Denver on the I-25, not the Flying H.

"Nah," he croaked. "I'm fine."

"Then why did you just drift over that yellow line as if you didn't even notice it?"

"I was thinking, but I'm all right now. You go back to sleep."

"If you're sure you're awake, I just may do that."

Only she didn't. Settling back into her corner, she swallowed a sigh. She'd been thinking about that other time when they'd been alone in the dark in the cab of a pickup truck, the time when she'd been wearing her sexy black prom dress. She'd had a hundred different reasons for what she'd planned to do.

She'd hated him for interfering in her life. She would get even by leading him on and then at the last minute humiliating him as he'd humiliated her.

Only it hadn't happened that way at all. They'd ended up in her bed, and at the last minute she'd forgotten all about her plans. Instead, she'd cried out his name and wrapped her legs around his naked hips, rising to become one with him at last.

In that blinding climb to physical rapture, she knew she didn't hate him at all. She adored him, she admired him...she might even love him.

And although afterward he didn't profess any great love for *her,* she was certain he must feel the same. He was so gentle with her, almost apologetic. He kissed her so sweetly and held her in his arms and swore to her that he'd never intended to let things go so far. But he hadn't been able to resist her, and if she wanted to make him suffer for what he'd done by telling her father, he'd offer no defense, although the thought of betraying Big Tom...

"Oh, Shane, don't be silly." She'd touched his face with her hands, the way she'd been wanting to do for so very long without realizing it. She brushed the dark, silky hair away from his forehead and kissed his eyelids, reveling in his acceptance. And she pressed her breasts against his chest in a way that had never actually occurred to her to do but now felt perfectly right.

They lay in the dark on the narrow bed in her pink-and-cream room, exhausted, the sheets and blankets tumbled around them and spilling onto the floor.

"We can't let this happen again," he said, all the while

running one hand along the curve of her spine. "It isn't right, Dinah. I won't be able to look your father in the face as it is now."

"Shane—"

"No, I mean it. I wanted to protect you, protect your reputation from all those young studs. I should have been protecting you from *me*."

"What if I don't want to be protected from you? What if—"

They heard it at the same instant: the roar of a pickup's engine. Someone was coming. They both froze.

But it wasn't Big Tom; the vehicle drove on past to the bunkhouse. Shane was out of the bed in a flash, yanking on his clothes.

"I've got to get out of here before anyone realizes—"

"The light's on downstairs," she said reasonably. "We were just talking, okay?"

His groan came to her from within the deep shadows. "Only that's not what we were doing."

No, it hadn't been, and they hadn't been able to make their peace with that over the next few weeks. They'd agreed that what they were doing was dangerous, that if her father found out he'd feel betrayed by both of them. They agreed they were too young to make a permanent commitment, that neither was ready to settle down...nor could they find the strength to stay away from each other.

God knew, they'd tried, but the strain became too much, leading to an awful argument just before that ridiculous incident with the elk. Her father had been livid—

"Want to grab a bite to eat in Denver? It'll be about 3:00 a.m. when we get there. Once we turn west on 70—"

"Oh, God," Dinah murmured, completely disoriented. "Shane..."

"What?" He said it sharply, defensively.

"You ran. Why?"

There was a long silence, and at first she thought he hadn't understood.

But he had, for he said, "Damn straight, I ran." His voice was like gravel on glass. "You'd run, too, if you had a man with a shotgun after you—figuratively speaking, of course. I was wrong, Dinah, and I couldn't defend myself. You were through with me and I let your father down, so hell yes, I left."

"I...see." Only she didn't. He'd left over such a relatively little argument. Yes, they'd vowed to end their affair, but they'd fought and made up before.

The obvious conclusion was that he'd just been looking for an excuse to get out of a sticky situation. Sure, Big Tom was furious when he learned Shane had bulldogged an elk on Flying H property, then tried to ride it. But he didn't have to sneak out of town over it. Even after all these years, Dinah realized that the real reason he'd left was because of her.

Her father had died of a heart attack only weeks later, and her grief had cut through much of her heartache over Shane's departure. By the time she realized she was pregnant...

She shot a quick, guilty glance at the man behind the wheel of her pickup and prayed he couldn't read minds.

THEY PULLED INTO the contestants' parking lot at the Tall Timber rodeo grounds at midmorning. Crawling stiffly out of the pickup, Dinah looked around at the looming grandstands and wondered what she'd let herself in for.

The place already bustled with activity, and a figure broke away from the crowd to lope toward them: Shane's partner, Josh, no doubt. When he got close enough for her to really see him, she was surprised by his youth.

"Dinah," Shane began, "this is—"

"Josh," she said with a smile, offering her hand. "Hi. I'm Dinah." She let it go at that.

The boy, who couldn't be a day over nineteen, gave her a broad grin. He was a shade taller than Shane's five ten but he had the same lean and wiry build. "Glad to meet you. Uh, are you guys…?" He wiggled his fingers to indicate a couple.

"No!" they said together.

"Actually," Dinah explained, "I bought Shane at the auction at Lost Springs."

"That's right," Shane said. "She owns me. We'll tell you all about it over breakfast."

Breakfast was coffee, cold cereal and toast, taken in a travel trailer so small Dinah would have bet three people couldn't get into it. She'd have lost that bet. With a narrow bed at each end and a hot plate and miniscule sink in the middle, there was plenty of room—if you enjoyed sardine cans.

As they ate, they talked. Josh, eager as a puppy to please, brought Shane up to date on all he'd missed by going to Lost Springs, and Shane explained—carefully, making it clear that there was no personal relationship— the civic motives behind Dinah's winning bid.

Josh frowned. "But you're gonna miss out on a lot of big money by tyin' yourself up over the Fourth of July."

Shane shrugged. "Hey, it's for a good cause. You'd do the same."

Josh shook his head. "I don't think so. You sure that's a good idea?"

Dinah held her breath, realized what she was doing and let it out. Shane would never go back on his word.

He didn't. He just shrugged and said, "It's done."

So everything was moving along just as it should. She

looked around from her perch on the edge of one of the beds for a place to set her empty cereal dish. "Well, guys, thanks for the breakfast, but it's about time I got moving."

"Don't go," Josh said quickly. He grinned a little self-consciously. "Stick around and watch us win top money."

"I'd really like to but—" An enormous yawn overtook her and she covered her mouth with her hand, surprised. "Excuse me! I'm tired, not bored."

Shane turned a steely expression on her. "You're not going anywhere until you get some sleep," he said in a tone that brooked no dissent—a tone she'd heard before and ignored.

"I'm only about three hours from home," she pointed out reasonably. "Believe me, I'm perfectly capable of—"

"Forget it, Dinah. We're talking mountain roads here. I won't let you take chances." He rose, the ceiling barely accommodating his not-too-overwhelming height. "Josh and I need to go check in and make sure everything's in order. You'll have this place to yourself, such as it is."

"But I really feel fine," she argued. "I don't need a nap."

"Dinah! *I* need you to take a nap, okay? I'm not going to let you go until you do."

That was Shane, looking out for her whether she welcomed it or not. "Oh, all right," she said ungraciously. "I'll see you both later, then."

They left and she slumped back on the bed, yawning prodigiously now that she was alone. She wasn't really tired. All she needed was a few minutes to rest and she'd be…

A SOFT KNOCK ON THE DOOR brought Dinah swinging up from the bed in confusion. Rubbing sleep from her eyes, she tried to get her bearings. A quick glance at her wristwatch showed that a good three hours had passed since she'd lain down.

Throwing open the door, she found Josh, not Shane, standing there with a big grin on his face. "Time to rise and shine," he said cheerfully. "Shane said for me to buy you a hot dog and get you all primed for the good stuff—us!"

"Where is he?"

"He had some business to take care of. He'll track us down later."

Josh led the way to the concession stands just inside the gate. There he bought hot dogs and soft drinks, then headed toward a low concrete wall where they settled with their sumptuous lunch. The crowd eddied and swirled around them: adults and kids, all in a holiday mood.

"So," she asked, flicking hot dog relish off her lap, "how long have you and Shane been traveling together?"

Josh chewed thoughtfully. "Almost a year. He'd kinda taken me under his wing, you might say, even before that. He's really helped me a lot with the finer points of this business, y'know? I owe him a helluva lot for that and…other stuff." He swallowed the last bite of hot dog. "Besides, it's cheaper on both of us, sharing expenses and all. When his last travel partner decided to drop out, Shane thought of me and, well, here we are."

She took a sip of her soda. "Do you like traveling all the time?"

"Heck, yeah!" His eyes sparkled. "I like keepin' on the go. Why not? I've got nothin' to go home for."

"Where's home?"

"Anywhere I hang my hat." He grinned and shrugged. "Hey!"

He pointed and she saw Shane approaching through the crowd streaming into the rodeo grounds. Her heart did a funny little flip-flop. He looked so good, so at home in these surroundings. *A license to avoid responsibility,* he'd said. Footloose and fancy-free with no wife or children to worry about…a perfect life?

Shane halted before them, pushing his black hat to the back of his head. She noticed that he'd replaced the championship belt he'd given to the boy at the ranch with one nearly as ornate.

"Get any rest?" he asked.

She nodded. "Plenty. Now that Josh has fed me, I really do need to hit the road."

Josh frowned. "You mean you don't want to hang around and watch us wipe out the competition?"

"Is that what's going to happen?" Smiling, she looked from one serious face to the other.

"That's our plan," Shane said soberly. "You don't want to miss that, now, do you?"

It surprised her to realize that she didn't. "I suppose if I leave a few hours later it won't really matter."

At least, she *hoped* it wouldn't. It was just a rodeo, after all.

DINAH HAD BEEN TO A LOT of rodeos, both large and small, but she'd never enjoyed one as much as she did this one. Sitting in the stands between Shane and Josh, she felt pampered and special as they went out of their way to include her in their conversation. They knew everybody and everything, it seemed: which cowboy was desperate for a trip to the pay window, which horse was likely to earn a high score for the man who could ride it, which pickup man really knew his business and which was trying like hell but was completely outclassed.

She listened, more impressed by the minute. Rodeo was

obviously an entire little world all its own and she felt privileged to be included in their insiders' talk.

A bareback rider hit the dirt three seconds short of the required eight and Shane groaned. "That old boy sure needed to make him some money in the worst way."

"Oh?" She watched the cowboy limp out of the arena, lifting his hat to acknowledge polite applause. "I guess everybody feels that way."

"Yeah, but Junior's a special case," Josh chimed in. "He's got a wife and kids and a big fat mortgage back home in Texas. His paydays lately have been few and far between."

So this man, at least, had not heeded Shane's rule for cowboy happiness: no wives and children to get in the way of the free-and-easy rodeo life.

Shane spoke suddenly. "He's got one of his boys here with him. Damn shame for a kid to see his old man bite the dust that way." He looked genuinely upset about the man's failure to make his ride.

"Happens to all of us," Josh pointed out, but he looked equally concerned. "He'll get 'em the next time."

"Yeah. There's always the next time." Shane stood up abruptly. "I think it's about time you and me head around back to get ready." He looked at Dinah. "Okay?"

"Sure." But she'd miss him—them, she corrected herself.

"You'll be here when we're finished?" Shane pressed.

She grinned. "You mean will I leave for home without saying goodbye? I wouldn't do that. Unlike someone I could name."

"Good. We'll see you later, then."

He turned and leaped from tier to tier to reach the bottom of the bleachers. Josh gave her a quick salute and followed. At the end of the bleachers, a kid approached and Shane listened, then nodded and reached for the piece of paper the boy thrust forward.

Another autograph-seeker, obviously. Shane treated them all with such courtesy. Now he was introducing Josh to the kid and handing the paper to his partner.

Trying to share the glory. That really wasn't the Shane she'd known. In what other ways had he changed?

In what ways had *she* changed?

BULL RIDERS HAD ALREADY gathered in the contestants' area behind the chutes by the time Josh and Shane arrived. One of the cowboys, rosining his gloves, flipped them a wave; another looked up from stretching exercises to nod. The rest ignored the newcomers, lost in their own preparations, some mental and some physical.

Shane recognized and accepted the wary tension in the air. Big rodeo or small, the same electricity was always present. No time to worry about that; he had to put on his spurs and chaps and the heavy rawhide gloves that protected his hands from the enormous pull on the bull rope.

The first set of bulls charged into the chutes and the gates clanged shut behind them. Shane, buckling on his chaps, felt the hair prickle on the back of his neck. He'd be the second rider out of the gates so he didn't have a helluva lot of time to psyche himself up.

Of course, with his experience, it shouldn't take all that long. All he had to do was breathe deep and clear his mind of *everything*—including the woman in the stands.

He hadn't expected Dinah to stay. That's why he'd sent Josh to see if she was awake. If he'd knocked on the door himself—

"Hey, you listening?" Josh shouted the question. "You're up next!"

Shane nodded. *Stick to business!* His draw wasn't the

greatest, but if the stars were right and both man and bull attended to business, they had a chance to finish in the money.

Climbing the rails, he dropped the end of his bull rope over the animal's shoulder. Josh reached through the bars and grabbed it with the hook. Automatically Shane accepted the rope and ran the end of it through the loop, pulling it tight.

"He spins to the right," Josh said, sounding worried. "You gotta be ready or he'll have you in the well before you can find your rhythm."

Shane nodded. He had no intention of eating dirt in front of Dinah. He tested the rope, pulling it tighter.

"Don't take him for granted, Shane. He's a sneaky bastard."

Maybe, but the big brindled beast stood in the chute, docile as a kitten.

"Hey, wake up!" Josh grabbed a handful of shirt and glared at his partner. "You gotta take care of business *here* before you start plannin' a celebration." A meaningful jerk of his head toward the stands made his meaning clear.

Shane emerged from his near trance. "Yeah, spins to the right. I got it."

He lowered himself onto the bull, settling well back over the animal's flanks while keeping his feet and most of his weight on the boards on either side. With his palm up, he slid his hand into the loop on the bull rope. Stick to business—yeah, he was in the zone where he belonged now.

Josh pulled sharply on the rope and the bull grunted but didn't move. Shane wrapped the loose end around his hand, gave it a twist and tossed it back over to the other side. He screwed his hat on tight, slid forward, tightened the grip of his thighs and nodded sharply.

Time to put up or shut up.

CHAPTER FIVE

THE BULL ROARED OUT of the chute and whirled to the right while Shane flailed away at the muscular shoulders with his spurs. The bull came out of the spin and was airborne, kicking his hind legs sky-high and stumbling a little on the landing.

Still firmly seated with the bull rope set just right, Shane was doing fine. He was several seconds into the ride now and all it took was eight. This old brindle was outdoing himself, and dollar signs floated through the cowboy's mind.

Concentrate...

The bull went into another spin, this one to the left. Not prepared for this aberration, Shane swayed, barely managing to stay upright. The book on this bull said everything went right, but Shane had survived that surprise. Almost there now—

From the corner of his eye, he caught a flash of red at the fence at the foot of the stands. Dinah? Had she moved down to get a better view? Was she worried about him or just excited by—

A quick move by the enraged bull ripped the rope from his hand. In the blink of an eye, Shane wasn't *on* the bull but flying over its head. He hit the dirt with a smack that knocked every scrap of air out of his lungs. Experience told him not to ponder the whys and wherefores at that particular moment. On hands and knees and powered by adrenaline, he scrambled for safety as the bullfighters sprang forward.

But nobody was fast enough to thwart that bull. Head down, he hooked a horn beneath Shane's ribs and tossed him high, following that with a charge that sent the cowboy rolling. Trying to protect his head, Shane heard shrieks from the crowd, smelled steam rising like a cloud from the mad bull.

One of the bullfighters grabbed Shane by an arm and dragged him across the dirt of the arena. The other bullfighter dashed past, clown costume flapping as he screamed and waved his arms to distract the rampaging bull. Something slammed into Shane's ribs and he gasped and saw stars.

His last unscrambled thought was, *All it takes is one mistake.*

SHANE CAME TO EVEN BEFORE they got him to the first aid tent. Dumped on an examining table, he groaned and tried to get his bearings.

"Well, well," the emergency medical technician drawled, "what have we here? If it's not ol' Shane Daniels, my favorite patient."

"Aw, you're just saying that, Curt." The effort to speak cost Shane plenty and he gasped with the pain. He hurt from armpits to waist. Unless he missed his guess, that bull had banged up his ribs pretty good this time.

Curt worked quickly and efficiently to strip away the shirt. He gave a low whistle. "Smart, cowboy. You're still bruised from last time."

"Just tape me up and turn me loose." Shane struggled to sit up. "I don't have time for this."

"You better take time or you're gonna wish you had." Curt touched a rib carefully and Shane flinched. "If you don't give those ribs a chance to heal completely this time, you're likely gonna puncture a lung and kill yourself.''

"That's what they all say," Shane scoffed, "but I'm still here. Why don't you just patch me up and I'll—"

Josh roared through the open tent flap, interrupting the conversation. He skidded to a halt, his eyes wide. "Whoa, that was a nasty crash."

"Was it?" Shane finally got into an upright position with his legs dangling over the edge of the examining table. He wrapped an arm around his ribs. "Dammit, Curt, can't you find the tape?"

"You need X rays."

"To hell with that. Just tape me up, I said."

Josh frowned. "Think that's smart? They told you last time that if you didn't—"

"I know what they told me, Josh." Shane licked dry lips. "What the hell are you doing here, anyway? You'll miss your ride."

"Yeah, I gotta get right back, but I wanted to see if you were dead or alive first. The way that bull tossed you around, I wouldn't have been surprised to find you all whacked up into little pieces."

"As you can plainly see, I'm fine."

"Yeah, sure." Josh wheeled around. "See you later, pal."

"Sure—uh, Josh?"

"Yeah?"

"Did I make the time?"

"Nope."

"Damn!"

If there was anything worse than being roughed up by a bull, it was having it happen short of eight seconds.

DINAH HAD AN AWFUL TIME tracking Shane down.

At first she'd been so shocked and horrified by what

she'd seen that her knees collapsed and she had to hang on to the wire fence to keep from falling flat on her face. Once she'd recovered, she had to figure out where the first aid tent was, then talk the guard at the entrance to the contestants' area into letting her in.

"You related?" he'd demanded.

"No, but—"

"Then you can't come in."

"You don't understand! I've got to get to the first aid station to find out how Shane Daniels is."

"I dunno. I'm not supposed to…"

"Please!"

Finally he'd waved her through and she'd hurried to the big tent marked Infirmary.

She didn't know what she'd expected, but it was not what she found: Shane sitting on the edge of an examining table buttoning his shirt. When he saw her, he grinned and picked up the can of soda beside him on the table.

"I told you it'd be fun," he said.

She didn't know whether to yell at him or collapse in gratitude that he could still joke. "I can't believe you're sitting there like nothing happened," she gasped. "When that bull hooked you…" She shuddered.

"Aw, it wasn't so bad."

She stared at the rapidly discoloring skin above his right eye. "You're lucky to be alive."

"We're all lucky to be alive." He swiveled toward the man writing on a clipboard. "That all, Curt? I'd like to see Josh ride if I can make it back in time."

"That's not all and you know it. Why don't you let Al run you over to the hospital in the ambulance for X rays? You really should—"

"Forget it."

Shane eased off the table and onto his feet. For a moment it looked as if his knees would buckle, but he grabbed the table and straightened.

Dinah stepped forward anxiously. "If he says you need X rays—"

"He says everybody needs X rays. He sounds like a broken record on the subject."

"But should you be taking chances?"

Shane cocked his head and grinned. "Afraid I won't be able to ride at Old Pioneer Days?"

"Shane Daniels!" She glared at him. "I wasn't even thinking about that. I was concerned for your health, that's all."

"Sure you were." He took a few hobbling steps toward the tent flap, drew a deep breath and straightened.

It looked like an act of sheer will.

The medical tech held out a small white packet. "Okay, hotshot, have it your way. You might want to take a couple of these if—make that *when*—you start hurtin' too bad. If the pills don't work, get your ass to the emergency room because there's nothing else I can do."

"Thanks, Curt." Shane took the package, extracted a couple of the pills and washed them down with his drink. "You've patched me up real good."

"Again."

"Whatever. You comin', Dinah?"

She nodded and stepped forward. After the barest hesitation, she slid her arm around his waist and looked up for his approval.

He caught his breath as if he was in pain, then stepped aside. "I'd love to have your arm around me, honey, but I've got this little twinge in my side," he said apologetically. "Guess I'll just have to gimp along on my own."

"Be my guest."

Stung and sorry she'd made the gesture, she stepped ahead of him to hold open the tent flap. He hobbled through and stopped to look around, his breathing shallow.

Regardless of what he might say, he was hurting. No longer affronted, she touched his arm lightly. When he looked at her, she said, "You scared me, Shane. I thought you were really *really* hurt—and I wasn't thinking about Old Pioneer Days."

"Hey, it's just a day at the office." He spoke lightly, as if such horrific spills happened every day. "Damn bulls can't be trusted." He gave her an insider's wink. "C'mon, let's go see if we can catch Josh's ride."

Together they hobbled toward the gate.

"Is Josh good?" she asked.

He gave her an incredulous glance. "Yeah, and he's gonna be better. As your pa used to say—" He stopped short.

"It's okay to talk about him," she scolded. "Besides, I bet I know what you're about to say—all it'll take is mileage."

They laughed together, moving through the gate and into the crowd. Shane, hobbling along with an arm wrapped around his ribs, drew a few sympathetic glances but no interruptions.

"That's right, Josh is a natural," he said with a smile. "If he stays healthy, he'll be one of the all-time greats before he's through."

"Better than you?"

He nodded. "Way better. But I'm good enough—most of the time, anyway. Today just wasn't my day. Tomorrow could be different."

They rounded one end of the grandstand. "You won't try to ride again tomorrow?" she asked in disbelief.

"I'll have to wait until tomorrow to decide—jeez! That's Josh out there."

He was right; she recognized the red chaps with flying fringe. The boy rode with a grace and style apparent to everyone, and the cheering section erupted with a roar of approval.

If everything had gone wrong for Shane, it was going right for Josh. Even the arm waving above his head was graceful. When the black bull bucked toward the fence, she saw that the cowboy was grinning.

The buzzer sounded. Josh hit the ground running, simultaneously lifting his hat to salute the crowd. He leaped up onto the fence and waved again. The crowd went wild.

Shane nodded approvingly. "That'll be worth eighty-five points or I miss my guess," he predicted. "Damn, that was a good ride!"

The judges agreed, giving the kid an eighty-six.

"That should take all the marbles," Shane said with obvious satisfaction. "I'm sure as hell glad one of us is makin' expenses."

Puzzled, Dinah followed him toward the back of the chutes. He'd seemed as proud of Josh as if he'd made the ride himself.

He'd changed, all right. The question was...in how many ways?

JOSH BOUGHT COLD DRINKS to celebrate, then lifted his paper cup with a broad grin. "Here's to the good bulls, bless their little hearts."

"You bet!" Shane agreed.

Dinah took a sip. "My favorite part," she said to Josh, "was how you managed to get off without falling flat on your face—or anything else."

He laughed. "I liked that part, too. Hey, let's go out

tonight and really celebrate. What do you say, the three of us?''

"But I've got to head for home,'' Dinah objected. "I've already hung around longer than I should have.''

"What's your hurry?'' Shane frowned. "Why not stay over and leave bright and early tomorrow?''

"Because—''

"That just makes good sense,'' Josh interrupted. "I think you brought good luck.''

"Maybe to you.'' She smiled. "I didn't do much for Shane.''

Josh grinned back. "Every man for himself. For me, you're good luck. C'mon, Dinah. It'll be fun.''

"Well…''

There really was no reason for her to rush back. She'd planned carefully and left everything in good shape. Whether she got back tonight or tomorrow wouldn't matter—or shouldn't, anyway. She glanced at Shane but he didn't react at all.

"You can sleep in the trailer,'' Josh persuaded. "Me 'n' Shane often sleep in the back of the pickup, anyway, when the weather's good. You'll have all the comforts of home.''

If that was true, she'd hate to see his home. She glanced at Shane but he wouldn't meet her eyes.

He didn't seem to care one way or the other whether she stayed, which got her back up. "Let me call home and check on a few things,'' she said, more out of spite than anything else. "If everything's all right, you just might have a date, Josh.''

Annoyed, she walked away a few steps before pulling her cell phone out of her leather shoulder bag. Hitting the redial button, she waited for a response on the other end.

"Hello?''

"Georgia? Hi! Is B.D. around?"

"Uh-huh. I'll call her, but first, how's it going, hon? Will he do it?"

"Looks like." She pushed aside disquieting memories of the way Shane had grimaced when she'd touched his ribs.

Big sigh. "That's a relief."

"Yes. So how's B.D. been doing? I hope she hasn't caused you any trouble."

"That little girl is a real corker, but she hasn't been a lick of trouble." Georgia's voice contained a smile. "Here, I'll call her. Will you be home later today?"

"I was thinking…maybe tomorrow, if that's not a problem for you."

"No problem at all," Georgia said happily. "Honey, she can stay with me another week and I'll like it just fine. Hang on, I'll get her." Her voice rose. "B.D., it's your mother!"

SHANE STARED AT DINAH, who was standing ten feet or so away with her back to them. Who had she been so hot to call?

Josh looked disgusted. "Cat got your tongue? You act like you don't want her to stay."

"I want her to stay."

"Then why didn't you speak up?"

"Because that would have been the quickest way to scare her off. Haven't you noticed? Dinah trusts me about as far as she can throw me."

"Yeah." Josh sounded puzzled. "She does seem to doubt your motives. I just figured that's because she knows you."

Shane had to laugh at that one. "You could be right.

Anyway, I hope she stays, because we still haven't worked out all the kinks in this Old Pioneer Days deal.''

"Don't do it, Shane.''

Wary, Shane glanced at his friend. ''C'mon, we're talkin' about some old broken-down bull in front of a few hundred people in a little backwater mountain town. What could go wrong?''

"You don't know?'' Josh sounded disgusted. ''I heard what Curt said about those ribs. Why take chances?'' He amended that by adding, ''At least when you have nothing to gain, including money.''

"I promised,'' Shane said. ''Bushwhack's paying good money to Lost Springs for my services. I can't very well back out now.''

Josh grunted disapprovingly. ''I guess not. That being the case, why don't you just go on back with Dinah and hole up there until the Fourth? That'd give you a chance to heal before you climb on another bull.''

"Because—'' Because why? Actually, that wasn't such a bad idea. The glance he gave Josh said as much.

Josh nodded. ''Look,'' he said, ''I need to go by the trailer and stow this gear.'' He waved his bull rope, and Shane's, in the air. ''Tell Dinah I'll catch up with the two of you later, assuming she hangs around.''

"I'll do that.''

Josh walked away. Shane hesitated, then took a few casual steps toward the woman holding a cell phone to her ear. Her back was still to him, but as he drew closer, he began to catch her side of the conversation.

"You're sure you don't mind if I come home a day later than I'd planned, sweetheart? Some friends have invited me out tonight....''

Some *friends?* That covered a lot. Was she trying to hide the identity of those ''friends''?

"Uh-huh…that's right." Light teasing laughter. "Of *course* I'm not having a good time without you…. You *know* I love you, sweetie. Do you love me?"

Jeez, Shane thought with disgust, this was enough to turn your stomach. She must be really crazy about this guy to carry on so shamelessly.

She wasn't wearing a ring on that left hand, so naturally he'd just assumed… How wrong could you be?

"Okay, I'll see you tomorrow, then. We can—" She looked up, saw Shane standing there and nearly choked. Snapping the cell phone closed, she asked sharply, "Where's Josh?"

"He had some things to do. He'll meet us later…that is, if you've decided to hang around." At that particular moment, he didn't much care how she responded.

So why was he so pleased when she said, "Yes, I've decided to stay."

THEY WENT TO the Bon Ton Café for dinner: big steaks with onion rings and corn on the cob all around. When the two men ordered beer, Dinah decided to join them. Not much of a drinker, she did occasionally enjoy a cold brew, and this didn't look like a chardonnay crowd.

In fact, the place was packed with rodeo competitors and fans. The atmosphere was one of camaraderie and good cheer, everybody treating everybody else like long-lost friends.

This was one aspect of small-town life that Dinah could appreciate. She'd never lived in a big city and never intended to. She was a small-town girl and that was all she wanted to be.

At the moment, she was a small-town girl seated at a table with the two best-looking men in the room—maybe in town. Both were dark and sexy and had a certain dangerous air that gave them an added attraction. So did the humor they brought to everything they did. Even serious matters were dealt with lightly, at least on the surface.

Serious matters like the pounding Shane had taken that day. A huge purple bruise decorated his forehead, and he moved with such care that she suspected the worst part of his injuries was concealed by his bright turquoise shirt.

A middle-aged man who looked like a rancher stopped by their table. "I watched you eat dirt today, Shane Daniels, and it wasn't a pretty sight. Glad to see you out here among 'em tonight."

"Takes more than one loco bull to keep a good man down, Charlie." Shane winked. "Especially if there's a pretty girl anywhere around."

Charlie grinned at Dinah, who was pleased at the backhanded compliment despite herself.

"Keep his motor revved up and he'll be back in the saddle by tomorrow at the latest," Charlie predicted. Laughing at his own humor, he departed.

"Stock contractor," Josh said, reaching for the ketchup bottle. "No wonder he's in a good mood. It was his bull that dumped old Shane."

Shane aimed a fork at his two-inch sirloin. "No hard feelings. I'll get him next time."

Dinah shuddered. After what that bull had done to him, she couldn't imagine any sane man putting himself at such peril again. But as Shane said, it was a day at the office for him.

How did a rodeo wife stand it?

Nevertheless, she enjoyed the meal and the company. Everything was loose and easy, with diners frequently dropping by to say hello, to congratulate Josh, to commiserate with Shane.

Over a piece of apple pie, Josh said, "Where'll we go next, the Thirsty Buzzard or Antelope Trails?"

"I've always been real fond of the Buzzard," Shane said. "It seems to have the best bands."

"Then it's settled." Josh looked at Dinah. "Okay with you?"

"Sure." She shrugged. "What do I know? I put myself in your hands."

Josh laughed. "You'll never regret it," he said. "Will she, Shane!"

Shane didn't look nearly as certain.

BY TEN O'CLOCK, the Thirsty Buzzard was packed with jeans and Stetsons and high-heeled boots. The decibel level had reached a piercing high that no one seemed to notice except Dinah.

Even so, she was having a good time. She'd been inside very few honky-tonks, the Bushwhack Saloon being an exception. The Thirsty Buzzard was jumping with a mob three-deep at the bar and every table taken.

A three-piece band played at one end of the room beneath revolving red lights. A couple of women in tight jeans danced alone on the small hardwood floor, but slowly other couples joined them.

A woman with long blond hair leaned over their table and stared into Shane's eyes. "Hi, honey. Sorry to see you take that spill today."

He shrugged. "Win one, lose one."

"And you, big fella—" She turned her smile on Josh. "You looked great out there. You looked so-o-o-o good I'm gonna let you dance with me."

"There's an offer I can't refuse." Josh surged to his feet. "Don't let anyone have my chair." He and the blonde headed for the dance floor, laughing together.

Dinah watched until they were swallowed up by the ever-growing crowd. "He's a nice guy," she said.

Shane shrugged.

"How did you two get together?"

Shane swirled foam around in his beer glass. "I was looking for a partner. I'd been on the road with Hoby Jones but he quit."

She frowned. "I've heard that name, I think."

"He was real big in rodeo there for a while. Rode all the rough-stock events—saddle and bareback as well as bulls."

"I didn't think it was possible to quit. I figured they sent the rodeo police after defectors or something." She gave him an impish grin.

"Cute," he said, his mouth turning down at the corners instead of up.

She sobered. "I hope he wasn't hurt or anything."

"No more than usual. What happened was his wife got tired of livin' that way and told him to choose, her and the kids or rodeo."

"I guess married guys are away from home a lot."

"Like all the time. And you never know how the money's gonna be. Hoby was good, but he was never gonna be a big-money guy." He stared down into his foam-flecked glass. "Hoby was about to lose his ranch," he said so softly she could barely make out his words, "so he took a job at his brother-in-law's gas station. I think it just about killed him, but he had to do it."

"That's tough, Shane."

"Yeah, well, it's the way the game is played. He had to make a choice and he did. I bought out his half of our outfit and looked around for somebody else to share expenses. There stood Josh, and if ever a boy needed guidance, he was it. Just chock-full of natural talent but green as grass.''

''Judging by today's results, he's learning fast.''

''I told you, the boy's got a world of talent.'' Shane stood up suddenly and held out a hand. ''Dance with me, Dinah.''

''What about your ribs?'' But she was already standing.

''Three beers and they're feelin' almost as good as new.''

He gave her that crooked little grin and she was lost.

If he could stand it, so could she.

She went into his arms gently…eagerly.

CHAPTER SIX

DINAH HAD NEVER DANCED with Shane before.

Incredible as that seemed, the truth was that they'd never gone out as a couple, never publicly acknowledged the irresistible attraction between them. With the exception of gossip at Bushwhack High School, nothing had linked them romantically in the public mind.

In his arms beneath the swirling lights at the Thirsty Buzzard, she felt a sense of disbelief, almost as if this were happening in a dream instead of in a honky-tonk in Tall Timber, Colorado.

Despite the sore ribs, she sensed no hesitancy in his movements. He was a professional athlete and she'd expected him to be a good dancer, which he was. He held her at just the proper distance with just the proper firmness, leading her smoothly through a good old Texas two-step.

She found herself smiling, really getting into the dance and the occasion. Her life had been a series of catastrophes for years and there'd been few opportunities to let her hair down and just have fun.

And this *was* fun. Her hand and her waist tingled beneath his light hold, and she could no longer attribute her breathlessness to just the exertion of the dance.

"Ladies' choice!" the leader of the band announced into the microphone. Almost before she realized what was happening, Dinah felt a light tap on her shoulder. Looking around, she saw a smiling woman standing there.

The smile was for Shane, of course. The newcomer said, "Excuse me!" and stepped in front of Dinah. With a shrug, Shane took the woman in his arms and whirled her away.

Annoyed, Dinah turned to walk off the dance floor. A cowboy standing nearby gave her a crooked smile.

"Looks like we both been dumped," he said cheerfully. "Care to have a go around the dance floor with me?"

"Sure!" Dinah accepted his invitation gladly. To heck with Shane and his admirer.

The cowboy danced with more enthusiasm than skill, but he was a cheerful guy with a broad smile so she didn't mind. At the conclusion of the number, he thanked her, adding, "Sorry my date made off with your fella. Bull riders!" He rolled his eyes. "They're the rock stars of rodeo, I reckon, always havin' to fight the women off with a stick. I should be so lucky."

Dinah had to laugh at that. Bull riders *were* the glamour boys, probably because what they did was so incredibly dangerous that just being in their presence was a thrill for many.

Not her, of course.

Josh touched her arm. "My turn?" he asked hopefully.

"Sure."

Over his shoulder she saw Shane holding a short, curvy brunette. Dinah looked quickly away as an almost perverse pleasure washed over her.

Half the women in this saloon might be looking for a chance to dance with Shane, but he was going home with her. Even though there was nothing between them now and hadn't been for a very long time, she didn't have to stand in line for his attention.

Eat your heart out, girls.

THE BUZZARD GREW progressively louder and by eleven-thirty reached a dull roar. Shane had to shout in order for Dinah to hear him.

"Having a good time?"

"Yes!" She grinned. "I'm not used to wild nightlife, though."

"You call this wild?" He arched his brows, remembering how much fun it had always been to tease her. "Hell, we haven't had a single fight yet."

"Ah, the thrilling life of a rodeo cowboy." Her lips curved invitingly and she had that devilish little shine in her eyes. "Doesn't it ever get old, though? Do you really enjoy constant traveling and strange towns—strange people?"

"They're not so strange after the first time," he objected, choosing to leap over the part about traveling. Because to tell the truth, that *was* getting a trifle old.

"A license to be irresponsible." She reminded him of his own words. "I guess it all depends on what you want out of life."

He gave her a nod and a thumbs-up, but inwardly, he had to admit that irresponsibility wasn't nearly as attractive at almost thirty as it had been at twenty. More and more he was starting to think about getting a little place of his own where he could raise horses and maybe a few cows, do a little stock contracting. That's why he guarded his Someday Fund so carefully. He wouldn't be able to take this wear and tear for another ten years, that was for sure.

For the moment, though, he was in tall cotton. Hell, yes—this was what he wanted out of life. He leaned forward to tell her so but a shout from the dance floor interrupted him.

"I *said,* what the hell do you think you're doing with my wife?"

Josh turned the blonde loose and took a hasty step backward. He held up his hands to placate the angry man in scruffy jeans and a black leather jacket. "Wife? Hey, I'm sorry. I don't mess with *anybody's* wife."

"No?" The man slammed a flat hand into Josh's chest and shoved. "You're messin' with mine."

The woman, a picture of fury, looked from one man to the other. "John Rogers, I haven't been your wife since last Thursday. You've got no right to come in here and—"

"You shut up, Sharla. I'm talking to this big, mean bull rider." He gave Josh another shove. "Think you can come in here and take over all the women because you're a big rodeo star? We don't need your kind around here, mister."

"Aw, hell," Shane said softly.

Dinah gave him a questioning glance. "Shouldn't you do something?"

"What?" He spread his hands. "It's already too late. That idiot is gonna prod Josh one more time and that'll be all she wrote."

"But—"

The ex-husband prepared for another shove. "What's the matter, big man? Cat got your tongue?"

And for the third time, he laid both palms flat on Josh's chest.

He didn't get a chance to push, though. Instead, Josh looked him right in the eye and said very clearly, "You made me do this."

A quick upward shove and the man's arms flew wide. Josh reached out, caught the man beneath the chin with a cupped hand and flung him staggering backward.

"Why, you—"

The man righted himself; Sharla screamed; Josh's chest rose in a massive sigh. "Why do these things always happen to me?'' he inquired just before the man roared forward and plowed into his chest.

Josh stumbled and hung on to the other guy for balance. Then he pushed his assailant upright and hauled back his fist to end the fight right there. Unfortunately, someone behind him caught his arm. John Rogers saw his chance and took it, landing a solid right to Josh's jaw while his arm was pinned.

"That does it." Shane stood, hitching up the waistband of his jeans. "Sorry, Dinah, but—"

"Don't apologize," she shouted. "Do something!"

DINAH, JOSH AND SHANE RAN through the dark back streets of Tall Timber, Colorado, laughing so hard it was difficult to keep moving. They'd slipped out the back door of the Thirsty Buzzard just as the cops came through the front. Because they'd walked the few blocks into town from the rodeo grounds, their only means of escape was by foot. Which was just as well, for vehicles of all descriptions screeched around in the parking lot, generally getting into one another's way.

It hadn't been much of a fight but had all the makings of a first-class riot between those trying to get closer to the action and those trying to get away from it. Dinah didn't think Josh and Shane would have had much trouble handling the opposition if the bar hadn't been so crowded. Most of the men seemed to be getting into the spirit of the occasion, unfortunately, and fists were flying at random.

It had obviously been time to bail. Grabbing Dinah between them, they'd made their break.

Stopping next to a Dumpster near a dark corner, the three leaned over and struggled to catch their collective breath, although laughter made that difficult. Josh flung an arm over Dinah's heaving shoulders and another over Shane's.

"Thanks, friends," he declared. "Why do these things always happen to me?"

"Just lucky." Shane cleared his throat and straightened gingerly, shaking his head in disbelief. "Josh, you might want to consider giving up dancing. You always seem to pick the girls with jealous boyfriends."

"They pick me," Josh objected. "I wouldn't mess with a married woman, you know that." He shook his head for emphasis.

"I believe you," Dinah assured him. She patted his arm. "All's well that ends well. Besides, that was more fun than I've had in a month of Sundays."

"You know, you're all right," Josh said approvingly. He turned back the way they'd just come. "Don't wait up for me, okay?"

She stared after him as he moved beneath a street lamp. "Where in the world are you going now?"

"Back to the Buzzard," he said cheerfully. "I wanna see how it ended up."

Dumbfounded, she watched him walk quickly away until he was lost in the shadows. "Do you believe that guy?" she asked.

"There was a time I'd have done the same," Shane said with a shrug. "Now all I want is to go to bed."

That word shot right through her: *bed*. She shivered. "Good idea. I'm tired, too. I'm not used to these late hours."

"You're too young to be one of those early-to-bed types." Sliding an arm around her shoulders, he guided her toward the street. "But then, Bushwhack isn't exactly the entertainment capital of Colorado."

She probably ought to pull away from his loose embrace, but that would doubtless be construed as a hostile or cowardly move. After dancing with him, drinking with him, running away from the cops with him, she could at least let this comfortable camaraderie last a bit longer. She didn't think he'd misunderstand.

"Don't you bad-mouth Bushwhack," she said lightly. Then, because it was more comfortable to do so, she wrapped an arm loosely around his lean waist. He didn't flinch so she mustn't have hurt his ribs. Or maybe they were anesthetized by the beers.

If she'd hurt anyone, it was herself, she quickly realized. They were in a walking embrace, and she felt a thrill dart up her arm and settle somewhere in the vicinity of her heart.

He looked down at her as they walked along. "You've never lived anywhere but Bushwhack, have you."

"No. I never wanted to. It's home."

"I've never had a place I was willing to call home." There was no self-pity in his tone. Obviously he'd just made a statement of fact, to his way of thinking.

"That's not true," she objected. Stepping off a curb, she found herself partially turned so that the side of her breast brushed against him. They both gasped and she assumed she'd hurt him. Pulling back a little, she said, "The Flying H was your home. Dad treated you like a son."

"Your father was a good man. I was real sorry to hear about what happened to him."

If he was such a good man, why didn't you stay and face him instead of running? she wondered. But that was water under the bridge. She knew why he'd run: to get away from *her*.

They were approaching the rodeo grounds. Just on the other side of the gate was the field where trucks and pickups and trailers were parked. She stumbled over an uneven patch of ground, and he tightened his grip until she could catch her balance.

She was more breathless than she should have been but still managed to say, "There are a lot of good men in Bushwhack, and good women, too. However you may feel about it, they consider you one of their own. They've followed your career and rooted for you all the way."

"I always appreciate a good fan."

They stopped in front of the small trailer, which was completely dark inside. Still touching, they faced each other.

"They're more than fans," she argued. "They're friends."

"Are *you* a friend, Dinah?"

She slid her hand away from his waist. "I...hope so."

He didn't take his own hand from her shoulder. "You could be more than a friend, if you wanted to. Things have changed. Our situation isn't like it was before."

"It sure as hell isn't." She felt a flash of temper but tamped it down. It was incredibly difficult to stand here and pretend that his touch wasn't tightening her stomach into a knot. "Just out of curiosity, what makes you think I'd ever want to be more than a friend?"

"This," he said, stroking the tense shoulder muscles between her neck and arm. "You're trembling like an aspen leaf."

"I'm cold," she said. "I'd better get on inside. You did say I could have the trailer, right?"

"Uh-huh. I'll sleep in the back of the pickup, unless..."

He'd reached her throat, her vulnerable throat, and it took a great effort for her to speak. "There's no 'unless' about it. Good night, Shane."

"Good night, Dinah."

And they just stood there staring at each other by the

light of a bare bulb suspended from a pole. She wanted to pull away, wanted to open the trailer door and walk inside with dignity, but she might as well be rooted to the spot. She couldn't move, she couldn't speak. She could only stare at him with wide eyes and parted lips and wonder why he didn't just go ahead and kiss her.

Then he did, leaning down until his dark shadow blotted out the light bulb and the parking lot and the whole darn world. His lips touched hers so lightly and sweetly that she sighed and, after a moment's hesitation, slid her arms around his neck.

Shane hooked one hand around the back of her head and the other around her waist. In a flash, she found herself plastered to his rock-hard body. Instinctively she angled her head to increase the contact of his mouth with hers. As she did, his lips parted and his tongue arrowed into her mouth with unerring accuracy.

She'd never been kissed so possessively in her life—not by Shane and certainly not by her late husband. This man took away her breath and her self-possession. She clung to him dizzily, eyes closed, slipping deeper into euphoria.

He left her mouth and nibbled his way to her ear. She shivered against the moist, warm rush of his breath and a tiny groan escaped her.

He sucked her earlobe briefly between his lips. "I could come inside," he murmured. "Wouldn't you like that, Dinah?"

She swallowed hard and forced her eyes wide. "I might...at the time. But I'd hate us both tomorrow."

"Why? We're not kids anymore," he argued between light kisses trailed down the side of her neck. "Why shouldn't we act like grown-ups?"

The hazy glow he'd created receded, letting in a ray of

reality. She put her hands on his chest and pushed back a fraction. "I don't think so," she said.

"Aah…," He sighed, his face magnificent in light and shadow. "And here we were getting along so well. It just seems a shame to call it a night."

She stepped back and he let his arms fall away. "Which isn't a nearly good enough reason to go to bed with someone." She was proud of herself for saying it lightly. "You've probably got time to go back to town and find someone a little more agreeable."

"I don't want anyone agreeable, I want you."

He said it so mournfully she had to laugh. "Sorry, I don't fool around on the first date." Or the second or the third, probably, although that was just a guess since she didn't actually date at all. Daringly she reached out to stroke his hard jaw. "Thanks for a…really interesting day and night."

"You're about to walk away from the best part." Turning his head sharply, he laid a burning kiss on her vulnerable palm.

She caught her breath. "It won't be the first time. See you tomorrow."

"Tomorrow."

He opened the trailer door, which hadn't even been locked, and reached inside to flip on the light. She moved up onto the one low step, and as she entered, she felt a pat on her bottom and heard a cheerful, "Good night, Dinah. Sweet dreams."

She probably should have been offended or angry, but instead, she found herself smiling. Who was she kidding? A pat on the fanny from Shane after a sizzling kiss was not to be confused with sexual harassment.

More like a sexual promise—one she didn't intend to investigate further.

SHANE PULLED AN ARMLOAD of blankets from behind the seat in the pickup and tossed them into the truck bed. Groaning, he wrapped one around him and settled down with another for a pillow.

He could hear water running inside the trailer. He grinned, thinking about Dinah maneuvering around inside the postage-stamp-size bathroom. A vision of her all wet and shiny and naked drifted into his mind and he closed his eyes for a moment the better to enjoy it.

Dinah had grown up real nice, but apparently she didn't spread that niceness around. Which was okay with Shane. He might be momentarily disappointed, but that was only a temporary setback, preferable to discovering that she'd turned into one of those damned buckle bunnies who occasionally made his life hell.

Not that he'd expect anything different from the daughter of Big Tom Hoyt. Big Tom's standards were high and he'd expected the same from those around him. That attitude had sure as hell influenced the young Shane Daniels, which was why he panicked when he heard Big Tom was after him.

Shane had trifled with the rancher's daughter, and he'd have been willing to pay for that in any coin Tom selected, save one: Shane simply couldn't bear the man's disappointment. Tom had believed in Shane, given him a chance to prove himself, and how had he been repaid?

At the time, Shane figured leaving Dinah without a word would be easier than facing her angry father, since her last words to him had been something on the order of ''And if I never see you again, it'll be too soon!''

And all because he'd tried to do the right thing by cooling a relationship he wasn't ready to take to its next logical conclusion: marriage. Besides, Big Tom's heart was set on seeing his daughter off to the University of Colorado in the fall, and already she'd been making noises to the contrary.

The lights went off inside. Shane shifted on the hard truck bed, stifling a groan. The evening hadn't been easy on his injured ribs, but it had been worth the pain. Only now, with no distractions, was he ready to admit how much he was hurting.

Gravel crunched beside the vehicle and Josh appeared at the open tailgate. He jumped in, the pickup rocking beneath his weight.

"Any more excitement in town?" Shane asked in a low voice. No need to disturb Dinah.

"Nah." Josh wrestled with a blanket. "Cops didn't arrest anybody, just warned a few. There was no real damage to the Buzzard, either, just a little bit of broken glass. I gave the bartender a hundred bucks to defray the cost."

"Damn decent of you."

"I thought so." Laughter underscored Josh's words. He sat down and leaned back against the cab. "She asleep?" He jerked his chin toward the trailer.

"Probably."

"She's a good sport."

"She always was."

"She's got you in a bind, though."

"How do you figure?"

"She's got you goin' back to that little burg for the Fourth of July, which is gonna cost you a small fortune."

"I got myself into it, Josh. It's not her fault."

"Yeah, I know."

"Okay, what else is on your mind? Spit it out."

There was a long silence and then Josh said, "That was a real nasty wreck you had out there today."

"You're not gonna blame that on Dinah!"

"Sort of. You lost concentration, my man. Why would

an experienced bull rider on an average bull do that unless his mind was on something—or somebody—else?''

"Yeah, well..." Shane couldn't defend himself from his buddy's charge. "I won't make the same mistake twice," he promised lamely.

"I hope not." Josh sounded anything but sure. "Harm's already done, though. I heard what that ol' boy in the first-aid tent said to you about those ribs." Another silence. "You oughta draw out tomorrow."

"Nah, I don't want to do that."

"Man, you're in no shape to ride."

"So *then* what do I do, sit around and watch you and everybody else take home the bacon?"

"I've been thinking about that." Josh slid down until his back was rounded against the cab, his chin on his chest and his hat pulled low. "You could go back to Bushrod, or whatever the place is called, with Dinah. Somebody would put you up and you could live like a king until it's time to do that exhibition ride. After that, you'd know for sure if you were a hundred percent and ready to come back."

"No way could I—" Or could he? They were only talking about a couple of weeks, give or take a few days. If what Dinah said was true, the city fathers were so hot to get him back that they'd probably go along with anything he wanted.

What he wanted was Dinah. If he couldn't get her in *that* amount of time, he was losing his touch.

Still... "I'll think about it," he grunted, pulling the blanket up over his shoulder. "Gotta see how I'm feeling tomorrow."

"Okay. But if you crawl on a bull tomorrow and he chews you up and spits you out, you'll have nobody to blame but yourself."

Shane never had anyone to blame but himself. He took full responsibility for all his decisions, the bum ones as well as the good ones.

Like his decision to kiss Dinah earlier that night. At the time, he'd honestly thought it could lead to a whole lot more. He should have known better. She was, after all, Big Tom's daughter. She'd make him work for anything he got this go-around.

Staring up at a sky full of stars, listening to the occasional sound of an engine as someone drove in or out of the parking lot, he tried to will himself to sleep—and failed. Josh might have a point, but Shane hated to draw out and waste an entry fee.

Anyway, if he went back to Bushwhack early, what would he do with himself besides eat and sleep?

And chase Dinah…

He fell asleep with a smile on his face.

BY THE TIME DINAH AWAKENED the next morning, Shane and Josh were up and gone. She figured they'd be back before she was ready to pull out, since she needed to get a few things straight with Shane.

She had to find out when the mayor could expect the star attraction to arrive, how long he'd stay, and whether or not he'd reconsider claiming Bushwhack as home. Arrive on the third, take part in the rodeo and parade on the fourth and leave on the fifth, she thought hopefully. Nothing good could come of having him hanging around town any longer than that.

She dressed, brushed her teeth and combed her hair. All she'd brought inside yesterday was a small flight bag, and she tossed her nightgown and yesterday's clothing into that. When they still hadn't returned, she fixed herself a bowl of cereal and poured a glass of orange juice from the can inside the miniscule refrigerator.

Opening the trailer door, she sat down on the threshold with her feet on the step to watch the world go by while she ate. Contestants milled around, singly and in groups, some loading, unloading or leading horses while others shook out ropes, polished saddles or worked on other gear.

The air hummed with a sense of expectancy. Dinah enjoyed being a part of it, even for a few minutes. She got an occasional curious glance, but other than that, those who passed by simply smiled and waved and continued on their way.

As if it was nothing unusual for Shane and Josh to have a strange woman show up in their trailer?

She frowned and concentrated on her cereal.

Someone called out Shane's name and she looked up quickly to see him and Josh approaching. While Shane paused to speak to one of the cowboys, Josh walked on over to her.

He stood before her, grinning. "Looks like you had a good night's sleep."

"I did. Thanks for giving up your bed."

"No problem."

Shane joined them. "You about ready to go, Dinah?"

That surprised her. She'd expected him to try to talk her into staying longer but apparently not. "Just about."

"Well," he said, "slow down, okay? I'll throw a few things together and be with you in a flash."

"You'll…?" She stared at him. "Be with me where? For what?"

"Be with you on the road to Bushwhack."

She shook her head. "Wait a minute. You're going back with me now?"

"That's right."

"Aren't you supposed to ride today?"

"I was."

"Then—"

"I drew out."

"Which means?"

"I withdrew."

"Shane! Were you hurt that bad yesterday?"

"Hell, no. I'm just a little bruised, that's all. But I figure I could use a little rest and relaxation. Since the good citizens of Bushwhack are so all-fired determined to use me, I might as well use them for a few days in return, right? Josh here says they're sure to treat me like a king."

"Oh, yeah." Josh nodded. "Like a dang king."

"Well," Dinah said uncertainly, "I suppose it'll be all right—I mean, of course it will. Everyone will be thrilled."

"Including you?"

"Me?" She stared at him, taken aback. "What difference does it make if I'm thrilled or not?"

"Because," he said with a completely charming grin, "I'll be your guest at the Flying H, Dinah. Is this gonna be great or what?"

CHAPTER SEVEN

"BUT—BUT—BUT—" Dinah stammered to a halt, staring at the brash cowboy standing before her with his thumbs hooked through his belt loops. "You can't stay at the Flying H!"

"Why not?" He cocked his head and grinned at her. "It wouldn't be the first time."

Unable and unwilling to formulate her real reasons for refusing his presence at the ranch, she gave a resounding "Because!"

"'Because' is no kinda reason." He leaned down and took the cereal bowl from her numb hands.

"Because you can't, that's all."

"Dinah, Dinah, Dinah..." He shook his head sadly. "You *do* want me to come to Bushwhack, right?"

"*They* want you to come."

"But you're the one who went all the way to Wyoming to get me."

"Only because they ganged up on me," she flared, then was sorry she'd told him that.

"You mean you weren't dying to see me again after all those years?" His brows shot up as if that possibility astounded him.

She couldn't tell if he was offended or just teasing. "Actually, I wasn't. The mayor and the president of the chamber of commerce and everyone else in town thought I'd have a better shot of talking you into it since you'd worked at the Flying H."

"Well, that hurts." He gave an exaggerated sigh. "It doesn't change anything, but it hurts."

"You're right, it *doesn't* change anything." She'd ignore his perceived "hurt," since that was undoubtedly laid on for her benefit. "Old Pioneer Days only runs July 3 and 4." Jumping up, she darted inside the trailer.

He followed. The interior was so cramped that she backed up quickly and sat down hard on the bed she'd already made up into its alter ego, a couch.

He put her cereal bowl in the sink and removed his hat before motioning for Josh to enter. Then they really *were* crowded.

"Sorry, honey." Shane looked genuinely regretful. "I've decided I need a little vacation and I'd just as soon not have to pay for it. Since I've got to be in Bushwhack soon, anyway, it makes sense to go early and let the locals entertain me in a style to which I'd like to become accustomed."

This was definitely not a contingency Dinah or the Bushwhackers had planned on. She'd set out to buy his services expecting to have trouble getting him there for a mere two days. Now he seemed determined to move in early, lock, stock and barrel. She licked her lips and cast about for an escape route. "I'm sure everyone would be delighted to have you come early," she said carefully. "Mayor Woodruff has a great big house and he could put you up without any problems. But you *can't* stay at the Flying H." She shook her head decisively. "It's out of the question."

"Care to tell me why?"

"Can't you just take my word for it? It would be really inconvenient, that's all."

He shook his head. "You've got to do better than that."

"Well then, because—" She cast about for a reason other than the real one: she didn't dare let him back into her house because she wasn't sure she'd be able to keep him out of her bed.

Then there was that other reason, the one that could screw up a lot of lives, his included.

"You can't and that's all," she said, annoyed at being put on the spot this way. "I don't have the time or interest in putting up somebody who's looking for a vacation. The ranch may not be what it once was, but it still keeps me plenty busy. Would you prefer a motel? The Bushwhack Trail is really nice and—"

"No motels."

"All right, then it's Mayor Woodruff's house."

"Dinah, you don't seem to get it." Bracing an elbow on the corner of the counter, he leaned forward with a charming smile. A lock of dark hair fell across his forehead, adding to his rakish air. "It's the Flying H or nothing."

"Then it's nothing," she retorted hotly. She couldn't, she just *couldn't* let him into her home…into her life.

"Don't you think you better check that out with the folks who put up the money to buy me? I don't think they'll be too happy if I don't show up at all, especially when they've already got flyers out sayin' I'll be there."

Reaching around to his hip pocket, he pulled out a sheet of paper, which he unfolded before offering it to her. She looked at it and gasped. *World champion bull rider and hometown boy Shane Daniels will be the grand marshal and featured guest at Bushwhack's Old Pioneer Days July 3 and 4.*

She groaned. The planning committee had certainly had

more faith in Dinah's powers of persuasion than she had. "Where in the world did you find this?"

"One of the guys who just got in gave it to me." He took the flyer from her and handed it to Josh. "I expect it'd be pretty embarrassing if I didn't show up at all."

"You know it would." She resented having to admit the obvious.

"In that case, why take chances?" How could he look so innocent? "I'll just go along with you now and you can keep an eye on me right up to the moment I'm needed."

Josh refolded the flyer and handed it back. "That sounds fair to me," he declared.

"Nobody asked you!" Dinah gritted her teeth, searching for a way out when there was none. Shane was right; if he went back now, no one would have to worry about whether or not he'd show up when needed. Okay, "no one" wasn't exactly what she meant; *she* wouldn't have to worry. "I've got to call the mayor before I commit to anything." She resented having to bargain but saw no other way.

"Take your time." He looked downright satisfied. "I've got to pull my stuff together, anyway."

She jumped up off the couch. "All right. I'll go outside and use my cell phone." Josh stepped aside and she stalked through the open door.

Shane watched her go, then turned to Josh with a huge grin. "I've got her," he said.

"Looks like." Josh took the couch she'd vacated. "This is the right thing to do. You'll take a hit in the standings, but maybe by the time you come back, you'll be healthy again."

"That's the plan."

Josh grinned suddenly. "Just don't get your hopes up too high where Dinah's concerned." He glanced toward the door through which she'd disappeared. "That one's got a mind of her own."

"Yeah, and don't I know it."

Shane turned to drag a duffel bag from a cabinet above the rear bed. This, he told himself with absolutely certainty, was gonna be a whole helluva lot of fun. Rest, relaxation, good food, a little bit of real cowboying...and Dinah Hoyt.

Might even come close to making up for all the prize money he was forfeiting.

DINAH WALKED FAR ENOUGH AWAY from the trailer until she was sure they wouldn't hear her before dialing Keith Woodruff's telephone number. He picked up on the second ring.

"Keith," she said, "it's me, Dinah."

"Dinah! Are you calling from the Flying H?"

"No, I'm in Tall Timber." Damn, she hated to tell him that. It would be all over town ten minutes after she hung up: *Dinah took a little detour with Shane Daniels—how little we don't know.* "Look, a problem has developed with Shane."

"What problem?" His jovial tone changed to one of alarm.

"He wants to come back to Bushwhack with me now. He—"

"You call that a problem?" Keith's glee bubbled across the line. "That's great! By all means, bring him back with you. We can come up with all kinds of extra events—picnics, ice cream socials, maybe he'll give a speech. Do you think he'd—"

"How would I know? Let me finish, okay?" She didn't like the way this was going at all. "He wants *me* to put him up at the ranch. I just can't do that, Keith."

"Okay, he can stay at my place, then." His tone said he didn't see the difficulty. "I'll be glad to do it. I can have a party for the town leaders. Yeah, a party. Shane can say a few words, maybe sign autographs. Do you think he'd mind? No, of course not. And—"

"Will you slow down?" Exasperated, she switched the phone to her other ear. "I suggested your place but he says it's the Flying H or nothing."

"Then it's the Flying H. What's the big deal? We'll make up any expense his visit may cost you."

"I'm glad you mentioned that, because I had to put in a hundred and fifty dollars of my own money to get the bid on him. You already owe me."

"Having him around all those extra days will more than make up the difference."

"But not at the Flying H!"

There was a long silence and then Mayor Woodruff said reproachfully, "Dinah, don't be a big baby. You know your daddy would have done it."

"Well, sure," she admitted uncomfortably, "but that's different."

"Dinah Anderson, there's no difference whatsoever. It's not as if you live alone out there. For the good of the town, you've got to keep Shane happy." *And there's no more to be said on that subject,* his tone implied. "When will you get back into town?"

"Later today, but—"

"But me no buts. I'll arrange a little reception for tomorrow and get back to you later at the ranch. This is gonna be great, Dinah, great. We're about to put Bushwhack back on the map!"

He hung up and she stood there, despairing. Now she'd have to tell Shane an abbreviated and whitewashed version of things she hadn't thought he'd ever need to know.

Damn! This wasn't going to be easy, starting with the ride home. But then, nothing had been easy since she'd laid eyes on Shane Daniels again at the Lost Springs Ranch for Boys.

SHANE HAD JUST ONE MORE THING to do before he climbed into Dinah Hoyt's pickup truck. Leaving her with Josh, he set out toward the stock barns.

It took a while, but he finally found the man he sought. Junior Davis, a rough-stock rider from Texas, had finished out of the money in every event the previous day. Shane had noted the man's problems with deepening concern.

Junior was a good ol' boy with a wife and kids to support. The way things were going, he wouldn't even have enough in the kitty to go on to the next rodeo, let alone send something home. It was an especially bad situation because he had his ten-year-old son, Clay, with him. A man didn't want to look like a failure in front of his kid.

Junior traveled and slept in an old minivan, which Shane spotted on the edge of the unpaved parking lot. As he approached, the boy climbed out of the van, stretched and looked around. At the sight of Shane, Clay's face lit up and he came running.

"Dad, Shane's here!" He threw himself at the cowboy for a big hug.

Shane winced with pain but didn't pull away, just patted the boy's wild hair. "How's it goin', Clay?" But his gaze was on Junior, limping around the front of their van.

"Not so good." The boy looked up with a trusting expression on his sun-browned face. "Dad didn't do so good yesterday, but he's gonna take it all today."

"I'll just bet he does."

"Anybody can have an off day," Clay said a bit defensively.

"You're preaching to the choir, boy." Shane grinned at the kid, then added to the father, "I came to say goodbye. I decided to draw out and move on."

"Sorry to hear that, Shane." Junior looked sympathetic; he'd been there. "That was a real bad wreck you had yesterday."

"Yeah, well, it happens." Shane shrugged. "Say, Clay—" He fished in his pocket, pulled out a wad of bills and extracted a five. "Think you could run over there to that concession stand and get us all a lemonade?"

"Sure, Shane." The boy took the bill and set off at a trot.

His father watched him go. "That's a good boy," he said. "Been a long time since he's seen me win."

"Hey, it'll happen. You gotta quit pushin' so hard, Junior. Look—" Shane pulled several bills off his stash. "I just remembered I borrowed some money from Linda that last time we were all in Seguin. I thought I better pay it back before I take off."

Junior's fingers curled, no doubt with the desire to snatch the bills from the outstretched hand. "She didn't say nothin' about that to me," Junior said dubiously.

Shane laughed. "That's no surprise. She said you'd probably kill her if you found out what she'd done."

"You're sure about this?" Junior couldn't resist the pull of the bills and took them into his own hands. He flipped through the stack, then caught his breath and frowned. "Linda never loaned you this much money. She never had this much together at one time in her life."

"Well," Shane said, "it's been drawin' interest, naturally." He touched the brim of his hat. "I better get a move on. I'll meet Clay halfway for my lemonade." He hesitated. "About your draw today, Junior…"

"Yeah?" The man looked up, frowning.

"Keep your chin up real high. That animal throws his head back worse than any bull I've ever seen. If you're leanin' forward when he does that, you're toast."

Junior nodded. "Thanks, Shane. I'll remember that."

"You do and you'll ride that sucker to day money. I've seen him score real high."

Satisfied, Shane walked into the crowd in search of little Clay.

Dinah, who'd witnessed the whole scene, stood on the other side of the battered van in a state of confusion. First the boy with the championship buckle at Lost Springs, now this.

She was seeing a Shane she'd just as soon not know about.

The old lone wolf Shane had been irresistible to her when she was a kid. This new nice guy Shane was going to test her maturity to the limits.

DINAH DROVE SLOWLY AWAY from the Tall Timber rodeo grounds. A quick glance in the rearview mirror gave her a glimpse of Josh, waving his hat in farewell.

She grinned.

"Something funny?" Shane asked, sprawled on the bench seat beside her.

"I really like Josh. How old is he, Shane?"

"About the same age I was when I started to rodeo."

"Where's he from?" Dinah turned onto the road that would lead her back to Interstate 70.

"Texas. He's a good bull rider and a helluva nice guy."

"He speaks highly of you, too."

He shrugged. "We get along."

Apparently Shane got along with everyone, judging by the reactions of fellow rodeo performers and the public. She remembered the expression on the face of the wary cowboy as he accepted Shane's money. It had been part relief and part remorse that he had to do it.

Shane shifted slightly and she heard him draw a sharp breath. Glancing his way, she saw him grimace.

"Ribs bothering you?"

"A little." He straightened, moving carefully. "I'm okay."

"Rodeo's even more dangerous than I realized."

"Tell me about it."

"Have you been hurt before?"

"Hasn't everyone?" His tone was negligent. "You can't ride in as many rodeos as I do every year without the law of averages catching up with you sooner or later."

"Why not cut back?"

He gave her a cynical glance. "You think they pay me just because they like me?"

"But you won the championship last year," she argued. "That's based on winnings, right?"

"Right."

"So you must have made a lot of money. Looks to me like you could cut back the next year."

His laughter was incredulous. "Dinah, do you know how rodeo works?"

"I think so."

"Just in case you've got the wrong idea, let me spell it out for you. Professional rodeo cowboys pay all their own travel expenses and they pay to enter events. If they don't place, they don't make a penny for their efforts."

"But you're a champion." She said it in a gently teasing tone, to let him know she didn't *really* believe it was all that easy.

"Past tense. I'll be lucky this year to make the top fifteen moneymakers. If I don't, I won't even get to the finals."

That startled her. "I don't understand."

"You saw what happened yesterday. I lost concentration. And sometimes the bull's no good. The score is based part on the bull, part on the ride." He grimaced. "This isn't the first time I've had to draw out this year, either." His voice became brooding and introspective. "Sometimes I wonder—" He clipped off whatever he'd intended to say.

"Wonder what?" she prodded.

For a moment, it didn't appear he would answer. Then he said, "Bull riding is a kid's game, or should be. Ten years of it and a man's lucky to be alive and in one piece."

"You wonder if it's time to quit," she guessed.

"Hell, no, that's not what I mean." He brushed a hand across his face as if clearing his head. "I'm not thirty yet, no way near ready to give up that big adrenaline rush when I drop down on the back of some big brute and ride him to the whistle. I don't know that I'll ever be ready to give that up."

She listened with a sinking feeling—not that she'd expected anything else. "Where do you call home?" she asked suddenly.

"The trailer back there in Tall Timber." He spoke flippantly. "That's the only home I want."

"Won't you want to settle down *someday?*"

He sounded cynical when he said, "You mean when I'm too old to do the damn fool things I've been doing? I don't know—maybe. Yeah, sure, I want a place of my own someday. I've got some savings but they aren't growing near as fast as I'd like."

Dinah knew why; he kept giving his money away. "What does a cowboy do when he's on a losing streak and can't afford to go on?"

"If he's lucky, his friends will come through for him. If he isn't lucky…"

"Maybe the lucky ones are those who face the inevitable and just go home."

"If they've got a home. Speaking of which, how are things at the Flying H, Dinah? It must have been hard for you to hold everything together when your father died."

There it was, the opening she'd been waiting for—and dreading. She took a deep breath, uncertain what to say but knowing she had to say something.

Before she could find out what was on the tip of her tongue, an antelope darted across the road directly ahead of her. With a startled cry, she whipped the steering wheel to the right and jammed on the brake. The truck skidded into the ditch and slammed into a low earthen embankment.

The engine didn't even die. Dinah sat there, shaking so hard her hands wouldn't stay on the steering wheel.

"That was close," Shane said calmly. "Are you all right?"

She nodded. "It shook me up, that's all. I should be used to dodging wildlife by now, but it's always such a shock when an animal runs into the road like that."

"Want me to drive for a while? I don't think the truck's any the worse for the jolt."

Well, why not? Why should she have to prove her toughness by carrying on? She wasn't trying to impress him, after all.

So she nodded. While he hopped out and went around to the driver's door, she scooted over and fastened her seat belt. She was feeling better already. There was something nice about having a man around to baby her.

SHANE LOVED ROCKY MOUNTAIN days like this one.

Driving through canyons and passes, he admired the mountains and forests and rushing streams that were Colorado. If he *had* to pick a home state, it very well might be this one. He'd choose it for its beauty and majesty, however, not for the people.

He darted a glance at one of those people. He'd told himself over the years how lucky he'd been to escape that loop of domesticity she'd nearly tossed over his head. Dinah had obviously liked the life of a rancher's daughter then, and seemed to like the life of a rancher now. He'd never heard her say a word to indicate she aspired to anything else.

Must be nice to know your place in the scheme of things.

She sighed.

He glanced at her but didn't say anything. She looked so deep in thought that he didn't think he should. He enjoyed looking at her, to tell the truth. She'd been pretty as a kid, but she was a beauty now.

It astounded him that she'd never married. He'd checked the ringless third finger of her left hand right away. She wore an Indian turquoise ring on her pinky, nothing else.

What was wrong with the men in Bushwhack?

He laughed and she glanced his way but didn't speak. Actually, she looked worried.

"Hungry?" he asked to break the silence. "We can stop to eat whenever you want."

She shook her head. "We can eat at home—unless *you* want to stop, of course."

"I can wait." Unless his stomach started growling, which was a definite possibility. "Does the radio work on this truck?"

"No. Why? Are you bored?"

He wasn't, but he said, "You're not exactly keeping me company here."

"I was thinking."

"Obviously."

"What about?"

"Oh, lots of things." She sounded evasive.

"Anything you'd care to share?"

"No." She said it quickly, then sighed. "But I guess I've got to. You'll find out, anyway."

A little shot of apprehension darted through him. "This sounds ominous."

"No, not at all." She spoke so self-consciously that he knew it was a lie. "It wouldn't have been necessary to say anything if you were just going to be in town for a day or two, but now..."

"Ah." He breathed the exclamation. "Is this where I find out why you don't want to put me up at the Flying H?"

"Yes. I mean, no." She chewed on that luscious lower lip. "It's personal stuff and has nothing to do with you."

"Personal stuff... Like, you robbed a bank and they're gonna come take you away? You've sold the Flying H and moved into town? You're married?"

"You're getting warmer."

His stomach flip-flopped. "You don't look like a fugitive from the law, and I think they'd have to carry you off the ranch feet first, so that only leaves—jeez, you're married? But—but you're not wearing a ring. You wouldn't be here with me now if you were married, would you?"

"I'm not married."

"Then what the hell?" He glared at her.

"I'm a widow." She bowed her head to look at the hands tangling in her lap.

He felt both shock and relief. "Jeez, I had no idea. I'm sorry." Sorry someone was dead, not that she was foot-loose and fancy-free. "Is that all?"

''No.'' She scooted around on the seat as far as the seat belt would allow. She looked dead serious.

A sinking feeling hit him hard and he could barely get the words out. ''Okay, hit me with your best shot.''

Dinah sighed. ''I have a daughter.''

CHAPTER EIGHT

DINAH HAD DREADED SAYING those words ever since she'd accepted the fact that she would have to take him home with her.

But actually, that wasn't quite accurate. She'd dreaded it much longer than that—ever since she'd realized on that long-ago day that she was pregnant and the father of her child was gone.

Shane looked stunned, his hands tightening over the steering wheel until the knuckles went white. He said, "You're kidding!" and his shocked voice matched his body language.

She forced a slightly quivering laugh. "Certainly not. I have a beautiful daughter who's the light of my life. I just wanted you to know so you wouldn't be too surprised when you meet her."

"A daughter."

"There's nothing difficult about the concept." He was so overwhelmed by her news that it steadied her by contrast. "Lots of married women have children."

"Lots of *un*married women have children. I'm still struggling with the fact that you were married. Who—"

"Mike Anderson."

"Mike Anderson of the Box A? The Box A right next door to the Flying H? Mike Anderson who was your father's friend?"

"One and the same."

"But—he must have been fifteen years older than you."

She had never seen Shane look so completely befuddled. What did he think, that just because *he* wasn't interested, she'd never find a man willing to marry her? "So he was a few years older," she said shortly. "So what?"

"So...so he was a helluva good man, but jeez! What happened?"

"Cancer."

He groaned. "Damn, that's a tough way to go. I'm sorry."

"Thank you."

"I'm still surprised, though." He shook his head. "I thought Mike was a confirmed bachelor."

She shrugged and straightened in her seat to look out the front window. The play of emotions across his face was dizzying and she didn't want to be looking at him when he started putting the pieces together. "Obviously, he changed his mind."

They rode for a few minutes in silence. Finally Shane said very calmly, "Exactly how old is your daughter?"

There: the question she'd been waiting for.

"Eight," she said quickly, shaving a year off B.D.'s age. Why take chances? B.D. was small for nine, anyway, and no one was going to go around spouting out her birthday in the short time he'd be there. And no one *ever* called her by her full name: Blossom Danielle. Danielle for Daniels, not one of Dinah's smarter moves.

"Eight," Shane repeated softly.

She could almost hear his mental calculations; she *could* hear his sigh of relief, which infuriated her.

"Under the circumstances," she said tartly, "I'd appreciate it if you'd watch your mouth and your attitude while you're a guest in my home."

"Absolutely."

The numbers had added up in his favor. She wanted to scream with frustration. Obviously, he was still a rolling stone with no interest whatsoever in settling down.

TO SAY SHANE WAS STUNNED by Dinah's announcement would be an understatement. In fact, he felt as if he'd just dodged a bullet.

It could easily have been him instead of Mike Anderson, all roped and tied. His stomach lurched at that realization.

On the other hand...

Would it really have been so bad? Good-lookin' woman, a thriving ranch, a kid of his own...

He pulled such unfamiliar introspection up sharply. He was a loner, a rolling stone. He'd never be happy tied down to one place, even with a woman like Dinah. But a kid would add a whole new wrinkle.

He could envy Mike that. Shane didn't figure he'd ever have any kids himself, since he was so determined to avoid romantic entanglements of a lasting nature, but he sure did like kids. He thought of little Eli Dodge, the proud owner of Shane's big gold-plated championship buckle; he thought of Clay Davis and the boy's fierce loyalty to his father.

To have a son...

A daughter would be okay, too. A pretty little girl to climb up on his lap and give him the hugs and kisses he'd have given to his own mother, if she'd been around to accept them.

Jeez. He was going way too far afield here. He glanced at Dinah, seeing her in a whole new way. "I'm real sorry about Mike," he said, meaning it.

"Thank you." Her face was calm and expressionless. "I don't know what I'd have done without him after Daddy died."

Shane frowned. "When did you say you got married? Your dad died not long after… I mean…" He didn't want to think she'd had eyes for Mike when she was fooling around with him.

"I know what you're getting at," she said sharply, as if she resented the question. "You mean Dad died not long after you left. Actually…it was much later before Mike and I…got together. But as Dad's friend, he was right there when I needed help."

"Okay, don't bite my head off." But that answer pleased him in a way.

He wouldn't want to think their brief but intense love affair had meant so little to her that she'd turned to the first available man.

It also pleased him to have another explanation for the sweet talk he'd overheard. She'd been talking to her kid on the cell phone, not a boyfriend.

Well, he thought with satisfaction, what do you know about that!

Now it was out in the open…sort of.

Dinah nearly breathed her own sigh of relief. Shane seemed satisfied with her explanation. It was unlikely he'd hear anything different from anyone in Bushwhack.

But Dinah knew the truth. She'd realized she was pregnant only a few days before her father's massive coronary, which had occurred a few weeks after Shane left. Mike, who found Tom Hoyt collapsed over his tally books, had remained at his friend's side until the end. Then he'd stayed to support his friend's daughter.

The first time she turned green and ran out of the room, he put two and two together in a big hurry.

"Was it Shane?" he'd asked, his square white teeth

nearly grinding with anger and frustration. "If that young whelp did this to you..."

She'd collapsed in tears, completely terrified. She had no idea how she'd be able to go on, to face all the daunting tasks before her. The ranch, a baby, no husband to help with either. *I'm only eighteen,* she'd wanted to cry. *I'm not ready for this!*

With Mike, she didn't have to say a thing. "There, there." He'd patted her shoulder awkwardly. "It'll be all right. I'll figure something out, don't you worry."

And he had.

"Dinah, I've thought this over from every angle and there's only one thing to do," he said not long after her father's funeral. Tom Hoyt had been laid to rest in the family plot at the Bushwhack cemetery, with Mike Anderson among the pallbearers. His mother, Georgia, had remained at Dinah's side throughout to offer unstinting support.

"Oh, God, tell me." She'd done nothing but grieve for her father and worry about her own predicament for days. She wasn't capable of running the ranch on her own, of having a baby and bringing it up all alone.

Mike patted her shoulder. "We've got to get married," he said. "Right away, so no one will know it's not my baby."

She understood immediately that this was the most wonderfully unselfish thing anyone had ever offered to do for her. Unfortunately...

"Oh, Mike," she whispered, tears in her eyes. "I couldn't let you do that. It wouldn't be fair."

His broad grin was like sunlight through clouds. "Dinah, I would be honored to be your child's father. I've always liked kids and regretted I didn't have any of my own."

"But…you don't love me. I mean, we don't love each other."

"We like each other, don't we?"

"Yes, of course we do, but—"

"That's a good beginning. Besides…" he grew more solemn. "Your baby deserves a father. The real one took off for parts unknown, which is a good thing because I'd probably wring his neck if I could get my hands on him. But that's not important now. What's important is you and your baby."

"But—" He was her father's friend. He'd been in his midteens when she was born. She'd known him her entire life.

He took a deep breath. "I'm asking you flat out, Dinah Hoyt. Will you marry me?"

He would almost certainly be the object of gossip if they did this, yet he was looking at her clear-eyed and sure.

So she said yes.

They were married at a small private ceremony attended only by Mike's slightly befuddled but supportive mother. Then he moved to the Flying H, joined their two ranches together and took over day-to-day operations.

When Dinah's baby girl was born, Mike was as delirious with joy as she was.

"My little girl," he bragged, holding little Blossom Danielle up to be admired by his adoring mother, Georgia. "I'm gonna teach her to ride and to rope, and I'm gonna buy her pretty pink dresses, and I'm—"

Gonna love her, Dinah realized. From that moment on, her admiration and respect and *liking* for her husband turned into a kind of love that eventually made it possible for her to go to his bed with a full and loving heart.

"I never thought this would ever happen," Mike murmured after they'd made love the first time, when B.D.

was almost six months old. "You were just a scared little girl when I married you, but now you're a woman." He kissed her forehead. "I guess that makes it all right."

"It's all right because I love you, Mike, I really truly love you."

And she had, right up until his death three years ago.

But now was not the time to reminisce, rolling down the road beside the man who'd unknowingly turned his back on his child. Dinah rarely allowed herself to dwell on the past. All that did was remind her of her mistakes.

"Take the next turnoff," she instructed, suddenly realizing where they were.

"I know the way," Shane said. "Don't worry, Dinah. I've been here before."

There were lots of places he'd been that he'd never be again, including in her bed. More and more she was realizing how hard it was going to be to keep her distance over the next couple of weeks. She'd do it, though, because if Shane Daniels ever got close enough to figure out her secrets, her life and B.D.'s would turn upside down.

She wouldn't let that happen, not ever.

SHANE PULLED UP IN FRONT of the Flying H ranch house and killed the engine. The two-story frame structure looked the same as he remembered it, except the paint was peeling now and the once-neat yard was in serious need of a good watering.

The rest of the place looked pretty fair, though. The barns and corrals appeared to be in good shape, and the stock they'd passed in the pastures on the way in was good stuff.

He glanced at Dinah, sitting beside him quietly as if waiting for him to make the first move. From the looks of things, she'd turned into a real rancher, no longer just the rancher's daughter—or the rancher's wife, he reminded himself. Apparently she took care of everything else before expending time or money on the house.

"Looks good," he said. "Not too many changes. That corral's been rebuilt and the trees between the main house and the bunkhouse have doubled in size. Other than that…"

She smiled. He'd noticed how much more at ease she was once they were on Flying H land.

"It's home," she said, as if that explained everything.

It didn't explain a damned thing to Shane, so he just grunted and threw open the door. Stepping out, he was met by a wiggling black border collie, who licked his hand in a spasm of delight before galloping around to greet Dinah.

"Nice dog," he said, turning to pull their stuff from the pickup bed.

"This is Maxie, B.D.'s dog."

"B.D.'s your daughter?" Jeez, he hadn't even asked the kid's name.

"That's right." She straightened. "She's with her grandmother. Did you know Georgia Anderson?"

"Not to talk to. I knew her when I saw her." She'd looked like a nice lady, too, exactly like a mother or a grandmother should look, with a kind face and a merry laugh. He hoisted his duffel over his shoulder and picked up her suitcase. "Lead the way, lady."

She missed a step. "You know the way to the bunkhouse."

His incredulous laughter cut her off. "You think I'm about to move into the bunkhouse? Think again."

Her eyes flew wide. "Surely you don't think I'll let you stay in the house with me and B.D.!"

"I sure do." He softened his stance in the face of her

consternation. "Hey, I'm an honored guest. You can't stick me in a bunkhouse."

"But I can't let you—" She stopped and took a deep breath, then her shoulders slumped. "Shane Daniels, if you take one step out of line…"

"Best behavior," he promised, recognizing victory when he saw it.

"In that case…" She looked as if she was about to say something more, then whirled and started for the house. But she'd made it crystal clear that she wasn't looking forward to having him inside her home.

At all.

"I'M NOT PREPARED for guests," Dinah said tightly. She stood at the top of the stairs, effectively blocking his way. Now that the time had come for him to actually move in, her cold feet had turned into blocks of ice.

"Don't think of me as a guest," Shane suggested with a grin. "Think of me as…"

"As what?" She grimaced. She didn't know *what* to think of him, or what to make of him, or what she was going to do with him.

"An old friend?"

She raised her brows. Hardly that.

"I sure wasn't an old enemy."

"You're getting closer," she said, trying not to smile.

"Okay, smarty, just think of me as a visiting celebrity."

"Bigheaded," she teased. "The thing is, this house has only three bedrooms."

"And there are three of us, right? You, me, B.D." His brows rose. "If we're short a room, I'd be willing to sacrifice myself and—"

"Don't even think about it." She gave him a quelling glance. "It's not numbers, it's content. I've taken the big bedroom that was my father's, and B.D.'s got her own room, of course. That only leaves my old bedroom. I'm afraid it's a little—'' she regarded him uneasily ''—feminine.''

''Yeah, pink frills and lots of lace.'' The silence dragged out and then he added, ''This won't be the first time I've been in that room. I can probably handle it.''

She caught her breath and suddenly she wasn't feeling quite so resigned to having him here. He'd brought the past up deliberately. ''If you'll give me a few minutes,'' she said stiffly, ''I can move in there myself. You'd be much more comfortable in the big room.''

''Uh-uh.''

''It's really no trouble.'' It was, but what would he know?

''I'd rather be in the room where you slept alone—or with me—than in the room where you slept with your husband. Call me old-fashioned, but that's how I feel.''

''Dammit, Shane.'' She clenched her hands into tight fists. ''I don't want any more references to—to you and me. We were a couple for about fifteen minutes and then you took off, so don't try to put me on the defensive about it.''

''Do you feel defensive, Dinah?'' He tilted back his head and looked up at her on the step above him. ''Hey, lighten up. This will only be for a few days. What are you afraid of?''

''Nothing. Not a damned thing.'' Turning jerkily, she led the way down the hall, past her room and B.D.'s, pausing finally at the last door on the right. She opened it and stepped aside to let him enter first.

He did, swinging his duffel bag off his shoulder and onto the twin bed. He stared down at the pink-and-cream coverlet with a frown. "I didn't remember that bed being so narrow," he remarked.

Her jaw tightened. "See? That's exactly what I mean."

He looked incredibly innocent. "What is?"

"I don't need snide little references like that. As far as the world is concerned, you've never been inside this room before. As far as I'm concerned—" She stopped short, biting the inside of her cheek. For the life of her, she couldn't say, *I wish you never had.*

"Okay, okay!" He tossed his hat on the bed, then looked around. "Jeez," he said. "I only saw this place in the dark—sorry!" He raised his hands defensively, palms out. "What I mean is, you weren't kidding when you said this is a girly room."

"Possibly because I was a girl when I lived here." She also looked around, seeing all the feminine touches: personal mementos and photos tucked and taped to the large dresser mirror, a stack of three small wooden boxes she'd decorated during her crafts phase, dolls piled in baskets in one corner, a ragged white teddy bear at the head of the bed.

She'd lived in this room her entire life, until she'd moved into the larger bedroom with her husband. This room held her life in many ways.

She pursed her lips. "You can still change your mind. You'd be happier in the big bedroom."

"I like it here."

"But you'll not only have to put up with all my junk, you'll have to share a bathroom with B.D." She made a face. "The other room has its own bathroom and is much bigger. Here—" She started forward, intent upon lifting his bag from the bed. "Why don't we just move you right on down there now."

He reached out to stop her. For an electric instant, his

fingers rested on her forearm like tiny embers. She jerked back, catching her breath.

"I'll be happy here," he said softly. "You run along and take care of your own unpacking and I'll just get organized."

She'd lost that one. She could only hope there weren't any incriminating personal items still floating around.

With no other choices, she gave in. "All right. After you get settled, come on down to the kitchen and I'll find something to feed us both."

"Don't go to any trouble on my account," he said. "As you could probably tell, Josh and I don't usually eat too high off the hog."

"I did notice. I'll try to do better than that."

Holding her back rigid, she walked out of the room, closed the door and collapsed against it. She felt as if she'd been holding her breath every second she'd been inside those four walls.

SHANE STOOD THERE for several minutes after she'd gone, just trying to get his bearings. He might have made light of it, but he felt downright peculiar being in her bedroom again.

Then a good feeling began to creep over him. This was where she'd lived when he knew her. These were the things she'd looked at, the things she'd used. Wandering over to the dresser, he examined the items on the shiny wooden surface: a brush, a mirror, a small glass jewelry box that tinkled out a cheerful tune when he lifted the lid. Inside lay a tumble of costume jewelry, all tangled up with her white graduation tassel.

A photograph caught his eye and he picked it up. Big Tom Hoyt beamed from the leather frame, his arm around a pint-size version of Dinah. She was grinning, too, despite the fact that one of her front teeth was missing.

When Shane's baby teeth started falling out, he hadn't grinned for about two years. He did now, though, recognizing on paper the love he'd seen in person between father and daughter. How he'd envied her that.

Something struck him then, something that made him put the photo down and back away from it.

Something that made him wonder for the first time if he'd made a mistake when he left her all those years ago. But he'd been scared and now he admitted it: scared of what Big Tom would do to the guy who'd messed with his daughter, but scared of something else, too.

He'd been terrified by the intensity of his feelings for Dinah Hoyt…feelings that hadn't gone away in the years they'd been apart.

WHEN HE ENTERED the kitchen, Dinah looked up cautiously. She couldn't imagine what had taken him so long but was afraid to ask. Had she left anything incriminating in there?

"All settled?" She picked up the pitcher of iced tea.

"Just like home." He pulled out a chair and sat down at the small table. "Nice kitchen."

She glanced around, automatically registering all the familiar features of the room: an old-fashioned electric stove with built-in bean pot, a refrigerator that spit out ice cubes only when it felt like it, a floor covered with yellowing linoleum. A small wood stove stood in one corner for those really icy winter mornings.

"Thanks," she said, and set the glass of tea before him along with a long-handled spoon and a thick ham sandwich.

He reached for the sugar. "Where is everybody?"

Bringing her own glass and plate with her, she sat across from him. "Ruben's around somewhere. I don't know why he hasn't already shown up to see what's going on. He mostly hangs around headquarters, cooks for the hands when there are any to cook for, runs errands and makes small repairs, stuff like that."

"Jeez," Shane said, "Ruben's still here? He must be seventy if he's a day."

Dinah nodded. "I'm sure he'll be at the Flying H until the day he dies. He got dragged by a horse a couple of years ago, so although he still rides, he can't do a day's work in the saddle anymore."

"Damned shame." He gulped his tea, then asked, "How many hands?"

"One full-time, but he's gone all this month to visit his parents in Texas. I've got a couple of kids here over the summer break."

He frowned. "Is that enough? Between this place and the Box A, you've got a lot of land to worry about."

"Actually…" Her lips tightened. "I sold the Box A last year. It was more than I could handle."

"Still…"

"This isn't the same operation it was when you worked here," she said, trying not to sound defensive. "I've also sold off a lot of the stock since Mike—" She bit down on her lower lip hard. "I'd be interested in hearing what you think about our operation, if you get a chance to look around."

"Always glad to give an opinion." He cocked his head, his mouth quirking up in an almost grin. "I get the feeling you think I plan to spend my time here sittin' on my butt eating strawberries and cream. In case I didn't make it clear, I'm looking forward to getting my hand in again with some real ranch work."

"Strawberry season's about over, anyway," she said with a grin. "Everyone will be delighted to have you aboard, I'm sure."

"With the possible exception of the boss lady."

"Hey," she said lightly, "a deal's a deal. I'll take just as good care of you as I know how. But speaking of people being glad to have you here, I think I should prepare you for one possible exception."

His brows rose. "No! You mean I'm not universally loved?"

His mocking attitude threw her slightly off balance. Didn't he realize how much of a celebrity he was in this small western town? But the person she had in mind was not anyone who'd ever known him.

"I think I should warn you not to expect instant rapport with B.D. She tends to be a little standoffish." And a little spoiled, too, but Dinah hadn't been able to find the strength to crack down on the child since Mike's death. B.D. hadn't been the same since.

She showed her unhappiness in myriad ways; sometimes she was meek as a lamb and other times she'd sass her mother and just about anyone else—with the exception of her grandmother, who brooked no such nonsense.

Shane grinned. "I won't hold that against her. Even a good horse can get cantankerous once in a while. I'll have her eatin' out of my hand before you know it."

"You may be the one eating your words." Dinah looked at him dubiously. "Just don't take it personal, okay?"

"Kids like me, Dinah."

"I understand that, but B.D. isn't just any kid. She's a little girl who still isn't over losing her daddy, and maybe never will be. I'd appreciate it if you'd cut her some slack, that's all."

"For you," he said grandly, "anything."

And that's where they left it—until Ms. B.D. Anderson came charging through the front door forty minutes later.

CHAPTER NINE

"MAMA, I MISSED YOU!"

B.D. rushed inside, pigtails flying. The heels of her cowboy boots banged against the wooden floors as she threw herself into her mother's arms. She wore her usual jeans and checked shirt, tails flapping outside her belt.

Dinah's arms had ached for her child and she held her fast, breathing in the little-girl scent of wind and sunshine and clean hair. "I missed you, too," she murmured. She held B.D. away and smiled. "Have you been good for Grandma?"

B.D. made a face. "She makes me."

Dinah laughed and looked up at the beaming woman who'd followed the girl inside. Georgia Anderson was a plus-size version of B.D. in boots and jeans, a chambray shirt and a Stetson perched on her gray curls. Her smile included them all.

"*Has* she been good?" Dinah asked sternly.

Georgia's grin grew even broader. "You know she's always good for me, Dinah. We never have a minute's trouble."

"And if you did, you'd never tell me."

"Honey," Georgia said, "I've been handlin' kids longer than you've been on this earth. Don't you worry about me and my granddaughter. We have an understanding."

"Yeah," B.D. piped up. "Our understanding is, Grandma's never wrong!"

They laughed together, even Shane, who'd entered the living room behind Dinah but remained in the background. Dinah had no idea how her unpredictable and high-strung daughter would react to having this stranger in the house, but there was no time like the present to find out.

Releasing the girl, Dinah gestured Shane forward. "This is Shane Daniels." She darted Georgia a questioning glance. "Did Mayor Woodruff call you about—"

"Oh, yes, I know all the details." Georgia thrust out a callused hand. "I remember you very well, Shane. You were a wild young thing!"

Shane grinned. "I remember you, too, Miz—"

"None of that, now. Everybody just calls me Georgia."

"Except me," B.D. said. "I call you Grandma. And Mama calls you Mom, even if you're not her mama for real."

"I'm her mama in every way that counts," Georgia said firmly. "B.D.? Remember what I told you?"

The little girl nodded. Squaring her shoulders, she thrust out a slender tanned hand exactly as Georgia had done. "Welcome to the Flying H," she said clearly to Shane. She darted a glance at her grandmother and added in an obviously unauthorized rush, "And will you teach me to run barrels while you're here? I saw girls do it at a rodeo and it looks fun."

"B.D.!" Georgia scowled. "I thought I told you not to spring that on him in the first ten minutes."

"Well…" The little girl thrust out a pouting lower lip. "Nobody will help me."

Shane shook her hand solemnly, his blue eyes sparkling. "I'd be glad to help, but I've only run barrels once. I got my butt—" he glanced quickly at Dinah "—my tail…I lost *bad* to some sixteen-year-old girl. It was embarrassing, that's what it was."

"Sixteen's pretty old," B.D. said, perfectly serious. "I just guess if you can ride bulls you can run barrels."

Shane's expression nearly made Dinah laugh; he seemed to consider carefully and then agreed with a nod.

"You got a horse?" he asked.

"Yes. He's not too good, though."

"You got any barrels?"

She nodded. "They used to be full of...full of..." She glanced at her mother for help.

"Oil drums," Dinah supplied. "They're in the pasture behind the barn."

"Then we're in business." Shane turned to Dinah. "Okay if I go take a look now? I want to roust Ruben out, anyway."

"Take your time. Dinner won't be for another couple of hours."

He nodded and turned back to B.D. "Lead the way, kid."

Oh-oh, here it comes, Dinah thought. Like most kids, B.D. hated being called that.

Unless, apparently, the caller was Shane. She took his hand, looked up trustingly and said, "Follow me." And she led him from the house.

Georgia watched with a faint smile. "My word," she said, "that boy is *good* with children."

"He is." Dinah couldn't dispute that for a minute. Turning, she walked back to the kitchen.

Georgia followed. "Keith told me you were fit to be tied, having Shane at the Flying H."

"Do you blame me?" Dinah snatched an apron from a nail near the back door. "I have my hands full around here without him underfoot." She tied the apron in place. "Would you like a glass of tea?"

"No, thanks. I need to get back home. I do have a message from our mayor and the Old Pioneer Days committee, though.''

"Oh, boy.'' Dinah rolled her eyes. "Now what?"

"They'd like you to bring your houseguest to a picnic reception in Rustlers Park tomorrow evening, say five o'clock. They're all set to give him a grand welcome.''

"Hope he's up to that,'' Dinah said dryly.

Georgia looked surprised. "Who wouldn't like to be welcomed home as a conquering hero?''

"That's just it, Bushwhack isn't his home and so far he's adamantly refused to pretend it is.''

Georgia grinned. "Surely he'll like the hero part.''

Dinah considered. "Actually, I think it will embarrass him.''

"Nevertheless, you'll get him there, right?''

"I'll do my best—yes, sure, I don't think it will be a problem. Just tell everybody not to get their hopes up that he's going to suddenly turn into Mr. Congeniality.''

"Will do.'' Georgia turned toward the door. "Tell him goodbye for me, okay? He seems like a real nice boy— heck, anyone who likes my granddaughter is all right in my book.'' She waved. "I'll see you tomorrow at the reception—and my granddaughter was perfect, no matter what you think.'' With an exaggerated wink, she was gone.

Sighing, Dinah sat down at the table and propped her head on her hand. Georgia had to be the best grandmother in the world. B.D. was a very lucky little girl to have her— luckier still because they didn't share any blood relationship at all.

For the umpteenth time, Dinah's guilt took over. Georgia should have been informed long ago that B.D. wasn't Mike's natural child, no matter what lies had been told. At first Dinah had been too insecure and overwhelmed to share the truth with anyone except Mike; later she'd thought they'd have plenty of time to find just the right opportunity to tell Georgia. Unfortunately, there was one thing they couldn't anticipate: Mike's untimely death.

Now Dinah doubted she'd ever have the heart to reveal the truth. And although she was convinced she was doing the right thing, she couldn't stop feeling guilty for lying to a woman she loved enough to call "Mom."

RUBEN HICKS AND SHANE DANIELS squatted in front of the bunkhouse to watch B.D. Anderson wrestle the fat little pinto into a turn, her elbows and heels flapping in a futile attempt to get a little speed out of the stubby legs. A fast, hard trot seemed to be about all the pint-size horse could manage.

Ruben shook his grizzled head. "Like tryin' to get blood out of a turnip," he said sorrowfully.

Shane threw back his head and laughed. "She's a good rider, though," he said. "What she needs is a *horse,* not that barrel on legs." Maxie the border collie lay in the dirt beside his boots, panting and watching the proceedings. Shane reached over to scratch the dog's ears.

"Try tellin' that to Dinah. I picked up a real nice little mare a while back, mouse-colored roan on her way to the glue factory—"

"They still do that?" Shane asked, astonished.

"I don't really know," Ruben admitted. "She mighta been on her way to one a them horsemeat factories. Wherever she was headed, I saved her bacon. Brought her back here, fattened her up for B.D., but Dinah wouldn't hear of it." He let out a disgusted whistle of sound. "She babies the girl," he confided in a stage whisper.

This bit of news did not surprise Shane. "I guess she's got cause," he said mildly. "Woman alone with a kid to raise and all—must be tough."

"Hell," Ruben scoffed, "that's by her own choice. There's plenty a men around here would be glad to take up the slack. But that's not my point."

"Shane!" B.D. hauled the heaving pony to a stop in front of the two men. "How do I make him *go?*"

Shane uncoiled his legs and rose. "Honey bunch, I'm not sure you can. That poor little crow bait is never gonna be a barrel horse and you might as well stop pestering him about it."

The girl's pink lower lip came out again and this time it trembled. "I'm sick of this pony!" She glared down at the hapless creature. "He was okay when I was a baby but now I want a big horse! Shane—" She looked at him with unsubtle expectation. "You *tell* Mama, okay?"

"Tell her what, shortcake?"

"That I need a real horse to ride!"

He chuckled. "I can tell her I *think* you're ready for a real horse, but she's your mama and what she says goes."

"Ruben told her but she didn't listen," B.D. said with a sigh.

Ruben stood up, his knees creaking. "We better put Peanuts away now," he said. "Your ma'll be callin' you to supper soon."

"You do it, Ruben." B.D. threw her right leg over the cantle and slid to the ground. Obviously she was not accustomed to doing her own scut work.

"Hold it, kid." Shane took the little animal's bridle. "You ride him, you put him away. Come on, I'll help you."

She frowned. "But I don't like to do that stuff." Suddenly she grinned. "You'll help me?"

"Sure. I'll be the boss."

She laughed and reached for the reins. "I bet you think I don't know how," she challenged.

"Well…" He didn't know why he enjoyed teasing her so much but he did. He also liked that ornery little sparkle in her blue eyes. "An old pal of mine used to say I shouldn't believe anything I hear and only half of what I see. I haven't seen a thing so far that makes me think you know how to take care of this animal."

"You're just trying to make me do it—I know that! Come on. I'll show you."

B.D. set off toward the barn at a trot, Peanuts following sluggishly behind and Maxie roaming around them in eager circles. Shane trailed behind the trio, a grin on his face. B.D. sure was one strong-willed little lady.

Just like her mother…

AFTER DINNER, DINAH SENT B.D. to tidy the mess in her room, an ongoing bone of contention. On her way out, the girl gave Shane a significant glance and whispered something her mother didn't catch but figured she ought to know about.

"Okay," she said when B.D. was out of sight, "what are you two up to?"

"She wants a horse. She thinks I can talk you into letting her have one."

"That again?" Dinah picked up a plate and stacked it on top of another.

"She's about to wear that poor old pony down into a little pool of tallow."

Dinah let out a spurt of laughter at an image of Peanuts melting like a stick of butter. "I don't think it's quite that bad."

He shrugged. "It is for a girl all whipped up to run barrels. Besides, Ruben says he's picked up a real nice little mare for her."

Dinah shook her head. "That horse was being sold for slaughter. How good could she be?"

His eyes darkened. "I don't think you meant to say that, Dinah. There are a lot of animals in this world, including human ones, who don't need anything but a chance."

He wasn't talking about horses all of a sudden, he was talking about the boys at Lost Springs Ranch—about himself. "Oh, Shane," she said quickly, "I didn't mean—"

"I know you didn't." But his expression remained intense and unyielding.

"I'm sure she's a fine little horse but..." Dinah hadn't seen that mare since a day or two after Ruben brought her here. She hadn't wanted to because she had no intention of letting B.D. anywhere close to the animal.

"Dinah." Shane looked into her eyes, his own finally warming. "I'm not trying to tell you how to raise your kid or anything. I just think eight's old enough to get out of the pony business and on to the real thing."

Eight—her heart leaped with apprehension. This was not an area in which she wanted him to delve. "Okay, I'll think about it," she said hastily. "It's just—God, it's hard to raise a child. There's always something."

He gave her a sympathetic look. "Which is why I don't have any," he said, his tone teasing. "A kid'll tie a man down worse than a woman."

She managed a smile but it was a stretch. And she'd foolishly begun to wonder if she'd misjudged him.

Time to change the subject. "Before I forget, Georgia says there'll be a big welcome-home-Shane picnic reception tomorrow evening in Rustlers Park. The city fathers would appreciate the pleasure of your company."

He did not look pleased. "Yeah, sure, okay. They bought me, they can boss me around, I guess."

"They're not trying to boss you around, Shane." She

was appalled he'd suggest it. "They're proud of you and looking forward to having you back."

He gave her a glance that would curdle milk. "Whatever you say. They want their money's worth and I don't blame them. Just don't expect me to lick anybody's boots."

He was getting her dander up. "What if somebody licks *your* boots, oh, mighty world champion?"

His quick grin sliced through the gathering tension. "I've been mucking out a horse stall with your kid so I wouldn't advise it." He rose. "If you don't mind, I need to talk to Ruben again. See you later."

"Okay. Later."

He disappeared out the back door and she pulled the kitchen curtain aside to watch his progress across the yard. He moved with an easy grace that she remembered too well. He always seemed in such complete control of his universe.

Dinah frowned. She wasn't in control of anything, her pulse included.

"LA-DIES and gentlemen—"

Mayor Keith Woodruff let the murmur of the crowd die down before he went on. He'd been pacing nervously next to the bandstand when Shane, Dinah and B.D. appeared a half hour late. Without a word, he'd hopped up to do his mayoral duty.

"—friends and strangers, children and our distinguished guest." Keith patted his expansive middle beneath a white shirt stretched to the max. He nodded toward Shane, who didn't indicate in any way that he was aware the mayor meant him.

Dinah shivered with a kind of dreadful anticipation. Shane looked like a champion. Instead of the usual faded jeans and run-down boots, his footwear was custom-made and shiny, his jeans new and cinched in place by a gold-and-silver buckle almost, but not quite, as big as the one he'd given away at Lost Springs.

His shirt was a bright red, and even the handkerchief around his throat was special—blue silk, which moved gently whenever he did. The only carryover was the black Stetson tipped at a jaunty angle.

When he'd come downstairs, even B.D. had done a double take. And it wasn't just Shane's exterior that had changed. On the drive to Rustlers Park, he had been downright taciturn. Even B.D., wedged between them on the truck seat, finally stopped chattering. Apparently Shane dreaded what was to come more than Dinah had realized.

The mayor took his time looking over the throng assembled in the park on this beautiful summer evening. His smile was beatific.

"Yes, friends, we have a very special guest here tonight. Let's put our hands together for our own...our native son...the pride of Bushwhack...."

Shane whispered in Dinah's ear, "I think I'm gonna upchuck."

"The world champion bull rider, Shane Daniels!"

Applause erupted around them. Shane assumed a stiff smile and nodded, turning in a full circle to acknowledge the tribute. When the sound grew louder instead of fading away, he summoned up a wave but didn't look too enthusiastic about it.

"Yes, ladies and gentlemen, Shane Daniels...grand marshal of Old Pioneer Days. Come on up here and say a few words to your fans, Shane!" Nodding, Keith began clapping again, urging everyone to join him. Soon a chant arose: *Shane...Shane...!*

B.D. looked at him with wide eyes. "Gosh," she yelled over the applause, "I don't get it!"

"Me, neither!" Shane yelled back, but Dinah knew better.

He got it, he just didn't like it. She leaned over and shouted in his ear. "You might as well go on up. They won't let you off without it."

He muttered an unrepeatable word in her ear, grabbed her hand and started forward.

She resisted. "Wait a minute. What are you doing?"

"If I gotta go up there and make a fool out of myself, you're gonna be right there to share it."

"Shane!" But he wouldn't listen, so she grabbed B.D. with her free hand, and he dragged them both up the steps in his wake.

"Speech! Speech!"

The mayor shrugged as if it was out of his hands, despite his coy grin of approval. "Say a few words, my boy!" he invited.

Shane nodded and stepped forward. Dinah held her breath. Silently she prayed that he wouldn't say anything to upset these people. She glanced down at her daughter. B.D., at least, was enjoying all the attention enormously. She smiled and waved happily to friends in the crowd, even to her grandma, who stood on the side of the bandstand with a curious expression on her face.

The crowd finally quieted down and Shane began to speak. "As the mayor says, I'm Shane Daniels. I ride bulls for a living, which no sane man would do. I used to work for Big Tom Hoyt at the Flying H so I know some of you and some of you know me."

He let that sink in and Dinah could see brows beginning to crease at the emphasis he'd put on the last two words.

"I left Bushwhack a long time ago and most folks around here were damned glad to see me go."

This was not proceeding as the mayor had planned. He

cast Dinah a panicky look but all she could do was shrug; she had no idea where Shane was going with this.

"I don't know why you people sent Dinah Hoyt—excuse me, Dinah Anderson—to bid on me at the Lost Springs Ranch for Boys. You didn't like me much when I lived here, so why you're so all-fired glad to see me now is—well, it's a mystery to me."

"Hold on," the mayor huffed, stepping forward. "That's no way to talk to your friends."

"I'm not talking to my friends," Shane said reasonably. He rocked back on his heels, still speaking to the crowd. "While I'm here, I'll do every damn—every *single* thing I can so you folks won't regret spending all that money on me. I owe a lot to Lost Springs and I don't want any of you to think you wasted your money."

He looked around the now-quiet crowd with critical eyes. "I'll ride in your parade and I'll ride a bull for you at the rodeo but—"

"Hear that, folks!" The mayor gave a couple of noisy claps. "Shane always was a good sport!"

"Hoo-ray for Shane!" someone shouted, and the crowd was off again.

Shane watched with an expression Dinah categorized as disgust. When the noise quieted down, Keith jumped in before Shane could continue.

"And while we're on the subject of things you're gonna do for Old Pioneer Days—heh-heh-heh," Keith chortled, "here's one more surprise. Boys, will you bring that sign up here?"

Oh, no, Dinah thought. *Don't spring that on him.* B.D. strained to get a better look and Dinah leaned down to whisper in her daughter's ear. "Why don't you go stand by Grandma?"

"No!" B.D. said, pouting. "I can see real good up

here.'' Pulling her hand free, she darted forward to stand beside Shane, who absently laid a hand on her shoulder.

Keith grabbed one end of the blanket covering what was obviously a small sign. ''Picture this on every street leading into our fair city,'' he boomed, yanking the covering away.

B.D.'s voice pierced the sudden silence as she read, ''Bushwhack, Colorado, home of World Champion Bull Rider Shane Daniels. Elevation 7,462 feet.''

Shane looked at the sign and shook his head. ''Mayor,'' he said, ''I'm not Bushwhack's favorite son, as you said earlier, and Bushwhack is not my home and never will be. My home is anywhere I hang my hat.''

His expression grim, he grabbed Dinah's hand and dragged both her and B.D. back down the steps again.

SHANE MIGHT HAVE DRAGGED THEM all the way to the pickup truck and right on out of town if he hadn't been waylaid almost immediately by a whole swarm of boys. Boys from six or seven all the way up to teenagers, with older males drifting over to linger on the fringes.

He didn't want to slow down but he had to; he always stopped for kids. When the first one thrust out a scrap of paper and said, ''Can I please have your autograph, Shane?'' it unleashed a torrent of similar requests.

Naturally, in order to sign he had to turn B.D. and Dinah loose, and that meant all hopes of early escape were out the window. Might as well take it with good grace.

''What's your name, kid?''

''Zach.''

''Wanna be a bull rider when you grow up?'' Shane scribbled, ''To Zach—Ride 'em, cowboy! Shane Daniels.''

''Nah,'' the boy scoffed. ''My mom won't even let me

ride my bicycle on the street. She *sure* won't let me get close to a bull.''

"Hey, hang on to your mom. You only got one a them and bulls are a dime a dozen.'' Shane patted the boy on the head and turned to the next one.

Surrounded by all those eager and impressionable young kids, he couldn't very well tell the city fathers where they could take their reception line when they appeared to pull him away. That meant shaking hands and grinning at people he'd hoped never to see again, people like Larry Woodruff, the mayor's son, and Greg Wells, Dinah's prom date on that long-ago night. Both acted as if they were long-lost buddies.

He must have been gripping and grinning for an hour when a lady he vaguely recognized as the cashier at the feed store arrived to cut him some slack.

"That's it for today,'' she announced. "We're about to starve our guest of honor to death. Now, don't worry, he'll be around until the Fourth of July so you'll get another shot at him.''

"Aw, Miz Sherman!''

"I mean it, boys.'' She smiled at Shane. "Come along with me, now. I filled a plate for you, and Dinah and B.D. are saving you a place.''

At the picnic table, they had to scoot over to make room for him to sit down before an overflowing plate of food and a paper cup of beer. He slid in, his thigh rubbing down Dinah's.

"Sorry,'' he said, giving her a slight smile that said something else entirely.

"Sure you are.'' She rolled her eyes and tried to scoot over to give him more room, of which there was precious little.

A middle-aged man, dressed like a rancher and seated

across the wooden table next to Georgia, half rose and held out his hand. "I'm Ray Porter and this is my wife, Pat," he said, indicating the pleasant-looking woman on his other side. "We bought the Box A from Dinah last year."

"Ray…Pat." Shane shook hands.

"We're real big rodeo fans," Pat said. "We've seen you ride many times."

"That's good to hear." Shane looked down at the food on his plate: fried chicken, potato salad, coleslaw, several yeast rolls and pats of butter, a couple of ears of corn.

Ray buttered his own roll. "We've looked forward to meeting you, Shane."

"Yeah?" Shane gave the couple a slanted glance, then turned to Dinah, sitting beside him. She'd changed his life yet again. He should be in Utah now, or maybe Oklahoma—somewhere with a rodeo that paid real money. Instead he was cornered here in the heart of good old Bushwhack, literally as well as figuratively, for boys were beginning to gather again, although at a discreet distance.

Pat smiled. "We've heard so much about you!"

Beside him, Dinah stirred; he could feel it through the leg she couldn't quite get far enough away. She gave the Porters a warning glance, which neither of them seemed to notice, so she stood up, uncoiling her legs from beneath the table. "Excuse me, I have to talk to our mayor."

Shane watched her go, frowning. Then he said to the Porters, "Whatever you heard, I'm sure it wasn't good." He picked up a chicken leg and took a bite.

"Depends on your point of view," Ray said, laughing. He leaned forward on his elbows. "Way I hear it, you were up for riding anything on the Flying H that had four legs."

"Just about." Shane didn't like the direction this conversation was going. He looked over at B.D. on his left. "How you doin', shortcake?"

The little girl pursed her lips. "I'm okay, but those boys *bug* me. What do they want your autograph for, anyway?"

"Beats me."

"Well," she said, "I just wish they'd go away! I don't even *like* boys."

Pat Porter smiled at the child. "You'll feel different in a few years," she predicted.

"No, I won't. Boys are troublemakers," B.D. argued. "They don't play nice."

"Boyish pranks."

Her husband Ray nodded. "Why, you like Shane, here, and he was famous for his pranks."

"Me?" This was news to Shane.

"Why, sure. Everybody's heard about the time you bull-dogged that elk and then tried to ride him. If that's not a first-class prank, I'll pay for lyin'!"

Stunned, Shane stared at the man. Nobody was supposed to know about that escapade except for Ruben Hicks, who'd been there, and Big Tom, who'd somehow got wind of it. It was one of the most closely guarded secrets of Shane's life and here it was, coming back at him from total strangers.

CHAPTER TEN

MESSING WITH THAT ELK had been a damn fool thing to do, not to mention illegal and dangerous. Shane knew it at the time, but there were extenuating circumstances. He'd been riding along in a fog, still brooding over a recent fight with Dinah, which he fully believed marked the end of their secret love affair.

The elk had jumped right in front of Shane and the bay took off at top speed in pursuit. What else was Shane to do? Without giving it a second thought, without making a conscious decision, he'd hurled himself recklessly down atop the fleeing elk, sending them both crashing to the ground.

Still on automatic pilot, Shane clamped a leg over the animal's back. When the fully grown elk sprang to its feet, there he sat without a prayer of hanging on more than a couple of jumps.

Actually, he'd lasted about three before parting company with the elk. He hit the ground and rolled over, coming to his feet and laughing maniacally. He'd lost his hat in the brief encounter so he picked it up and dusted it off before replacing it on his head.

Ruben, who had witnessed the whole thing, had predictably given Shane forty kinds of hell. In the end, though, they'd agreed that no harm had been done; the elk had taken off like a shot and was obviously in good shape.

"No need to mention this to Big Tom, I reckon," Ruben finally conceded. "It'd just get him all worked up."

Relieved, Shane had nodded. Big Tom would go on the warpath for sure if he heard about the elk incident. Hassling wildlife was practically a hanging offense on the Flying H. *Riding* one would probably get a man fired.

How had any of this become public knowledge? Shane looked at the smiling Ray Porter and snarled, "How the hell did you hear about that damned elk?"

Ray looked taken aback. "Why...I don't know. It's common knowledge, I guess. I'll bet I wasn't in town a week before I heard that story." He observed Shane anxiously. "Did I say something wrong? I'm just repeating what I heard."

"Sorry to jump on you that way." Shane put down the piece of fried chicken, his appetite gone. "I just didn't realize everybody knew about that."

"Oh, yeah." Ray nodded vigorously. "They all know."

"But don't worry," Pat piped up. "It just adds to your legend."

"Ma'am," Shane said, "I don't *want* a legend." What he wanted was to get out of here. He wasn't comfortable with all these people staring at him, not just the ones at the picnic table but those gathering around for more autographs.

Hardy Guthrie made his way through the crowd. He greeted everyone at the table with his usual debonair smile, then got down to business. "Shane, I wonder if we could prevail on you to sign a few more autographs? For the kids, you know..."

"Sure thing, Hardy." Shane rose, pulling his legs through the small opening.

Hardy's smile grew even wider. "Then we'd appreciate it if you'd sign a few T-shirts we want to auction off during Old Pioneer Days.'' He winked. "Anything for your fans.''

The "few" T-shirts turned out to be five dozen, but Shane tried to keep smiling as he scrawled his name across the pristine white surfaces. They'd paid good money for his presence here and he didn't want anyone to say that Shane Daniels didn't hold up his end of a bargain.

But he wished Dinah had hung around.

"Just another dozen and then you're through," Hardy said in that gratingly cheerful voice. "Then we'll give you your schedule for the celebration, where you're supposed to be and when, that kind of thing.''

Still ashamed of his reaction to the city limits signs, Shane didn't groan, although he sure wanted to.

OVER NEAR THE BANDSTAND, Mayor Woodruff handed Dinah a check for a hundred and fifty dollars—the amount she'd had to put in to buy Shane at the auction. At the same time, he was ripping into her for the guest of honor's earlier remarks. He ended with "And we are *not* going to repaint those city limits signs. It's up to you to get him to change his mind.''

Dinah glanced over at Shane, bent earnestly over a stack of gleaming white T-shirts. What did they want from the man, blood? "He's been cooperative in every other way," she protested. "You shouldn't have hit him between the eyes with those signs before he even got a chance to feel comfortable here again." If, indeed, he ever had been comfortable in Bushwhack. She was starting to wonder.

"That's water under the dam now.''

"That's water *over* the dam, Keith.''

"I don't give a care where the water goes," he snapped. His jowls quivered with outrage. "All I know is, we paid big bucks to get him here and he's not gonna turn prima donna on us now."

"He hasn't done that. He's been totally cooperative except on that one point." She pursed her lips in frustration. "Did it ever occur to you that it's not possible to shove a hometown down anybody's throat? I know *I* wouldn't stand for it for a minute."

"You don't have to," the mayor said. "You're not world champion of anything, Dinah, if you'll forgive me for pointing that out. Now, here's what I want you to do—"

"I've done too much already," she objected.

"This is just part of the job you took on when you agreed to make the bid for us. You've got to get Shane to change his mind, simple as that." He nodded for emphasis. "I'll say nothing further on the subject, but when the time comes for me to announce our new city limits signs, I expect your boy to nod and say thank-you."

She groaned. "I don't have that kind of influence with him, whatever you may think. Why don't you just drop that part of the celebration?"

"Not a chance. Now, go do your duty."

He walked away and Dinah sat down on the edge of the bandstand in disgust. She'd known from the beginning that she was jumping—or rather being pushed—headfirst into something she wanted no part of. She'd persuaded Shane to come here, she'd taken him into her house. Now she was supposed to convince him that Bushwhack was his hometown?

She'd better learn hypnotism in a hurry!

B.D. trotted up. She'd been at Shane's side, apparently enjoying all the attention, most of which she seemed to think was for her.

"Shane says let's go home," she announced.

Dinah's heart lunged, then began to bang into her ribs. It wasn't his home! But all she said was, "All right. I'm ready."

THEY PARTED SOMEWHAT stiffly that night.

Shane hadn't said a thing about the picnic in the park and neither had Dinah. B.D. had rambled on at length but hadn't required a response beyond an occasional "Uh-huh" from one or the other of her listeners.

B.D. always went to bed at nine o'clock, summer or winter. As that time rolled around, Dinah felt her anxiety level rise. Shane had gone outside to sit on the front steps of the house. She opened the screen door and stuck her head out.

"I'm about to tuck B.D. into bed and then I think I'll turn in myself," she said. "Is there anything else I can do for you?"

A long silence and then, "No, I guess not. See you in the morning."

"Uh…you can put your laundry in the hamper in the hall bathroom."

His low laugh came out of the shadows. "Forget it, Dinah. I'm not gonna let you wash my underwear."

"Don't be silly," she said a little breathlessly. "I washed my father's and my husband's and I certainly—"

"—won't be washing mine," he said in a that-concludes-this-conversation tone. "I know how to run a washing machine. Besides, I'm not used to having a woman do for me. None ever did, which is what made me such an independent cuss."

"So you've got no use for women," she suggested.

She could hear the smile in his voice when he said, "Now, I didn't say that, did I?"

She felt a little catch in her throat but managed to say

negligently, "Do what you want about your laundry. Good night."

"Good night, Dinah. Sweet dreams."

OVER OATMEAL AND ORANGE JUICE the next morning, Dinah asked, "So what do you want to do with your day?"

She was speaking to Shane but B.D. answered. "I want to run barrels." She glanced quickly at Shane. "Did you talk her into it?"

"Into what?" Dinah asked.

"A new horse," B.D. said impatiently. "I really need one, Mama. Peanuts is too old and short and slow for a girl who's—"

"B.D., we've had this conversation before," Dinah interrupted quickly. Her daughter had been about to say "for a girl who's nine years old," and that revelation was to be avoided at all costs. "When I get around to it, I'll look for something else for you to ride. At the moment, I don't have anything handy."

Shane stirred his oatmeal. "Have you looked at Ruben's roan?"

"Not since he brought her here last winter. Have *you?*"

"No, but I'm inclined to take his word for it. Ruben's forgot more about horses than either of us are ever likely to know."

"That was true once, but now…"

"Ruben's getting old," B.D. piped up.

"B.D.," her mother scolded, "it's rude to refer to a person's age."

"Then why does everybody say, 'How old are you, little girl?' Just because I'm a kid—"

"Whoa!" Shane threw up his hands. "I hate it when women fight." He winked at B.D. "Maybe your mom won't mind if we at least take a look at Ruben's mare later. In the meantime, I've got to get a move on.''

"What are you going to do?" Dinah asked in surprise. She'd had visions—horrible visions—of him hanging around the house underfoot all day, expecting her to fetch and carry. Just because he hadn't been at all demanding to this point didn't mean—

"I'm helping move that herd to the new pasture," he said, looking surprised she didn't know. "Ruben said you told him to see it was done."

"Well, yes, but I didn't say *you* were to do it. After all, Shane, you're a guest and—"

"Knock it off, Dinah." He shoved back his chair and stood up. Gone were the dress-up clothes he'd worn to town yesterday. If anything, he looked even better in wear-bleached denim and well-worn work boots. "I don't intend to sit around here day after day twiddling my thumbs. I'm looking forward to doing the work I usually just play at."

"Can I go, too?" B.D. jumped up, her glance beseeching her mother. "Pu-*leeese?*"

"This is work, honey, not play." Dinah began stacking plates. "You can stay here and help me, okay?"

"But—" The lip shot out and the eyes clouded up.

"If we get everything done, we can ride out later and see how everything's going," Dinah bargained. "Okay?"

"Okay, I guess."

"Cheer up, shortcake." Shane knocked lightly on the top of her bent head with gentle knuckles. "Be a good girl and I'll expect you later."

"Okay, Shane!" The smile she gave him didn't reveal a hint of the pettishness of seconds earlier.

Dinah turned away quickly. This was awful, the way B.D. had fallen for him. When he left, what would it do to her?

SHANE SADDLED UP and rode out with Dinah's teenage hands. Ken was nineteen and a student at the University of Colorado; Linc was only seventeen and a senior at Bushwhack High. Both came from ranching families and it didn't take him long to realize they were good, reliable boys.

At first they regarded Shane with awe, but as they rode along through another brilliant high country summer day, they soon began to loosen up. And talk…

Shane knew he shouldn't pump them, but he'd already seen enough to whet his curiosity. When questions about the glamorous life of a professional rodeo cowboy tapered off, he saw his opportunity.

"This place looks about the same as when I worked here almost ten years ago," he said, "but the differences I've seen haven't been to the good. You fellas happen to know what's been going on around here?"

Ken and Linc exchanged furtive glances. Then Ken said, "It's been hard on Dinah since Mike died, I guess."

"Yeah?" Just enough to keep them talking.

"The price of beef's been in the toilet for years," Linc told him. "Mike was just about to start turning this ranch into a stock-contracting operation—you know, rodeos and shows and stuff like that. But then he died and I don't think he'd told Dinah any of the details of what he planned to do. Leastwise, she's never followed up on any of it. In the meantime, most all the beef ranchers around here are trying to diversify."

"Yeah," Ken agreed. "The Bar O is running sheep, the Lazy M has brought in a few buffalo, and my dad says an old boy over to the west is ranching ostriches." He shook his head in wonder. "Does that beat all? Herding birds!"

As Shane listened to the two boys, he found himself feeling just a tad sorry for Dinah. She'd lost her dad and

Mike had stepped in. But then she'd lost him, too, and who was going to fill that gap now?

Not me! Shane kicked his horse into a lope. If he was a marrying man, sure. He couldn't imagine a nicer package than Dinah, this ranch and B.D., who appeared to need a daddy almost as much as her mama needed a husband. Shane didn't mind a little "pretend" now and then, but that was no long-term solution for the females of the Flying H.

"I THOUGHT SINCE WE WERE coming out, anyway, I might as well bring you all some lunch." Dinah slid down from her horse and untied the saddle strings, which held a large cloth bag lumpy with the food inside. "You men hungry?"

"As a wolf." Ken stepped forward to help with the bag. "Heavy," he said approvingly.

Linc followed Ken over to a broad rock, where they deposited the sack. Dinah glanced around for Shane and found him waiting for B.D. to arrive, her heels flying in an attempt to coax more than a sluggish trot out of Peanuts the pinto.

When girl and animal arrived, Shane reached out and plucked her from the saddle. He gave her a hug before setting her feet firmly on the ground.

"Ham sandwiches!" Ken waved a wax-paper-wrapped slab. "And apples. Thanks, Dinah."

"You're welcome. Dig in, everybody."

They needed no further urging. She turned to Shane with a smile she was determined to keep impersonal. "How about you? Are you hungry?"

"I'm always hungry," he said. "Back at Lost Springs, they used to call me a bottomless pit."

"Then help yourself," she invited, indicating the food spread over the rock by the boys. "You, too, B.D."

They ate in the sunshine, sitting on the ground and talking easily about the cattle they'd collected over near the fence.

"They look to be in good shape," Shane said. "Big Tom always did have a good herd—" He stopped short. "I keep forgetting this is Mike's doing now, not Big Tom's."

"That's all right." Dinah looked down at her sandwich. "They really were very much alike in the way they approached ranching. Mike tried to do what he thought Dad would have done."

Shane took a swallow of water from his canteen. "Is that what you've tried to do, Dinah?"

She sighed. "To the best of my ability. I don't enjoy the business end of it, though. The truth is—" She gave a little laugh. "I'd rather stay home and bake a cake than try to balance the books. I'd rather work in my garden than try to figure out which cattle need to be where, and how we're going to get them there."

"Still," he said, "I can already tell you're doin' a good job of it."

"If you mean I'm surviving, I guess I am. If you mean am I enjoying it, the answer would have to be not much."

Alarm leaped into his eyes. "You're not thinking of selling!"

She let out a disgusted breath. "No...not yet, at any rate. This place meant so much to my father and my grandfather that I'd hate to do that. At some point, I may have to. It's not easy to be a rancher and a mother, too. If I have to choose, I've pretty much decided I'll have to go with B.D." She gave him an impish smile. Wadding up the wrap from her sandwich, she tossed it back into the bag.

"Well, boss lady—" He stood up and brushed himself

off. "While you're here, want to take a look at what we've gathered so far?"

"Sure. B.D.?"

The girl pouted. "I want Shane to help me run barrels."

Leaning over, he grabbed her by the back of her collar and lifted her easily to her feet. She gave him an outraged glance that quickly changed into a self-conscious giggle.

"After the work's done," he said sternly. "Work first, play second."

"Play first, work second!" she challenged, but she was laughing. Running to Peanuts, who was dozing in the shade, she literally jumped into the saddle. The pony threw back his head in surprise but didn't take so much as a single step.

Mounting her bay, Dinah told herself it was time to face a few facts. Even if B.D. wasn't ready for a new mount, Peanuts sure was ready for a new rider—preferably one about four years old who'd be content to cling to the saddle horn and amble around a nice fenced yard without barrel racing options.

"PLEASE, SHANE," B.D. BEGGED. "Let me ride Ruben's horse."

He shook his head slowly and emphatically. "Can't do that, shortcake. Until your mama says it's okay, you're stuck with Peanuts."

Grumbling under her breath, she turned away, shoulders slumping dejectedly. But she didn't argue, didn't cry, didn't try to talk him out of his decision.

The kid was learning.

While she maneuvered Peanuts into position, Shane looked over the course with approval. Three fifty-five-gallon drums had been arranged in a triangle. The pair must circle each barrel in a cloverleaf pattern, riding for the quickest time. The professionals turned in times below twenty seconds, riding hell-bent for leather on a fast horse.

B.D. and Peanuts would be lucky to break five minutes. Shane brushed a hand across his mouth to hide a smile that simply wouldn't go away. When he had control again, he yelled to the pair, "You ready?"

"Uh-huh."

"Ruben, you ready with that stopwatch?"

"Ready!"

"Then let's do it. B.D., remember to go completely around each barrel without knocking it over, okay?"

"Okay!" She leaned forward in her stirrups.

Shane let his bandanna fall. B.D. shrieked and banged her booted heels against Peanuts' fat sides. The pinto jerked himself upright, looked around wildly and took off—to the right instead of straight ahead.

B.D. sawed on the reins, yelling at the top of her lungs. Red-faced and panting, she managed to haul the confused pony around in the correct direction. Whereupon he took the bit in his teeth and ran left—or trotted swiftly to the left, which was just about his top speed.

Shane snatched his hat off his head and held it in front of his face, covering all but his eyes. Tears of laughter streamed down his cheeks. Not for the world would he hurt B.D.'s feelings, but the struggle between kid and pony was just about the funniest thing he'd ever seen.

Somehow B.D. managed to get Peanuts in the general vicinity of the first barrel. Hauling hard on the reins, she pulled the pony's head to the right. The confused little animal hauled himself around and banged his shoulder into the first barrel, which toppled and rolled.

Ruben collapsed against the corner of the bunkhouse, bent over and guffawing. Shane laughed so hard behind his hat that he could barely see through his tears. He didn't know who he admired the most for trying, the pony or the girl.

"What in the world...?"

Dinah's astonished exclamation brought him swinging around. "It's—she's—B.D...." He couldn't go on.

Dinah took in the scene and began to smile. Smiles turned to muffled laughter, and then she was leaning against him. His arms just naturally went around her, and then they were hanging on to each other, shaking with amusement.

B.D. didn't give up. She wrestled Peanuts around the last barrel and headed for home, yelling and banging her heels into the pony's fat sides. Laughter turned to cheers as the three adults realized what a heroic effort girl and pony put into that final dash.

"My gosh," Dinah exclaimed, wiping her damp cheeks, "she's actually got him into a lope!"

She did, too. Shane straightened and picked up his bandanna from the ground, ready to let it fly to mark their passage over the finish line. They thundered past and he called for the time.

"Four minutes and seventeen seconds," Ruben responded, waving the stopwatch above his head triumphantly.

B.D. leaped off the back of her heaving pinto. "Is that good?" she cried.

Shane nodded, struggling to control himself. "I figured anything under five minutes would be *great*," he assured her. He glanced at Dinah, whose cheeks were nearly as red as her daughter's. Was she thinking about those few seconds in his arms? "Dinah?"

She cleared her throat. "Yes?" It came out a croak.

"Think you're about ready to talk about a *real* horse for this girl?"

All of a sudden, she wasn't laughing.

B.D. was. "Yes! Oh, Mama, say yes!" She clenched her hands together in her excitement. "I'm too old to be riding a short horse. I'm already—"

"I know how old you are," Dinah said quickly. "It isn't that."

"Then what?" B.D. demanded. "I'm a good rider, huh, Shane?"

He nodded. "She's a real good rider. If you're worried about her getting hurt—"

"It isn't that," Dinah said again quickly. "It's…"

Everybody waited for her to go on, everybody except Ruben, who wandered up just about then. The old cowboy nodded.

"It's just that her daddy gave B.D. that pony," he said wisely. "Mike picked it out special and taught her to ride on old Peanuts. Is that it, Dinah?"

She barely seemed to be breathing. "I…it's not… maybe…"

B.D. frowned. "I don't get it."

Shane did. He put his arm around Dinah's shoulder, propriety be damned. "You'll have to bite that bullet sooner or later," he said gently. "Unless you want her to be ridin' that pony with her feet dragging the ground."

"No, of course not." Sadness laced Dinah's laughter. "All right, I can see when I'm outnumbered. Ruben, about that little mare you're so all-fired excited about—"

"I can catch her up first thing tomorrow for a tryout," he offered. "She's real nice, Dinah, and just the right size for a barrel racer." He winked at B.D. "I call her Pepper. She's fat and sassy as a pup, but she's got a real nice disposition."

"Can I have her, Mama? Can I?" B.D. jumped up and down in her excitement.

"We'll have to wait and see how the two of you get along," Dinah said. She turned away, then hesitated. "It's time for you to take care of Peanuts and then I want everybody to wash up for supper, okay? You, too, Ruben. The boys have gone into town so there's no need for you to cook just for yourself. I hope you haven't already started anything."

"Nope. I was just a-waitin' for an invitation."

"Then come along."

The two men stood together, watching her go. Ruben turned a satisfied smile on Shane. "I knew all along what the burr was under her saddle," he said. "You shoulda seen Mike when he brought home that pony and set B.D. on top of him. She couldn'ta been more than two years old but she grabbed hold of the mane and hollered giddy-up just like a real cowgirl."

"Mike and Dinah…" How to phrase it? "They got along pretty well, did they?" Shane started after B.D., who was just disappearing into the barn with Peanuts ambling behind, his long tail brushing the ground.

"Like two peas in a pod," Ruben agreed, falling in beside Shane. "Never heard a cross word between 'em. And they both doted on B.D." He shook his grizzled head. "That was a real shame, what happened to him. But she cain't hang on to the past at that little gal's expense. Never heard of no successful barrel riders on *ponies*."

Neither had Shane. But he *had* heard of women who tried to hang on to something that was gone. He didn't think Dinah was that type, but you never knew....

CHAPTER ELEVEN

DINAH COULDN'T REMEMBER the last time she'd had so much fun at the supper table—even after having her true reason for depriving B.D. of a real horse shoved in her face. She sighed. She hadn't even formed the thought until Ruben said it: Mike gave B.D. that pinto. Replacing Peanuts was just another step in letting Mike go.

"Mama! Did you hear me?"

"I'm sorry. What did you say, honey?"

"That I ride in the parade every year, right? Maybe this year I can ride Pepper—can I, Mama? Peanuts can't hardly keep up, y'know."

Dinah did know but she wasn't about to make any rash promises. "We'll have to see how much I trust Pepper before we decide about that," she said. "It wouldn't kill you to miss one parade, after all."

B.D. frowned. "Shane says I can ride with him and he's the grand marshal."

"But they might want him to ride in a convertible, for all I know," Dinah said.

Shane shook his head, his grin devilish. "Not if I can borrow a horse. I can, can't I, Dinah?"

"You can borrow any horse we have on the place," she said with a smile, "even Peanuts."

B.D. laughed uproariously. "I'd sure like to see you ride Peanuts. Your feet would drag on the ground."

"Speaking of feet..." Ruben rose. "Mine had better hit

the ground and head back to the bunkhouse. Thanks for supper, Dinah. It was larrupin' good.''

"You're welcome, Ruben. Sure you can't handle another piece of peach pie? Good western slope peaches—''

The old man groaned. "Can I take a piece for breakfast?''

While she cut a slice of pie for him to take, and seconds for Shane, Dinah was struck by how pleasant the evening had been. Real family stuff.

She caught such thoughts up short. It wouldn't do to start enjoying Shane's presence in her life and her home. He wouldn't be staying. He hadn't the last time, and she knew that he wasn't a bit more interested in domesticity and home now than he was then.

But he was so good with B.D....

By the time Dinah refilled her iced tea glass and sat back down, he had their daughter—*her* daughter—screaming with laughter. B.D., usually standoffish with strangers, had taken to this one with the speed of light. Only Dinah knew why.

The secret was tearing her up. It seemed like a crime to keep the knowledge of his daughter from Shane, yet what would be gained in the long run if she told him? He still wouldn't hang around for long. He'd probably insist on sending money, which would only humiliate and infuriate Dinah. She'd gotten along just fine without his financial assistance—without *him,* for that matter.

Her heart constricted, despite the smile she kept plastered on her face. She missed having a man around the place; she had finally admitted that to herself. Once Shane was gone...

Her shoulders sagged. If she was ever going to find a man to share her life with, she'd have to go looking for one. Prince Charming was not going to ride up on his white steed and knock on her door. It was up to her.

And not just for herself, either. B.D. needed a father and would need a man's influence even more as she grew up. Having Shane around had already proved to Dinah how much she didn't like living on her own.

During a break in the conversation, she rose. "Who's going to help with the dishes?" she teased, expecting something less than a landslide of volunteers.

"Not me!" B.D. sang out. She looked expectantly at Shane.

"I will," he said. "Living on the road in that trailer, I've got pretty doggone good washing dishes. Josh always dries, though."

B.D. frowned. "I guess I could dry," she said, not sounding happy about the prospect.

Shane shook his head. "Nah, let your mom do it." He unbuttoned his shirt cuffs and began rolling up his sleeves.

B.D.'s eyes opened wide. "I guess I want to."

"I'll do it, honey," Dinah said, getting into the spirit of Shane's little game. "You go on upstairs and pick up your room. I'll inspect it when I get finished here."

"But I *want* to dry dishes." B.D. jumped up. "Please let me dry the dishes!"

Dinah and Shane exchanged amused grins. "What do you think?" he asked. "Want to give her a shot at it?"

"She did say please," Dinah mused. "I guess it would be okay. While you two do that, I'll have time to put a loaf of bread in the breadmaker for breakfast tomorrow. How's that?"

Shane whooped and hollered right along with B.D.

WHILE DINAH WENT TO TUCK B.D. into bed, Shane wandered out onto the front porch and sat on the top step.

There was nothing like a Rocky Mountain night, he thought, looking up at about a million stars. The air smelled fresh and loaded with pine; not a breeze stirred. B.D.'s dog, Maxie, came out of the darkness to look Shane over, then dropped at the foot of the steps with his chin resting on his paws.

Not a sound disturbed the quiet, not the whir of an insect or the croak of a frog. Not a sound…except Shane's sigh.

A guy could get used to this. A pretty woman, a bright kid, a ranch…and all of it another man's. Mike might be gone, but he sure as hell hadn't been forgotten. What did it take to inspire that kind of loyalty?

Footsteps inside told him Dinah had come back down from her motherly duties. Must be nice for B.D. to have someone who'd tuck her into bed each night. And if Dinah wasn't around, there was always her grandmother.

Shane almost envied B.D., even if she had lost her father too soon. Besides, Dinah was bound to bring a new one home someday. A husband for her, a father for B.D., some guy who'd appreciate all this.

Sitting there in the dark, Shane imagined Dinah wandering around the living room, picking up things and putting them back in their places, plumping the pillows on the couch. She seemed to enjoy the very tasks that so many women claimed to resent these days. An old-fashioned girl.

The radio came on, playing a country-western song about unrequited love, a subject Shane knew nothing about from personal experience. *Love* wasn't in his vocabulary. *Fooling around. Sleeping together. Sex.* Those were all words he knew and appreciated. But love?

Maxie rose and stretched, gave Shane a mournful glance and wandered off into the darkness. Shane watched the dog go, thinking that even owning a dog was more responsibility than he was interested in. He had enough trouble looking out for himself.

But this was a real nice setup for the right kind of man....

The music rose to a wailing crescendo and then an announcer came on to herald news on the hour. But first there were a few public service announcements. Shane listened with half an ear.

Old Pioneer Days! Something for everybody—

In Shane's experience, that usually meant nothin' for nobody.

Food, fun and excitement—games and thrills galore. Our amateur rodeo—

Amateur rodeos could be a lot of fun if nobody got hurt. But then, the same could be said of professional rodeos.

World champion bull rider Shane Daniels—

His interest perked up. He sat up straighter on the step and paid attention.

—will give a demonstration on what it takes to be the best. Yes, hometown boy Shane will ride recently retired Red Devil, a former Professional Cowboys Rodeo Association bull-of-the-year—

Shane's heart stopped beating and he forgot to breathe. Red Devil was one of the baddest bulls ever to buck out into a rodeo arena. He'd nearly killed Shane three years ago, broken a couple of ribs and an ankle. And Shane was lucky at that. He knew one cowboy who was crippled and another who'd lost an eye to that killer bull.

So far as Shane knew, Red Devil had been ridden only once, and that was considered a fluke by the cowboy community and not likely to be repeated. The bull had been retired less than a year ago because he was deemed too dangerous to ride.

Shane was already beat up from previous encounters

with bulls who looked like Mary's little lamb compared to this brute. He'd be a fool to get within ten feet of that killer.

And for free.

He rose and stomped down the steps, swearing under his breath.

DINAH HEARD THE CLATTER of his boot heels on the steps with surprise. She couldn't imagine where he was going, but he'd be back.

This time.

She shivered and continued sorting through the farm and ranch journals in the magazine rack. Had he heard the radio announcement touting Old Pioneer Days? It must feel strange to hear people you didn't know talking about you on the radio. He was probably used to it, though, the same way he was accustomed to people—especially kids—asking for his autograph.

Shane had such a wonderful way with kids. They all loved him, starting with the little boy at Lost Springs and continuing right on to B.D. He'd make a wonderful father.

He *was* a father.

She finished straightening the room and looked around, nervous as a cat. Having Shane anywhere in the vicinity was enough to keep her constantly on edge. She'd be glad when his stay was over, or so she told herself.

Wandering to the door, she looked out but could see nothing beyond the porch itself. She opened the screen and stepped out cautiously. Shane was nowhere to be seen.

Crossing to the railing, she leaned against it and looked up at a star-spangled night. Taking a deep breath, she closed her eyes.

"Smells better than a woman's perfume." His voice came out of the shadows.

Dinah started, then settled back down—although her pulse didn't. "It does smell nice," she admitted. "Is everything all right?"

"Everything's fine." He stepped back into the light coming through doors and windows. "Glad to see you. I could use some company."

"You could?" She sat down on the top step, smoothing her jeans over her knees. "Why?"

He shrugged, mounting the steps to sit beside her. "I think it's the quiet," he said. "It gets me to thinkin'."

"Not much time for that, traveling around the way you do," she guessed.

"Not if I play it right." He gave her a wry glance over his shoulder. "I guess it's being around B.D., but..."

"Yes?"

"It's got me to thinkin' about my own childhood, I suppose you could say."

"I don't know much about that beyond the fact that you were at Lost Springs Ranch for Boys."

"I don't talk about it much," he said. "Hell, I don't *think* about it much. But for some reason, tonight it's on my mind."

"I always wondered," she confessed when he didn't go on. "Dad did, too, but only because he thought there might be something he could do to help."

"He'd already done that." He turned his head to look at her. "Going to Lost Springs, and then coming here, were the best things that ever happened to me."

"It would have made Dad proud to hear that," she said.

"Meaning I should have told him when he was alive?" His gaze sharpened. "Back then, I wouldn't have known how, even if it had occurred to me."

"So now that it has occurred to you, tell me, Shane.

I'm interested, and I promise I'll never say a word to anyone.''

"You don't need to promise, Dinah. I know you wouldn't.''

His easy approval meant more to her than it should have, given the circumstances. She settled back with her shoulder against the railing and waited for him to go on.

"I hardly knew my mother,'' he said.

"I kind of guessed that. You don't seem too knowledgeable about mother-kid stuff.''

"That's because…'' He drew a deep breath. "They found me wandering around by myself in a laundromat in Los Angeles when I was four or five—I was apparently trying to eat detergent. She'd dumped me like so much dirty laundry.''

"You poor kid,'' she said, trying to keep her voice from choking up.

"Yeah.'' He shrugged. "The cop bought me a pack of those peanut butter crackers. I'll never forget it. Then he asked me about my mother. The funny thing is, at that age I should have remembered at least a little about her, but I didn't. I couldn't even tell them my age. I said my name was John Smith. Had she told me that? Had someone else? I don't think my name was actually John Smith, do you?'' He raised his brows as if he were being quite serious about it.

She forced a smile. "I doubt it. But if you didn't know your name, how did you turn out to be Shane Daniels?''

"Picked it myself,'' he said, his sudden laugh containing more bravado than humor. "The cops gave me to social workers, who stuck me in some institution with about a million other kids. There was a TV with two or three tapes and one of them was that movie, *Shane*. I really loved that flick—cowboys and guns and a little kid who always managed to be where the action was.''

"I like that movie, too. What about the Daniels?"

"There was a big kid there named Daniel who made the other kids play *Shane* over and over again. The next time the cops asked me my name, I told them it was Shane Daniel. They must have heard it with an *s* because that's what they wrote down and I've had the name ever since."

"And the police never located your mother."

"Nah, but they had a handicap, looking for the mother of John Smith or Shane Daniels. My guess is they wouldn't have found her no matter what name I gave them."

"I'm so sorry," she whispered.

"Yeah, thanks." He seemed embarrassed by her sympathy. "I was sorry for a long time, too—sorry for myself. It got me into a lot of trouble. I didn't think I had to pay attention to what anybody said. No wonder I was in and out of foster homes and public institutions for the next few years. By the time I hit ten, it wasn't a question of joining a gang, it was a question of which gang."

Maxie chose that moment to amble up the porch steps. Pausing before them, he cocked his head and lifted his left front foot the way border collies did. Without missing a breath, Shane shook hands with the dog, then patted him on the head.

"I was lucky I got that chance in a million. My social worker was a nice lady with a bleeding heart named Mrs. Romano. She sat me down and told me if I didn't straighten up I was going to juvie hall. If I thought my life stunk up to that point, wait till I saw juvie hall."

"That bad, Shane?"

He nodded. "And worse. But there was one alternative, a place willing to take in 'troubled youth.' That's what she called me, 'troubled youth.'" He laughed at what had to be a painful memory. "Mrs. Romano said it was a hard place run by hard men. I'd have to shape up or they'd throw me out and once I got thrown out of Lost Springs Ranch for Boys—" He sliced across his throat with a stiff forefinger.

"And you, being a smart kid—"

He laughed. "More like a smart-ass kid. The minute the word *ranch* left her mouth, I was jumping up and down and asking when I could leave. And that's how I ended up at Lost Springs."

"Where you didn't live happily ever after."

He gave her a brooding glance. "That wasn't really their fault. I went because I wanted to be a cowboy like Shane in that movie, not because I wanted to learn how to make beds and wash dishes and live in a dormitory with a hundred other boys. I wanted to ride horses and chase cows." He grinned at her. "Do you know how much trouble a kid can get into chasing milk cows?"

"I've got a pretty fair idea." She loved his smile. There was something warm and intimate about it that took her breath away.

He scratched Maxie behind one ear. "I didn't exactly turn into a model citizen overnight but I finally started to learn. To get what you want, you have to give a little."

"I'll bet you learned that the hard way."

"Don't you laugh at me, Dinah Hoyt—Dinah Anderson." He grinned back at her.

"What about Shane's last stand?"

He groaned. "You would bring that up."

"Naturally. So what was that all about?"

"Me. It was about me and the fact that there's no quit in me, never was, even when I first got there. Sam used to say I wouldn't back down from the devil himself."

"Sam?"

"Sam Duncan. He was the coach at Lost Springs, and as good a friend as a boy ever had. Anyway, I hadn't been there but a few months when I got into it with an older boy. It was winter and a bunch of us were spreading hay for the cattle. The bigger boys would shove the bales down from the hayloft, then us little guys would pull the flakes apart and spread them out."

"Sounds fair enough."

"It was, only one of the big boys thought he had to boss the rest of us. He kept pushin' me—just laying his hands on my shoulder and shoving me. I was new and half his size so I stood it as long as I could."

"Which was?"

He grinned. "About the third time he pushed me, he knocked me flat. I came up off that barn floor fightin' mad and went for him. I got him around the waist, and because of his heavy jacket and my heavy jacket, he couldn't knock me loose. All the other boys circled around us and they were laughing and screaming. Sam came in and pulled us apart. Hell, I was like a snapping turtle—I didn't want to let go.

"Sam said, 'What's going on here?' The boys all yelled, 'Shane stood up to that big bully Raymond.' And Raymond said, 'Yeah, and it's gonna be Shane's *last* stand if he ever tries that again.'"

She burst into laughter. "You poor little thing!"

"I sure didn't think I was at the time. I was struggling to get loose so I could light into him again, but Sam wasn't having any of that."

She looked at him from beneath her lashes. "But I don't suppose Sam could be everywhere at once."

"You got it. It took me four years, but I finally got that big SOB and I cleaned his plow but good. He was different after that. When he'd start picking on someone smaller and weaker than himself, I'd find him looking around to see if I was watching. When he saw me, he'd quit.''

"Always for the underdog," she murmured.

"Whatever. I guess it's no fun being a bully if you've got to watch your back. A few months later when he graduated, he took off and that was that.''

"Except for Shane's last stand.''

"Yep." He smiled. "Every time I'd find myself in a tough spot, one of the boys would say, 'Is this Shane's last stand?' Well, of course, I couldn't let that pass and I'd try all the harder.''

"I remember how it was when you first came here with that chip on your shoulder.''

"Hey, I never crossed *you*."

"You were jealous of me, though.''

"The hell I—'' He stopped short. "I guess I was.'' He looked at her long and slow. "How did you know?''

"I could see it. You were jealous because Big Tom was *my* father, not yours. Go on, admit it.''

He sighed. "Yeah, I might as well. It used to get to me because you seemed to take him for granted.''

"Children should be able to take their parents for granted,'' she said. "They should know their parents will love them no matter what, and be there for them no matter what.''

He let out a scornful bark of laughter. "Easy enough for you to say.''

"Actually—it isn't." She looked down at her hands in her lap. "My mother died when I was seven. Before that, she was here, all right, but she was always sick. When she *wasn't* sick, she was traveling to spas and resorts and health farms. I couldn't run and jump on her lap for a hug and a kiss so I turned to my father.''

"Whatever she had finally killed her?''

Dinah nodded. "In a manner of speaking. The plane carrying her to a new spa went down over the Rockies. I missed her...but not as much as I should have."

Maxie must have heard the sadness in her voice, because he put his chin on her bent knees and stared at her with soulful brown eyes. Dinah slid a hand over his head and he nearly groaned with appreciation.

Shane put his hand over hers, stilling the stroking motion. "How did you learn to be such a good mother yourself?"

"I'm not sure I *am* all that good, but I try. Georgia helped me a lot. She must have been the best mother in the world. I know Mike thought she was. But he had parent problems, too. His father played around on Georgia and everybody knew it. When Mike was about eighteen, his father was gored by a bull and eventually died of it. That's how Mike inherited the Box A."

"A lot of guys thought it was...pretty peculiar he never married."

She laughed. "He sure wasn't gay, if that's what everyone was worried about. Poor Mike was almost painfully shy around women. When his dad died, he was just starting to get a life of his own, but with so much to do, that fell by the wayside."

"He thought your father walked on water."

"That's because Dad helped him when he took over the Box A." She looked directly at Shane. "Big Tom befriended a lot of people in his lifetime, especially young people. He just liked to help."

"He helped me. That's why I was so sorry when—" He broke off abruptly, his expression suggesting he'd said too much.

"Sorry when what?"

"Nothing."

"But—"

"Hush." He put a finger across her lips, not his.

She went still, incredibly aware of the callused finger on her mouth. Everything around her seemed to have entered some state of suspended animation as she waited to see what would happen next.

He took his finger from her mouth and slid his hand around her neck beneath her braid. His grip was warm and commanding, but not in the least frightening.

"This is kind of like old times," he said quietly. "Thanks for listening to me."

"You told me things I've wanted to know for years."

"Really?" He sounded disbelieving. He exerted the slightest amount of pressure on the back of her neck. "There's something *I've* wanted to know for years."

"What?" Her heart thundered so loud in her ears she feared he might hear it.

"I've wanted to know what it would be like if we ever…got together again."

She swallowed hard, barely able to trust her voice. "Well, here we are."

"No, honey, *together*. As in intimately."

"Oh." She licked her lips. "We can't find out, Shane. Everything's different. I have responsibilities.…" The last word was little more than a groan, because in actual fact, she longed to simply melt into his arms.

"But I don't. No strings, no ties."

"Here today, gone tomorrow."

"But that means you wouldn't have to worry about getting out of any sticky situations. We could just have a real nice time with no messy complications." He pressed his thumb lightly against the throbbing indentation at the base of her throat.

"I don't think that would work for me," she whispered. "You're going to leave but I'll still be here."

"That's the beauty of it." Leaning toward her, he exerted pressure on the back of her neck to bring her face close to his. "You can satisfy your curiosity without it turning into a big deal."

It was already a big deal, she wanted to shout. Being here with him, having him touch her, was a very big deal indeed. If he kissed her, she didn't know what would happen.

So naturally, he kissed her. His lips met hers lightly, experimentally, as if he had all the time in the world. With a languorous sigh, she slid her arms around his neck and closed her eyes while he rained tiny kisses on the corners of her mouth, on her cheek.

At last he claimed her lips as she'd longed for him to do, but with a mastery that was new to her. Firm and commanding, the kiss led her step by easy step along the path to complete surrender. He touched her breast and she didn't pull away, never even thought of pulling away. By the time his tongue slipped past the barrier of her teeth, she was beyond caring about anything but getting closer to him and never letting go.

Somehow he had her on his lap, leaning back against one arm while the other fumbled with the buttons of her shirt. She should stop him but she couldn't. When his hand slid beneath the strap of her bra to cover a breast aching for his touch, she moaned into his mouth.

She hadn't felt this kind of crazy excitement since they were kids. Flaring passion scorched her, made her gasp for more—

Maxie shot to his feet, uttering a soft warning growl. Shane hesitated, his mouth inches away from her pebbled nipple. She held her breath, afraid to move.

The crunch of gravel preceded Ruben's voice around the corner. "Shut up, Maxie, you dang dog. It's just me, Ruben. I'm no threat to anybody or anything."

Except, Dinah thought, righting herself and fumbling for the buttons on her blouse, my love life!

CHAPTER TWELVE

DINAH SLID OFF SHANE'S LAP, tugging the edges of her shirt together to cover her breasts. He wanted to groan; he wanted to kill the old man ambling around the corner of the house and stopping short at the foot of the steps.

If there'd been no interruption... But there had been, and now she'd go inside and think about what had nearly happened and erect all those defenses women kept handy. He doubted he'd find her so vulnerable again.

Ruben did an almost comical double take. "Why, there you both are, just a-waitin' for me, looks like."

"Oh, yeah, just waiting," Shane agreed with a quick glance at Dinah. The buttons were safely fastened and there was nothing to give her away except the increased pace of her breathing...and the flush on her cheeks...and the vulnerable look she gave him.

"That's good, 'cause here's the deal." Ruben propped one booted foot on the first step. "That little Pepper mare is over in the south pasture. I'll go get her first thing, bring her back and get her all saddled up so she's ready when B.D. finishes breakfast. Does that sound okay with you folks?"

"Sounds good to me. Dinah?"

"Yes, of course. Just don't go to too much trouble, Ruben." She popped to her feet as if someone were pulling her strings. "If you two will excuse me, I think I'll..."

She didn't say what she thought she would do, just

turned and rushed inside the house. Shane twisted around on the step to watch her go, then turned back to the old cowboy. Ruben was looking after her with a frown.

"Dang," he said, "that was practically unfriendly."

Shane shrugged. "She's probably just tired."

"Still…" Ruben shook his head. "She's not mad about this horse business, is she? I mighta stepped over the line by pointin' out the obvious, about Mike givin' his baby girl that pony, I mean."

"Ruben, I'd bet dollars to doughnuts that she wasn't thinking about horses at all."

He looked relieved. "That's good. That's real good. Well, in that case I'll just—"

"Could you hang on a minute?"

"Sure. What can I do you for?"

"You can answer a question." A question Shane had been intent upon asking ever since the picnic at Rustlers Park. "How come everyone in town seems to know about the elk incident?"

"What elk incident?"

"You know, how I bulldogged that elk and then tried to ride the fool thing."

"Oh, *that* elk incident." As if it were no big thing, a cowboy riding an elk—or trying to. "Lemme think…"

"It happened just before I left," Shane said, trying to nudge the old man's memory. "Nobody was around but you and me, remember? I bulldogged the elk first?"

Ruben's eyes lit up. "I *do* remember that. That ol' elk tossed you good. It was downright comical to watch." He hesitated. "Now, what was you wantin' to know?"

"How come everybody in town knows what happened?"

Ruben screwed up his lined face in thought. "Y'know,

I don't recall. My memory isn't what it used to be. I just can't recall the details at the moment.''

"Think they'll come back to you?"

"Oh, sure. Always do, usually when I least expect it."

"When you remember, I'd like to know right away."

"Sure thing." Ruben nodded his head emphatically. "Is that all?"

"Yep. See you tomorrow."

Ruben ambled back around the house and out of sight, Maxie at his side. Looked like the dog was trying to make up for his errant growl, Shane thought, watching the animal stretch to lick the cowboy's hand.

Shane owed old Maxie a juicy bone for that one. If Ruben had walked in on them without warning, Dinah would likely have died of humiliation.

If Ruben hadn't walked in on them at all, Shane wouldn't be hunched over feeling like a bomb about to explode. The encounter with Dinah hadn't been planned by either one of them, it had just happened.

Or almost happened. After hearing about Red Devil, Shane sure as hell needed some loving. Looked as if it wasn't going to happen tonight, though.

Sighing heavily, he rose and went inside.

DINAH WAS WAITING FOR HIM.

She hadn't intended to, but she didn't seem capable of forcing her feet to move up the stairs. It had been so very long since a man had held her in his arms...stroked her breasts...kissed her. No, be honest, she raged at herself; it had been so long since Shane had done any of those things.

Her love life with her husband had been...mildly satisfying. She'd enjoyed making love with him but the emphasis was always just that: on love. With Shane she felt so wild and sexually charged and ready. Maybe he was right that a brief affair would end before either of them became inextricably involved.

Or maybe just one more sexual adventure with him would bring the closure she so desperately needed. When he'd left, she'd been deeply in love with him, although she'd never told him so. Since then, she'd grown up, gotten married, had a child and lost a husband. She wasn't the same person now. Shane's lovemaking couldn't possibly have the same impact on her, could it?

The murmur of voices outside ceased and she realized Ruben must have gone. She had to get out of here before Shane saw her and got the wrong idea. She'd just run upstairs and—

"You still up?" He sounded startled, as if he'd had no idea she'd be standing there in the middle of the living room.

"I was just going up," she said quickly. "Uh, what did Ruben want?"

"He's going to catch up the mare and saddle her for B.D. to try out right after breakfast."

Dinah let out her breath in an exasperated rush. "All right."

"Is it what he said—that B.D.'s father gave her the pony?"

"I suppose it must be. Peanuts is a good little guy, though. He deserves better."

"Hey, just because B.D. gets a new horse doesn't mean the pinto has to go to the glue factory." He started toward her.

She held her ground. "I suppose not, but a pony needs a kid. I don't want to just turn him out to pasture and forget him."

"Ever think of having more kids of your own?"

He was very close now, so close that she thought she

could catch the outdoorsy scent of him. "Before I have any more kids," she said, "I'll have to find a husband."

"Ah, you want to do it the old-fashioned way." He put his warm hands on her upper arms. His crooked little grin betrayed a tension not otherwise apparent.

"You're good with kids," she said. "Don't you ever want any of your own?"

He began to rub her arms, working his way to her shoulders. "I'm not good with kids."

"You certainly are." She held fast, although she couldn't control the trembling.

"Nah. Kids hate me. Why should I want any of my own? Kids are a dime a dozen." He touched the collar of her shirt, slid his hands down the lapels.

"You don't mean that."

He brushed his knuckles lightly over skin bared by the V-neckline, then reached for the first button.

"You see right through me, looks like." The button popped open and he moved on to the second. "Kids tie a man down."

"I remember what you said—almost as much as a woman does." Another button gave way, causing her to catch her breath.

He frowned at the last stubborn button. "Did I say that?" The button opened. He took the now-unfastened edges of her shirt in his hands and slowly drew them apart.

His sigh of pleasure sent equal pleasure skittering through her body. She took a deep breath, aware of the way it raised her breasts above the edges of her plain cotton bra. She wanted him to see and be pleased. Her breasts were much fuller now than before. "You know you said that," she gasped.

"Then you've heard the worst about me and you're still here." He drew her into his arms and she went willingly.

He buried his face in the curve of her neck. "Dinah, darlin', I want you so bad my teeth ache. I want you so bad *all* of me aches."

"Every last bit?" She slid her arms around his waist and pressed as close to him as she could get. She might as well admit she'd been thinking about being in his arms ever since Mayor Woodruff sent her bachelor shopping.

"Oh, yeah." It sounded a great deal like a groan. "You're not gonna leave me to suffer."

As if she could leave him, period. She whispered in his ear, "Maybe we should go upstairs and t-talk this over."

"You mean it?" He drew back to stare at her, his face dark with a passion held in tenuous control.

"I mean it."

He brushed a kiss across her lips. "I suppose in keeping with the occasion, I should carry you up the stairs like the guy in that movie you liked so much—what was it?"

"You know what it was. You're no Clark Gable, but I think it would be a very nice gesture on your part if—"

"Okay, you asked for it." Bending over, he hauled her onto his shoulder and straightened. "You all right?" He clamped an arm over the back of her legs.

Draped over his shoulder, she could barely breathe. "This is *not* the way Clark Gable did it."

"But you said yourself that I was no Clark Gable, so you can't be disappointed." He turned to the staircase and she gasped and gripped his belt for balance. She could feel the muscles of his back working beneath her breasts.

He took the stairs two at a time. At this more-than-mile-high altitude, he should be gasping, but he wasn't. He loped down the hall to her old room, now his, shoved open the door with one foot, carried her inside, kicked the door closed behind them and flopped her over onto the narrow bed. Leaning down, he switched the light on the bedside table to the lowest setting.

She hit the bed laughing. Covering her face with her hands, she shook with a combination of excitement and nervousness. She couldn't believe she was here, that she was doing this. On the other hand, it would have been the height of hypocrisy to pretend she didn't want him as much as he wanted her.

"Are you all right?" He caught her wrists and swung her hands away from her face, looking genuinely concerned.

She gulped and nodded. "B.D.'s asleep next door," she whispered. "She sleeps like a rock but we mustn't take chances."

"Agreed. No chances." Pinning her wrists lightly to the bed beside her head, he lowered himself over her. "Just a little bitty kiss to keep me interested," he said. His mouth closed over hers eagerly.

She fought to free her hands, not to resist but to grab him and keep him there. He held her still with such ease that she soon ceased struggling. If she couldn't *do* anything, she could at least concentrate on what was being done to her...all of it wonderful.

Her head spun. When he lifted his head to brush his lips across hers in tiny teasing caresses, she tried to draw him closer again.

"Not so fast." In the muted light, he smiled down at her. "Let's do this right, okay?"

She didn't care about right; she wanted *now*. But she swallowed hard and managed to nod.

He sat her up on the side of the bed, reaching for her blouse and helping her out of it. After unhooking her plain cotton bra, he pulled it off, sneered at it, grinned at her and tossed the bit of fabric aside.

Only then did he lower her back onto the pillows. "Oh, my," he said, gathering her breasts into his hands, squeezing gently. The dark head lowered so he could take a nipple into his mouth. The soft warm suction sent a sweet lassitude spreading like a wave of honey through her, leaving her limp and pliable.

He raised his head and his blue eyes gleamed like agates. "I got distracted," he said defensively, but he was breathing hard. "Gotta get you out of those jeans and boots before you come to your senses."

"I…" She had to swallow hard before she could go on. "I don't think you've got too much to worry about on that score." She reached for him and the snaps on his western shirt popped open in a wave. She touched his chest but he jumped up off the bed.

"Hold on a minute. Let's take care of you and then we'll worry about me." Grabbing her booted foot by toe and heel, he tugged. The boot inched off, taking its own sweet time. Before it hit the floor, he was pulling on the second one.

By the time he had the boots off, she'd unsnapped and unzipped her jeans. Grabbing them by the cuffs, he pulled as she lifted. In an instant, she lay there wearing nothing but white cotton panties.

He reached for the waistband but she stopped him. "Not until you've bared some flesh, cowboy." She lay back to watch with an arm bent beneath her head.

Muttering under his breath, he shed his shirt, his eagerness making that simple task a lot harder. He used the bootjack beside the closet door to remove his boots with a minimum of trouble. She smiled; the jeans came next.

In fact, everything came next. He discarded that denim with a flourish and she immediately saw two things: his ribs were black and yellow with bruises, and he had a raging hard-on.

She spread her arms wide and smiled. "Take me," she invited in a sultry tone. "I'm yours."

He pumped his right arm in the air and said "Yippee!" in a very soft, very triumphant voice. He hit the bed running.

SHE LET HIM DO EVERY damned thing he'd wanted to do to her since the minute she'd walked back into his life. She held back nothing, offering those soft hands and that sweet mouth and firm body for his pleasure, accepting the same from him and whimpering for more.

Poised at last above her, sheathed in latex and sorry about it, he felt a totally unexpected wave of tenderness sweep over him. Despite his raging need for her, he didn't want this encounter to end. More was at stake here than simply their mutual satisfaction.

What that might be he neither knew nor cared to examine. It scared him; for an instant he wavered. But she rubbed her fingers over his mouth and gasped his name and he was lost. He entered her hard and deep, arching his back to gain leverage, sliding, pumping.

Her breath came in short, frenzied pants and she moved beneath him like a wild thing. Every sense seemed heightened, every jolt of pleasure magnified, until all of a sudden they hit their peak in a shuddering, all-consuming climax.

DINAH HAD NEVER FELT so completely satisfied in her entire life. Even a whole chocolate cake couldn't give her this kind of bliss.

He flicked her nipple to get her attention. "What are you grinnin' about?" he asked, his voice filled with a lassitude she recognized.

"Shall I compare thee to a chocolate cake?" she paraphrased. "Thou art less temperate and even tastier."

"The woman's gone round the bend." Leaning over, he lapped at the nipple with his tongue. "I'm lovin' every minute of it."

She wished he hadn't mentioned love, even in jest. This feeling of oneness was not some accidental happening. She *did* love him, always had and always would. Even when she'd been angry at him for leaving her, she'd loved him.

Maybe he loved her. It didn't seem so impossible, lying here with him and filled with the kind of satisfaction she'd never encountered without him. Was it grasping at straws to hope he was here because he wanted to be with her? Maybe he'd stay this time. Maybe everything would be different.

He smoothed his hand down over the gentle curve of her stomach, cupping the nest of curls between her thighs. "Honey," he said with a sigh, "you are really something. If I still had my championship buckle, I swear I'd give it to you in a heartbeat."

She started to smile, and then, like a bucket of cold water, his meaning washed over her: he was comparing her to the buckle bunnies who chased him to hell and back every time he showed his face at a rodeo.

She sat up abruptly. "Shane Daniels," she said in a quivering voice, "you'll never change."

Still lying on his side on the narrow bed, he blinked at her. "What? I was trying to give you a compliment."

"I'll give *you* a compliment."

Putting both hands on his hip, she shoved. He rolled right off the bed and hit the floor before he knew what she was doing. Tossing the tangled bedspread on top of him, she leaped to the floor, grabbed the robe hanging from a hook on the back of the door and fled before he ever fought his way out from beneath all that chenille.

FACING HIM THE NEXT MORNING was one of the toughest things Dinah ever had to do. In fact, she lay awake most of the night planning how to handle it, finally deciding on aloof disinterest.

That lasted until she actually saw him at the breakfast table. He looked better than ever, which was curious given the fact that he looked exactly the same. This left Dinah with the uneasy feeling that she'd made a mistake of gigantic proportions last night when she crawled into bed with him.

"Mornin', honey," he said, eyeing her askance.

"Hush!" She glanced around quickly to assure herself that B.D. wasn't right behind him. "We'll have none of that. Nothing has changed, absolutely nothing."

He frowned. "Everything's changed," he objected. "You can't just pretend nothing happened."

"I can and I am." There. That should make her position clear.

He stared at her for a moment and then his frown disappeared and he grinned. "I get it. You don't want anyone to know. No problem, darlin', it'll be our little secret."

She waved a spatula in his direction. "Shane Daniels, that is *not* what I meant and you—"

"Mama!" B.D. rushed through the kitchen door, her hair straggling down around her shoulders. "Can I go see Pepper, can I, please?"

"Not until you eat breakfast and let me braid that hair," Dinah said sternly.

Her severe tone was for Shane, not B.D., but he didn't seem to realize it. He just sat down at the table and grinned at her like a cat with more than a passing familiarity with canaries.

THE TELEPHONE RANG just as Dinah reentered her kitchen an hour and a half later. Outside, B.D. rode Ruben's little mare, Pepper, in circles around the yard, her face one big smile. The horse was just as she'd been billed: small enough for a child, big enough for an adult, smart, well-behaved and sleek as a seal.

Only Ruben could have seen what lay beneath the surface of the sorry creature he'd brought home months ago. Dinah was impressed. Then she made the mistake of glancing at Shane. As he looked at girl and horse, she caught an expression that she wished she'd never seen.

But now Dinah had to clean up the breakfast table, left for later in B.D.'s rush to get outside.

As she reached for a sponge, the telephone rang again. "Hello," she said, looking out the kitchen window at the happy threesome.

"Dinah? Glad I caught you."

Mayor Woodruff. The man never seemed to bring good news. "Good morning, Keith. What can I do for you?"

"You can set my mind at ease."

Oh dear. "If I can."

"We haven't seen much of Shane in town since the picnic. In fact, we haven't seen him in town, period."

"Then by all means, set your mind at ease. He's still here." Outside the window, Shane stood beside the horse and rider, looking up to speak seriously to B.D., who nodded. Then he lifted his arms and plucked the girl from the saddle. For a moment he held her high, smiling into her laughing face.

Dinah felt a sharp pang of longing. The connection between them was so strong and they didn't even know...

"That's not what worries me," the mayor said. "I just heard that he got hurt at that rodeo in Tall Timber and had to withdraw. I figure that's why he came back with you early."

"Yes. And…?"

"Will he be in shape to ride? This is important, Dinah. We're advertising this all the way to Denver. We're selling rodeo tickets like hotcakes and I don't even want to *think* about what will happen if he doesn't come through for us."

Dinah flashed back on a picture from the night before: a tall naked cowboy with a raging hard-on and ribs the color of storm clouds. Her cheeks grew warm at the memory and she was grateful the mayor couldn't see her. "I'm…sure you have nothing to worry about."

Outside, Shane worked to adjust the saddle, B.D. nodding at his side. He was teaching her as Mike had taught her. While Dinah watched, he lifted the little girl and sat her back atop the roan. Dinah's throat closed on a floodtide of emotion.

"I don't like the way you said that," the mayor continued to complain. "You hesitated. I am not reassured."

"Keith, what am I supposed to do? This is your problem." And if she were pressed, she'd have to admit she wasn't at all sure she wanted Shane to ride, anyway. The memory of a furious bull tossing him around the arena at Tall Timber was still too fresh.

"Just double-check this for me, okay? I'm sure there's nothing to worry about, but why take chances?"

"What would you do if he said he couldn't ride? It's not likely you'd find a replacement at this late date."

"Wouldn't look for one," Keith admitted. He laughed ruefully. "But it would give me time to make up my mind whether to shoot myself or make a run for Mexico. Because if Old Pioneer Days doesn't break all records this year, my name around here will be mud. My neck is on the line, Dinah. Just ask him and make sure, okay?''

WHEN SHANE CAME THROUGH the back door, Dinah was up to her elbows in soapy dishwater. ''Did you see her?'' he demanded. ''What a girl!''

Dinah glanced at him without smiling. She mustn't give him any encouragement. ''I saw. She's doing great.''

He crossed the room to stand beside her at the sink, plucking a glass she'd just washed from the dish drainer. Filling it with water from the faucet, he drank. ''She'd like to ride out with me and Ruben this morning. We'll be trailing that herd to the new pasture and she won't be in our way.''

That drew a reluctant smile. ''She will, but if you don't mind, I guess it's okay with me. I have to go into town for supplies, anyway, and B.D. hates that.''

''Then it's settled. I'll watch out for her.'' He started to turn away.

''Before you go—''

He turned back, brows rising in question.

''Mayor Woodruff called. He heard about you getting hurt at Tall Timber and he's concerned that you may not be well enough to ride at Old Pioneer Days.''

His eyes narrowed with annoyance. ''Did you reassure him?''

''No.'' Her gaze held his.

''Why not?''

''Because I'm not sure myself—not sure you should try it, I mean. I—'' she licked her lips ''—saw how bruised and beat-up you are, remember?''

''Ah.'' Her explanation seemed to reassure him. ''You saw that and a whole lot more.''

Her cheeks burned. "Please, Shane, I'm trying to be serious. Keith is scared to death that you'll leave him and the town in the lurch, and I'm…" She worried her lower lip with her teeth. "I don't want to be responsible for getting you hurt again if you're not a hundred percent."

His temper flared. "If I only rode when I was a hundred percent, I might have to give up rodeo entirely," he snapped. "But don't worry, Dinah. Whatever I do will be because I want to, not because you talked me into anything. You don't have to feel responsible for what I do."

"I didn't mean it that way, Shane. I just meant—"

"Let it go—and tell the mayor he can relax. I do what I say I'll do, what I'm bought and paid for."

He stomped out of the kitchen and she watched him walk across the yard to rejoin Ruben and B.D., who were waiting in front of the bunkhouse. And she knew that if he got hurt at Old Pioneer Days, she'd feel responsible no matter what he said.

If he didn't ride, she'd feel responsible for that, too.

Talk about a rock and a hard place…

CHAPTER THIRTEEN

RELAX, SHANE HAD TOLD HER. *I do what I say I'll do, what I'm bought and paid for.*

Sure I do, he thought after he'd had time to cool down. *Everyone can relax except me, and I'll worry when the time comes. Hell, I'm feeling better every day....*

In the meantime, he was having too damned much fun to think about what the future might hold. Working with horses and cattle and the kid was just the vacation he needed. He woke up smiling every morning.

And went to bed scowling every night because it quickly became clear that Dinah had no intention of gracing his bed with her presence again. The first time she turned him down after their lovemaking, he'd been confused; the second time he was annoyed; the third time he started to get a little panicky.

This could easily have been any cowboy's dream vacation. Why'd she have to go and get all uptight on him now?

The day he nearly blew the whole thing, he was thinking of Dinah instead of the business at hand. One of the kid cowboys had brought in a black and a couple of bays that had been running loose since last fall and put them in one of the corrals. When Dinah announced she was going to ride the black that day, Shane put his foot down.

"Not until I work out the kinks, you won't."

"Oh, for heaven's sake." She planted her fists on her

hips and glared at him. "I know that horse and he's no bucker. A couple of hops and he'll settle down."

"We'll play it safe just the same."

The black rounded his back beneath the saddle but Shane got the cinch good and tight, anyway. He swung into the saddle, ready for a crow hop or two.

The horse just stood there.

"See?" Dinah said, looking annoyed. "It really wasn't necessary for you to—"

"Thank me later," he said as the black exploded under him. Unprepared, Shane lost a stirrup on the first jump; the saddle slipped on the second; and by the third, he'd have been airborne if the horse hadn't stumbled and crashed over backward, pinning his rider beneath him. Thrashing to get up, the animal rolled completely over the man before stumbling to his feet.

Breath knocked out of him and lungs bursting, Shane felt a blinding flash of pain accompanied by a tearing sensation along his spine. He might even have blacked out for a few seconds, because the next thing he knew, Dinah had his head on her lap and was whispering urgently, "Shane, are you all right? Please speak to me!"

"I'm fine." He managed to grate the words out. In fact, he didn't feel fine at all. What he felt like was a fool. He'd been showing off and he should know by now where that would get him.

If he didn't quit playing to the gallery, he was going to get himself killed. He struggled to sit up and nearly passed out again.

B.D. leaned over him anxiously. "Shane, are you hurt? That mean old horse—"

"It wasn't the horse," he groaned. "It was the idiot in the saddle." He tried to focus his eyes enough to look around. "Is he all right?"

"He's fine." Dinah's voice sounded strained. "It's you I'm worried about."

"Don't be." The worst of the pain was passing, or else he was getting a grip on himself. He struggled upright, ignoring his dizziness. The damned horse stood no more than ten feet away, head down and breathing hard.

"You *are* hurt." Dinah reached for the buttons on his shirt.

He never thought he'd see the day when he'd bat her hands away from his body, but that's what he did now. "I'm okay," he said in a ragged voice. "Just got the breath knocked out of me, is all."

B.D. grabbed his elbow. "Then let's go saddle Pepper and you can watch me run barrels like you said," she commanded, tugging hard.

He felt the pull down his torso all the way to his waist. It hurt like hell. Jeez, what had he done to himself this time? He should see a doctor, but with B.D.'s trusting blue eyes on him, what could he do?

"You got it, shortcake." He managed to get to his feet.

Dinah stepped into his path. "Don't, Shane." She looked frightened. "Let me drive you into town to see the doctor."

"I promised B.D." He wanted to brace his ribs with his arms but didn't want her to know how much pain he was in.

For a moment she frowned at him and then she sighed. "I don't guess I can force you. Just be a little more careful, okay?"

"Yeah, sure," he said, but he didn't mean it. He'd always believed that being too careful could get you killed almost as fast as being careless.

THE TELEPHONE RANG as Dinah entered the kitchen. Still distracted by Shane's spill, she was surprised to find Josh on the line.

"Just checkin' in," he said cheerfully. "Is Shane around?"

"You just missed him."

"Too bad. Maybe you can tell him I called. So how's it goin'?"

"It's going...fine."

"Dinah, you don't *sound* like it's fine. What's happening?"

She sighed. "Shane just lost a fight with a horse."

Josh laughed. "It's not like he's never been thrown before."

"This time the horse fell on him. I don't even want to *think* about what it might have done to his ribs."

No laughter this time. "Ribs bothering him, are they?"

"He won't admit it, but yes, they are. And this won't help."

"He's still got a few days until he has to do that exhibition ride," Josh said, sounding as if he were trying to convince himself. "He'll be okay by then. I mean, what're you folks gonna put him up on? Some old milk cow?"

"I'm no expert on bulls, but I think this one is probably a little rougher than that. He's a former rodeo bull of the year. One of the local ranchers bought him for breeding rodeo stock, but from what I hear, he's so wild he may end up as hamburger instead."

"Retired, huh. Must be old." Josh spoke with considerably less confidence than before. "You wouldn't happen to know that bad bull's name, would you?"

"It's...Red Dust...Red Dawn..."

"Red *Devil?*"

"That's it."

"Whoa!" No joking around now. "That's the bull that

gored Shane three years ago. Jeez, Dinah, didn't you know? Our boy Shane is in a world of trouble.''

"JOSH WAS EXAGGERATING," Shane said when she told him about the telephone call. He and B.D. had called it quits after only a half hour because his ribs were giving him holy hell. He was seriously considering a visit to old Doc Kelly in town if he could get away without raising suspicion.

"I don't think so." Dinah looked grim. Apparently Josh had scared her plenty. "He wants you to call him on the cell phone. He's someplace in Utah."

"Okay, when I get time." He straightened away from the kitchen counter where he'd been leaning. It took a real effort but he didn't think he'd given away how much pain he was in. A rib injury always hurt like hell even when it wasn't serious, he assured himself.

He didn't think she noticed anything amiss. He asked with elaborate casualness, "You need anything from town?"

"Ruben gave me a whole list of stuff." She raised her brows. "Are you volunteering?"

"Why not? I haven't been into town since the picnic. I could use a change of scene."

From her expression, she took that remark personally, as if she thought he was trying to get away from *her*. "The keys to the truck are on the nail by the door," she said.

"Can I go, too?" B.D. asked.

"Nah, you'd be bored." He'd like to take her but didn't figure he could, under the circumstances.

Her face fell. "Please, Shane? I'll be good, I promise."

"Can't," he said shortly, turning away because he couldn't stand to see her disappointment. "I'll bring you something."

"I don't want something, I want—"

He didn't wait to hear, just headed out the door. Behind him, he could hear Dinah take the kid to task.

"B.D.," she said severely, "don't be a baby. Shane isn't used to living with a woman and a child and I'm sure we're getting on his nerves in a big way. Why don't you just—"

Shane stepped outside the house, her voice mercifully fading away. She was right; he wasn't used to living with a woman and a kid. But she was wrong when she said they were getting on his nerves. Maybe he was even liking it a little more than he should.

Damned good thing he'd be getting out of here soon.

OVER THE NEXT SEVERAL DAYS, Dinah watched Shane insinuate himself ever deeper into the very fabric of life at the Flying H. His trip to town apparently did him a lot of good, because upon his return, he was almost his old self again.

The two teenage cowhands were eating out of his hand and unwilling to make a move that didn't have his stamp of approval. Ruben thought he'd hung the moon, and B.D. followed him around like a puppy.

Only Dinah tried to keep her distance. He'd be leaving soon. She wasn't going to let herself depend on him or grow too accustomed to having him around. She wasn't!

Was she?

The second night after his trip to town, she found herself out of busywork after the supper cleanup and impulsively decided to join him on the front steps. B.D. was in bed, Ken and Linc had gone into town, and Ruben had muttered something about starting a sourdough batter for breakfast biscuits.

They were alone.

When she lowered herself beside him, he glanced her way briefly but said nothing. After a few minutes, she cleared her throat.

"Did you ever get back to Josh?"

"No."

"Why not?"

"Nothin' to say."

She was horrified. "Good grief, Shane, that's no way to treat a friend."

"He knows where I am. He can call back if it's important."

Apparently friendship meant something different to him than it did to her. "All right," she said shortly. "It's none of my business, anyway."

"That's right."

His response took her aback. He seemed to have absolutely no interest in her presence. He hadn't even looked at her after that first cursory glance. A new concern struck her. "How are the ribs, by the way?"

"Fine."

"I was afraid you'd really hurt yourself when that horse—"

"Let it lay, Dinah." Irritation laced his tone.

"But—"

"Do you think I enjoy being reminded that I let a hay-burner like that throw me? Do me a favor and don't bring it up again."

She stood, stiff and resentful. "You men and your stupid pride. I was concerned that you might have been hurt, not— Oh, forget it." She turned angrily away. "I'll see you in the morning."

He didn't even answer her.

SHANE LET HER STOMP BACK inside, knowing that he didn't dare follow his instincts. Those instincts clamored for him to thank her for her concern, put his arms around her and carry her up those stairs again.

There were several drawbacks to that plan, however. In the first place, he didn't want to acknowledge that it felt kind of good to have a pretty woman worrying about the state of his health. In the second place, he wasn't sure he'd be *able* to carry her up the stairs, even slung across his shoulder like a bag of grain.

And in the third place—well, he wouldn't be able to do what he wanted to do once he got her alone without giving away a secret he'd worked hard to keep.

Straightening, he put a hand gingerly on his torso, feeling the stiff elastic bandage beneath the shirt. Doc Kelly had strapped his ribs and sent him on his way with a warning.

"This is serious stuff. You've got yourself a rib sprain, maybe even a sprain-fracture, but I can't be sure without X rays."

"No damned X rays."

"You already said that. Now, I'm telling you—it's gonna take a good six weeks for those ribs to heal, with or without fractures. Take it easy, Shane. Under no circumstances should you try to ride anything that isn't willing to cooperate. The next time you get bucked off a four-legged critter, be it horse, bull or pig, may be your last. A word to the wise…"

Shane didn't figure he was particularly wise but he was a man of his word. He didn't have to climb on that bull for five days yet. All doctors were alarmists. He had plenty of time to heal.

He hoped.

His cell phone rang as he walked into his bedroom— her bedroom, actually. It would be Josh, of course. Shane knew what his road buddy would say, so why bother going through the drill?

Shoving the phone beneath the pillow to muffle its sound, he ignored it.

"CAN I GO WITH YOU AGAIN today?" B.D. asked Shane at breakfast the next morning.

"Isn't this the day you visit your grandmother?" Shane glanced at Dinah for confirmation.

She nodded. "Grandma will pick you up before lunch, honey."

Going to Grandma's was one of B.D.'s absolute favorite things to do, yet now she looked torn. "But I want to go with Shane." Her face was a picture of frustration.

"I know," Dinah sympathized, "but you can't be two places at once."

B.D. frowned. "You don't get it, Mama," she announced. "Shane…will you be here when I get back?"

Dinah's heart stood still and she looked quickly at him to gauge whether or not he'd understood the real message: *You're going to leave me, but please, not yet!*

He had, and he looked stunned. "Sure, shortcake. You go have fun with Grandma. When you get back—"

"Tonight," B.D. said. "I'll come back tonight."

Dinah frowned. "Don't you want to spend the night at Grandma's? She said there's a movie in town you might like to see."

"No, I'll come home," B.D. said firmly. "Tomorrow I'll go out with Shane, okay?"

The adults exchanged troubled glances. "Okay," Dinah conceded. "But Grandma may be disappointed."

As indeed she was. Watching B.D. climb into her Jeep Cherokee, Georgia looked questioningly at Dinah. "Why doesn't she want to spend the night with me? I don't get it.''

Dinah sighed. ''It's Shane. She knows he'll be leaving soon and she wants to spend as much time as she can with him.''

Georgia looked thoughtful. ''She's really crazy about him.''

''I'm afraid she is, Mom. When he leaves...'' Dinah shook her head hopelessly. ''It's going to be hard on her.''

''On you, too.''

''Me?'' Dinah's eyes flew wide. Surely Georgia couldn't suspect—

''Ruben says Shane's worth ten men around this place,'' Georgia said easily. ''Ken and Linc have bragged all over town about the way he's taken hold.''

''He...has been a big help,'' Dinah admitted uncomfortably. ''But it's B.D. I'm worried about.''

Georgia nodded. ''I see your point. Isn't there any way you could get him to...'' She shook her head. ''No, I suppose not.''

''Grandma!'' B.D. waved from the passenger seat. ''Can we go now?''

''You bet, honey.'' To Dinah, Georgia added, ''I'll bring her back after supper.''

''Thanks for understanding, Mom.''

Georgia grinned. ''I understand, all right. I just don't have any good advice handy at the moment. Maybe something will occur to me, though. If it does, I'll be sure to pass it on.''

After they'd pulled out of the ranch yard, Dinah sat down disconsolately on the back step, propping her elbows on her knees. What in the world was she going to do about Shane?

Every day she realized more clearly the enormity of her

mistake. She hadn't told him about his child at the time for so many good reasons: they'd quarreled and he'd left Bushwhack to get away from her before she even knew she was pregnant; she hadn't known where he was for more than a year; she'd been numbed by her father's death; she'd been so frightened to be alone and pregnant.

She'd also been beholden to Mike, who'd known everything but was still a devoted husband and father. Their marriage was strong if not particularly passionate. Although Mike had left the final decision to her, he'd given his opinion when asked. Say nothing, he'd said. What could possibly be gained by creating talk and confusing B.D.? Mike was her legal father. Why complicate all their lives?

Dinah dragged a booted foot through the dust below the stair. Everything was different now. Mike had been here when she needed him, but now he was dead and she needed Shane—needed him like she'd never imagined needing anyone.

What would he do if she told him he had a daughter?

Groaning, she buried her face in her hands. Would he hate her for keeping it from him…or for finally breaking her silence? He liked B.D., that much was obvious. But he apparently liked all kids, and that hadn't been enough to make him want any of his own.

What would he do if she told him the truth? Would he stay? Her heart leaped at the thought. Or maybe he'd be so furious that neither she nor B.D. would ever see him again.

Maybe he'd understand. Maybe if she told the truth—

Maybe! Dinah jumped up and stood there gritting her teeth. The truth included a great deal more than just paternity.

It also included the fact that she loved him. But how

did you say to a man who'd be moving on in a matter of days, *I love you and I had your child. I just didn't tell you.*

Still, it had to be done.

THAT NIGHT THEY ATE LATE, just the two of them. Shane seemed distracted and rushed and the meal passed without much conversation beyond the pass-the-salt variety.

Still, she was determined to say what needed saying, even if her hands already trembled with dread. As he finished his second slice of pie, she began hesitantly, "Shane? There's something I've been meaning to…to mention. Well, actually, it's more than just mentioning. It's—"

His restless gaze lifted to the window. "I think B.D.'s back," he said abruptly. "That's Georgia's Cherokee or I miss my guess."

Dinah felt sick to her stomach. This had been a bad idea; what if she'd already told him and then B.D. and Georgia walked in before he'd had a chance to deal with it? God only knew what might happen then.

He pushed back from the table. "Sorry, you wanted to say something?"

"It's not important." She, too, rose, feeling numb relief. Obviously, she had to be more careful about choosing her time and place.

He shrugged and went outside to meet B.D. Dinah could hear her daughter's squeals of pleasure at the sight of him…pleasure and perhaps a little relief.

She tried again later that night, but just as she was about to work up her courage, Hardy Guthrie called about Shane's scheduled appearances. When Shane got off the phone he was grumpy as an old bear, so there was no talking to him about anything.

The next day offered no opportunities at all. When

Shane was around, so was B.D. When B.D. went to bed, Shane announced he had business with Ruben and disappeared. She tried to wait up for him, but when he hadn't returned by eleven, she gave up and went to bed.

Went to bed mad, actually. What the hell was going on here? She could no longer pretend that Shane wasn't avoiding being alone with her. What was he afraid of, that she'd try to get him back into bed?

Her cheeks burned with embarrassment as she stomped up the stairs. Apparently making love to her hadn't made much of an impression on him. He certainly wasn't in any hurry to repeat the experience—not that she'd let him!

No way was she going to level with him now. It just wasn't worth the stress and strain.

DINAH HAD A BURR under her saddle and Shane didn't want any part of it. She kept looking at him as if he were a snake about to strike. Whatever had put that expression on her face, he flat didn't want to know.

With his departure imminent, there was no point in getting any more involved in her business than he already was. It surprised him to realize that he was actually going to miss her and her daughter and this place when he left.

But he wouldn't miss them for long. As soon as he got back into the swing of rodeo life, he'd be fine. More than fine—he'd be happy again. Because he sure hadn't been happy here, not really. Oh, he liked the life, liked the work, liked the people he dealt with, liked B.D., liked—

Yeah, he liked Dinah, but she kept him so constantly off stride that he almost dreaded being around her. He couldn't look at her without wanting her in his arms and his bed, but he didn't dare let that happen again or he might never be able to leave.

Damn.

Shane looked down at the bridle he'd thought he was repairing. Instead of drilling a small notch for the tongue of the buckle, he'd bored a hole almost big enough to pull the whole buckle through. He tossed the bridle aside in disgust.

He'd come out to the barn right after supper in a futile attempt to distract himself. Today was July 1. Old Pioneer Days would kick off July 3. On July 4, he'd have to dude himself up to ride in the parade as grand marshal, then climb on Red Devil and pray.

If he survived all that, he'd have to find transportation to Oklahoma, where he'd hook up with Josh. Then life would get back to normal.

He devoutly hoped.

Leaning down, he picked up the bridle with a sigh. Now he was going to have to go into town to buy a new strap and—

He heard a vehicle pull into the ranch yard and cocked his head to listen. It wasn't Georgia's Cherokee, that was for sure. He frowned. It almost sounded like—

Jeez! As if he didn't have enough trouble.

With an exclamation of distaste, he walked outside to greet Josh.

Dinah and B.D. came out of the house at the same time. When Dinah saw who it was, she rushed forward to greet Josh like a long-lost friend. Shane hung back, watching her draw B.D. forward for introductions.

What the hell was Josh doing here? You'd think when Shane didn't answer his cell phone, that should have been some kind of clue.

Josh looked around then, saw Shane and waved. Nothing to do but face him.

Josh launched the first missile. "What's the matter, your cell phone broke?"

Shane strove for innocence. "You been callin' me?"

"Yeah, I been callin' you. Didn't Dinah give you my message?"

"I certainly did," she said, giving Shane an I-told-you-so look.

"Well," Shane said evasively, "I've been busy. What do you want? You should be on your way to Oklahoma right about now."

"I thought I'd skip Oklahoma and check out Old Pioneer Days." Josh grinned. "I hear it's gonna be a real rip-snorter."

Shane offered a sour smile. "You been winnin'? Is that why you've got rich pains?"

Josh shrugged. "Win some, lose some." He turned to Dinah. "Hope you don't mind if I park my rig and hang around a few days until Shane's finished. I figure we might as well pull out together."

Dinah's expression didn't change. "I don't mind at all. Just pick your spot. I'm sorry I don't have any more room in the house, but you're welcome to sleep in the bunkhouse if you'd like."

"Thanks. That'd give me more room than the trailer, if I won't be putting anybody out."

"Not at all." She wouldn't even look at Shane. She brushed her hands across the front of her thighs. "I'll bet you're hungry. How about I fix you a plate? It'll only take a minute."

"That'd be real nice."

"Okay. B.D., you can give me a hand."

B.D. shook her mother off. "Are you leaving, Shane?" She looked at him anxiously.

"Not right away." He patted her shoulder. "Why don't you help your mother get something for my friend to eat. I'd appreciate it."

She looked like she wanted to refuse. Finally, with a deep sigh, she gave in. "But don't go anywhere," she said before she turned away. "I'll be right back, okay?"

"Okay."

Shane watched her dragging steps. Then he turned to Josh and practically snarled, "So what the hell do you think you're doing here?"

Putting his fists on his hips, he waited for an answer he didn't think he was going to like.

CHAPTER FOURTEEN

JOSH EYED SHANE WARILY. "I just wanted to make sure you were pulling out of that exhibition ride, is all."

"Why the hell would I do that?"

"Because—" Josh's easygoing manner fell aside. "Because, dammit, if you don't, you're apt to get yourself killed."

"What the hell are you talking about?" Shane snarled. "That was the deal and you damn well know it."

"That was before you found out they're about to throw Red Devil at you."

"Jeez." Shane flexed his hands restlessly. "You've been talking to Dinah, I see."

"Yeah, but I also found this on my way here." Josh dragged a folded piece of paper from his hip pocket and offered it to Shane.

There it was, the two names linked on the page: Shane Daniels and Red Devil.

"You can't do this," Josh said flatly.

"Why the hell not? Just because that bull tossed me once before—"

"He didn't just toss you, he tossed you and then he stomped you. That bull's a killer."

"And I'm a world champion bull rider so it should be a fair contest."

"You *were* world champion. You know and I know that you're way behind in the standings this year."

Blunt, but accurate. "I'm still the champ until December," Shane rasped.

"Big damn deal. Hell, I'm ahead of you at this point and we both know I'm about half as good as you are when you're a hundred percent."

"I take it you've been winning."

"Yeah, but that's not the point. If you were healthy I'd say go for it, but you're not. You're still all banged up."

"I'm fine, Mother. Stop worrying."

"Sure you are."

Josh lashed out with lightning speed and whacked Shane in the ribs with the flat of his hand. Although the blow was light, Shane gasped and buckled over, belatedly protecting his torso with his arms. For a moment he thought he might black out.

The wave of dizziness passed and he straightened stiffly. "You son of a—" He saw the shock on Josh's face and quit talking.

"Jeez," Josh breathed. "I didn't know it was *that* bad. When Dinah told me you'd been tossed by a horse—"

"Well, hell. What's she trying to do, ruin my reputation?"

"She was worried about you, and so am I. Draw out. It only makes sense. If you're gonna risk killin' yourself, at least don't be dumb enough to do it when there's nothing on the line."

"There *is* something on the line. They're depending on me."

"From what you've told me," Josh shot back, "you don't give a hoot in hell about these people or their town or anything else around here."

"I don't."

"Then what…?" Understanding appeared on Josh's face. "Ah. It's Dinah."

Yeah, Dinah, but Shane wasn't ready to admit that. He glared back defensively at his friend.

Who nodded slowly. "I get it. Looks like you'll just have to tell the truth, then—that you're hurt."

"And sound like a damned coward? Hell, no!" All Shane's frustration was packed into those words.

For a long moment the two men stood there glaring at each other. B.D. broke the impasse by throwing open the screen door and leaning out.

"Mama says come eat!"

Shane waved at her and nodded. To Josh he said, "Keep your mouth shut about this. I don't want her to know."

Josh nodded. He didn't ask who "her" was.

JOSH SETTLED RIGHT IN.

Even if Dinah wanted to tell Shane all her secrets, she wouldn't be able to get him alone to do it. Although she liked Josh, she soon found herself also resenting him: he made Shane's coming departure so much more *real*. The two of them planned to leave together right after the bull ride on the fourth, without even hanging around for the big fireworks display, although no one had the heart to tell B.D. Dinah figured neither she nor her daughter would ever see Shane again after that, unless it was at some rodeo.

Predictably, July 3 was bad.

Shane and Josh took B.D. into town for the carnival and a couple of personal appearances, but Dinah stayed home. She'd run out of lies to tell herself, and all she could think about was Shane's impending departure. If she thought it would do any good, she'd risk anything…

They returned late that night and Shane carried a sleeping B.D. in from the pickup, then up the stairs to bed. By the time Dinah had tucked her daughter in, he'd gone over to the bunkhouse with Josh and Ruben.

Running out of time and determined to tell him everything, she fell asleep sometime after midnight on the living room couch. When she awakened and went on up to bed, it was after two and she didn't know if he'd come in or not.

WHILE JOSH DISTRACTED B.D. by watching her run barrels the next morning after breakfast, Shane quickly stowed his duffel in the trailer. They'd made their plans the previous evening. No point in getting B.D. all worked up before he had to. It would ruin the day for her.

Dinah watched silently. Only after everything was loaded did she confront him. "You are going to tell her goodbye before you go, I hope."

"Naturally. I didn't see any point in saying anything until—"

"You don't have to explain anything to me," she said coolly, turning away. "I just don't want her to be hurt any more by this than necessary."

"Dinah—"

She stopped short in the kitchen door but didn't turn around. "Yes?"

"You've been trying to tell me something."

"No, I—"

"Mama! Shane!" B.D. burst through the back door, her pigtails flying. "I'm getting better! It only took me two minutes and a few seconds this time. Josh says—"

Shane felt a twinge of jealousy, which he pushed back. He was leaving. No strings, no entanglements.

No responsibilities.

THE PARADE WASN'T TOO BAD. Shane rode in the back of a convertible, sitting up high with his feet on the seat and

B.D. beside him. The kid was in her glory, smiling and waving at everyone.

Occasionally she'd look at Shane with glowing eyes. She obviously thought the cheers from those lining the parade route down Bushwhack's main drag were for her.

Ah, to be so young and confident and eager....

He wondered if he'd ever felt that way himself. As a kid, he'd never ridden in a parade or heard people cheer for him. He'd heard police sirens and threats and even gunfire, but never acclaim. No wonder he felt so apart from all this now.

B.D. nudged him with her elbow. "You're supposed to wave," she informed him. "That's what you do in parades, Shane!"

"Okay, shortcake, whatever you say." He smiled and waved mechanically, wondering where Josh and Dinah were, wondering why he felt such an overwhelming sense of...*doom*. Nothing was right today, starting with sneaking around to deceive this child. Somehow he didn't think the day was going to get a helluva lot better.

They reached the end of the parade route at last. The convertible pulled into a parking lot near the entrance to the rodeo grounds, where they were to disembark. Shane thanked their driver and lifted B.D. out of the vehicle.

"Can we do it again?" She giggled, looking back over the route they'd just completed.

"Nope, but we can watch the rest of the parade while we wait for your mother or grandmother to show up," Shane suggested.

"Okay!" She skipped ahead, across the graveled lot toward the sidewalk.

Shane followed at a more leisurely pace. The crowd had

thinned out a block or so back so he didn't have any trouble keeping her under his watchful eye.

He saw Georgia walking at an angle to intercept him and slowed his pace. She greeted him with a big smile. "B.D. sure looked like she was having fun," she said, falling into step beside him.

"Yeah, she was." Shane felt a pride that was completely misplaced. "She was giving me orders all the way. Smile. Wave. She's a real smart kid for eight."

Georgia nodded. "Only she's not eight, she's nine."

"But I thought—" Shane stopped stock-still, feeling as if he'd just been hit by a lightning bolt. "Are you sure?"

"Of course I'm sure. I'm her grandmother, for goodness' sake." She looked at him curiously. "What is it, Shane? You don't look so good. Sun getting to you?"

He wasn't feeling too good, either. He licked his lips and lied through his teeth. "Yeah, that's probably it." He'd wait and talk to B.D. about this. Georgia was entirely too sharp to fool with.

They reached the girl, who was standing on the sidewalk clapping wildly for a group of young riders astride palomino horses. Georgia tapped her shoulder. "I've got some water in the car. Would either of you like a bottle? I don't know about you but I'm parched."

"Parched?" B.D. looked questioningly at her grandmother.

"Thirsty."

"Me, too!"

"Shane?"

"No, thanks. I'll wait here with B.D. until you get back."

Georgia nodded and headed toward the Cherokee on the other side of the lot. B.D. turned back to the parade.

Feeling an incredible sense of urgency, Shane leaned

down to speak in her ear. "I've been wondering. What does B.D. stand for?"

She didn't even look around. "My name is Blossom Danielle Anderson," she said, "but I like B.D. best. Don't you?"

Shane felt as if his life were flashing before his eyes. All he could do was nod, but that nod wasn't telling the truth. He liked *Danielle* best—as in Daniels.

He'd just learned something Dinah had never intended him to know.

Nine-year-old Blossom Danielle was *his* daughter, not Mike Anderson's. The question was, what did he want to do with that knowledge?

"GREAT PARADE," JOSH SAID when the last mounted rider had gone past. "Are you ready to go, Dinah?"

She nodded. "Georgia's meeting Shane and B.D., but I said I'd catch up with them as soon as I could." Even saying his name was an effort at this point, her feelings were so mixed.

Someone in the dispersing crowd jostled her from behind and a man's voice said, "Sorry, Dinah. I didn't mean to knock you down."

She turned with a smile, happy for the distraction. "Hi, Doc. I don't think you've met Shane's friend, Josh Kilmer. Josh, this is Doc Kelly, Bushwhack's favorite medicine man."

The two men shook hands and Doc said, "Yeah, and Bushwhack's *only* medicine man." His eyes narrowed. "How's our grand marshal doing?"

Dinah shrugged. "Fine, so far as I know."

"Did he withdraw from that bull riding exhibition?"

Dinah glanced at Josh, who didn't look nearly as surprised by the doctor's question as she was. "No. Why should he?"

"You don't mean to tell me—" Doc reared back and glared at her. "Why, that damn fool."

He was scaring her. "What are you talking about?" she demanded.

"I shouldn't say anything," Doc grumbled, "but I'm going to, dammit. I can give you two good reasons he shouldn't try to ride that bull. Number one, the only place I've ever seen ribs worse than his was in a barbecue joint. Number two, that particular bull is a man-killer." He glanced at Josh. "Have I got that right, young man?"

Josh's face suddenly wore a very serious expression. To her horror, he nodded.

"But Shane said you were exaggerating," Dinah cried. "Tell me he was right, Josh!"

"Red Devil's been ridden exactly once," Josh said soberly, "and that was only because the cowboy got lucky. Remember the bull that threw Shane at Tall Timber, Dinah?"

She nodded, although she didn't want to remember. That had been one of the scariest moments in her life.

"Next to Red Devil, he looks like somebody's pet calf."

"Oh, God." She crossed one arm over her waist, feeling sick.

Doc looked from one to the other. "There's still time to talk him out of it. He's not supposed to ride for a couple of hours, right?"

"Right." Desperately, Dinah turned to Josh. "You're his friend. You can talk him out of it."

"I've already tried. I got nowhere. You, on the other hand…" He eyed her critically. "Dinah, if you can't do it, it can't be done."

She felt a flash of confusion, unsure of his meaning but

too frantic to stop to pursue the point. "It's my fault he's even here," she said miserably. "If anything happens to him—" she shivered "—I'd never forgive myself."

"Is that your only reason?" Josh asked quietly. "Because if guilt's all you've got workin' for you, my advice is, don't waste your time or his."

SHANE BUCKLED ON HIS CHAPS, mad as hell and unwilling to confront the reasons why. Very soon he'd be risking life and limb, and for what? Because he'd given his word, because he was a professional, because...

Because, dammit, he'd been hoodwinked by a woman, a woman who'd had his child and kept the truth from him, a woman who'd lured him back here to bail out a little pissant town that he had always hated and still did.

The way he was feeling, he'd make hamburger out of that bull.

That is, he would if he didn't pass out first. All this deep angry breathing was not a good thing for a man whose ribs felt fragile as crystal. Even bending made him gasp for breath.

The amateur competitors in this pip-squeak undertaking were giving him a wide berth. He supposed his state of mind was readily apparent but he didn't give a damn. The only face he wanted to see was Josh's, because he was going to need assistance getting his rigging on that beast and himself on its back. He and Josh always worked together. Where the hell had the kid gone, off somewhere with Dinah?

Mayor Woodruff and Hardy Guthrie hurried up, one tall and broad, one dapper and trim. Both looked relieved to see him.

The mayor stuck out his hand. "There you are, Shane. You all ready to show us locals how it's done?"

Shane shrugged and regarded the two glad-handers with a jaundiced eye.

Hardy nodded his sleek silver head. "We've sold more advance tickets than even *we* dreamed," he said happily. "Folks are really looking forward to seeing you do your stuff."

"Whatever." It sounded surly even to him.

The two men seemed a little taken aback.

"Uh…" The mayor glanced at the chamber of commerce president. "There's just one other little thing." He licked fleshy lips. "About those city limits signs… We're hoping you changed your mind about lettin' Bushwhack claim you as a native son. It would just put the topper on Old Pioneer Days if you'd let us announce—"

"No." That's all Shane said, just *no,* but he said it with conviction.

Hardy frowned. "Could we impose upon you to tell us why? Because we don't have any idea why you feel so strong about this."

Shane started to tell them the subject was off limits, that he didn't have to explain jack. Then behind them, he saw Dinah hurry around one of the snack bars and every other thought flew right out of his head.

She saw him, too, and stopped short. She looked flustered and alarmed, but also determined. She started forward again and Shane turned back to the two men looking at him so anxiously.

"I'm doing what I said I'd do," he growled. "I rode in your damned parade and I'm gonna ride your damned bull, if he doesn't kill me first."

"Heh-heh." The mayor tried to make light of it. "Of course you'll ride him. You're a professional."

Shane wanted to tell him about all the professionals that

bull had already turned into little cowboy meatballs but there was no time for that.

"Will you at least say a few words over the public address system before your ride?" Hardy asked desperately. "You know, just to get the folks interested in what's—"

"Damn! You people want blood, don't you. Stop pushing me or..." He let the vague unspecified threat trail off.

The mayor put up his hands in a placating gesture, although he was obviously mystified by Shane's attitude. "Okay, okay, we can take a hint."

Shane would have groaned except Dinah arrived at that moment. She stood to one side, unsmiling.

Keith and Hardy walked away shaking their heads. Shane waited where he was for Dinah to approach. She did, after taking a deep breath.

When she spoke, her voice wobbled. "Shane, I have to talk to you."

"Not here." He looked around for a place they could have some privacy. The nearest was a kind of lean-to utility building that housed equipment for the sound system and announcers' booth. Grabbing her hand, he dragged her toward it.

She didn't resist. People scattered before his determined march. Reaching the open entryway, he hauled Dinah inside and swung her around to face him.

Lips parted, she stared at him intently, as if trying to decide how to proceed.

"I'll help you out," he said, his voice flat although his emotions weren't. "Yes, I'm going to ride. You want to make sure I don't back out, right?"

"God, no!" She licked her lips. "I came to ask you—to beg you, if necessary—*not* to ride. Please don't do it, Shane."

That threw him. "Why the hell not?"

"I know about that bull," she said.

"Ah." Josh had told her the truth. "You don't think I can do it, is that it?"

"I think there's a good chance you can't, because you're still hurt. Doc Kelly said—"

"Jeez!" He flung himself away from her so he didn't have to see the aching concern on her face. Furious with himself for being so damned soft, he tried to calm down. "Can't anybody keep their mouth shut around here?"

And then he remembered that of course *some* people could—Dinah, for one. She'd kept her mouth shut for years about her daughter's father. Shane didn't think he'd ever be able to forgive her for that. Should he throw his new knowledge in her face? Before he could decide, she spoke.

"Shane, I'm sorry. I knew you'd be mad, but I can't let you risk your life in a stupid exhibition."

"You can't stop me." He turned back, wanting to intimidate her, wanting to tell her that he neither trusted her nor believed her when the chips were down.

She wasn't ever going to tell him about B.D. If she'd intended to do that, it would already have happened. Thinking about that, he said, "There's only one thing you could say to me that would even give me pause. Since there's not a chance in hell you're going to do that—"

"But I am." Her unflinching gaze met his. "Shane—" she swallowed hard "—I love you."

"You what?" He stared at her stupidly. He'd thought that at last she was going to confess about B.D, and instead…

"I love you!" She hurled herself against his chest, throwing her arms around his neck and hanging on. "I'd die if you got hurt because of what I've manipulated you into doing."

He'd thought he was ready for anything, but he wasn't ready for this, for her words or for her body soft against his. Her voice had quivered with sincerity, but how could he believe her? Why hadn't she mentioned B.D.?

He looked down into her face, saw the trembling lips and the wide green eyes and felt some of the anger slipping away, to be replaced by a softer emotion that—

"Shane? Are you in there, boy? I got somethin' important to—"

Ruben came loping inside and stopped short. "Aw, hell," he said, "I'm interruptin'."

Dinah pushed herself out of Shane's arms. She didn't look at him, just hung her head and mumbled, "It's okay. Shane and I—" She didn't finish, apparently realizing that the only believable explanation would be the real one.

Shane's head still whirled and his ribs screamed for mercy. "What is it?" he asked the old cowboy. "You said it was important and it damned well better be."

Ruben blinked. "You're the one said so," he announced. "It's about that danged elk—you know, the one you tangled with? You asked me what I remembered about that and it just come to me."

Shane glanced at Dinah, who was standing with her back toward them. There was so much he wanted to say to her, to ask her, but first he had to deal with Ruben.

"Okay, tell me what you remember."

"It's like this. Another Flying H rider saw what you done. He come to me a week or so later and said he thought he ought to tell Big Tom, since harassin' wildlife is agin the law to start with and he was jealous of you, anyway. I thought I talked him outta doing that, but just then Big Tom walked in and he spilled the beans."

"Then...that's why Big Tom was on the warpath that day? Everybody in town knew he was looking for me but nobody said—'' Nobody said it was because of the elk. In his guilt, Shane had just *assumed*.

Ruben nodded. ''He was fit to be tied about it. He swore up and down he'd skin you alive for messin' with a wild critter. That's why he went lookin' for you, all right.'' The old man squinted thoughtfully. ''We always figured you heard he was on a rampage and that's why you left town so sudden-like.''

''Jeez.'' The awful truth washed over Shane with all the subtlety of a pie in the face. He wanted to put his fists through the flimsy wall, he wanted to howl at the moon.

Big Tom had had no idea Shane had trifled with his daughter. If he'd had the guts to hang around and take his medicine like a man, he would never have had to leave. He could have built a life here…a life with Dinah and their daughter.

A life that suddenly looked awful damned appealing.…

She was staring at him, her eyes wide and disbelieving. ''Do you mean to tell me that's why you left—because of the elk?'' Her voice rose. ''All this time, I thought it was to get away from *me*.''

''Dinah—'' He hated the pain he saw on her beautiful face. ''I—''

''Is Shane in there?'' The raised voice from outside belonged to Mayor Woodruff. ''I don't care what's goin' on, I gotta talk to him now.''

What is this, Shane wondered, the bus station? What did a man have to do to get a little privacy? At that moment, Keith charged in.

''There you are! It's time. Are you ready for us to introduce you?''

''No!'' Dinah stepped forward, arms extended protectively. ''You can't, Shane. Please don't.''

The mayor looked aghast. "Have you lost your mind, girl? He *has* to do it."

"Why? So the people in this town can sell a few more hot dogs and rodeo tickets?" She turned on Keith like an avenging angel. "He's hurt. If he rides in this condition—"

"What in the *hell* is going on in here?" This time it was Josh who ambled in. He took in the cast of characters and his eyes grew wide.

"You!" Shane turned all his confusion, all his anger on his friend. "You sure do have a big mouth, partner. Where do you get off, spilling your guts to Dinah about that damned bull?"

"Hey, the truth is the truth. I didn't make anything up."

Keith said anxiously, "It's time to go, Shane. Hardy's up there makin' small talk but everybody came to see you, not him." He took a step toward the exit. When Shane made no move to follow, he stopped. "You *are* comin', right?"

"Wrong." Dinah looked desperate. "Tell him you're not riding today, Shane. Please tell him."

"Is this up for a vote?" Josh inquired. "Because if it is, I vote—"

"Votin' on what?" Ruben looked around the room, obviously confused.

"*Shane—*"

It seemed as if everyone in the room said his name at the same time but each with a different inflection. Shane raised his hands defensively and stepped back against the wall. He was in a tough spot and he knew it.

The choice was his: put this woman he now admitted he loved first, or save face by doing what he'd promised to do, thereby risking any future he might have with her, not to mention his life.

Squaring his shoulders, he did what he had to do, the only thing he could do.

CHAPTER FIFTEEN

"MAYOR WOODRUFF," SHANE said into the taut silence, "I won't be riding today."

He nearly flinched saying it, half expecting a bolt of lightning to strike him dead. Going back on a promise went against the values he'd learned at Lost Springs and had been reinforced by Big Tom Hoyt.

The joy and relief on Dinah's face reassured him. He'd done the only thing that made sense. She was right; he was in no shape to ride. Even if he threw his life and health away to keep his word, it would be for nothing. He'd go flying on the first jump, worse than the rawest rookie.

Keith squawked like a plucked chicken. "You can't do this to us! We spent good money to get you here. We've pulled out all the stops, advertised your ride to hell and gone—damn, we *adopted* you even after you treated us all like—"

"I'm sorry about that," Shane said quickly. "I've been dealing with a…a whole lot of stuff—" what an understatement "—and I took it out on the good citizens of Bushwhack. I'll do anything I can to make up for this. I'll pay back the money, I'll—"

"Money won't help!" Keith looked around wildly. "What are we gonna tell all those people out there in the grandstand? They came to see a professional bull rider. How're we gonna tell them that our star attraction doesn't feel like riding today—sorry, but he's got *stuff* on his mind.''

"Shane, you been thinkin' about that elk?" Ruben put in suddenly. "Because if that's the stuff been botherin' you—"

"No, old-timer." Josh patted the man's shoulder. "He's thinkin' about all those folks who'll be disappointed."

"Yeah, and I hate it," Shane said fervently. "I don't want anyone to think I give my word lightly. Maybe I could just—"

"No maybes!" Dinah said fiercely.

"Then," Keith said, "what the hell are we gonna do?"

"I've got an idea."

Everybody looked at Josh with varying degrees of hope. He grinned and Shane recognized the cockiness; he saw it in his mirror every morning when he shaved.

"Anything," Keith pleaded, grasping at straws. "Anything!"

"*I'll* make the ride."

Keith blinked. "Who the hell are you?"

Josh made a great show of hitching up his jeans. "I'm number seven in the all-around professional bull rider ratings at the moment, which is nine places higher than the guy you're tryin' to get killed."

Jeez, Shane thought; Josh *had* been winning. Even so, Red Devil was a potential killer and it was Shane's duty to stop the kid before it was too late.

Everybody was looking at him to see how he'd take Josh's offer. He started to flatly reject the compromise then realized that would just insult Josh. A young up-and-comer deserved his shot, even at the expense of a fallen champion.

So what Shane said was, "Okay, Josh, I'm not your

daddy. If you think you can do this, go for it. I'll explain what's going on to the crowd and introduce you.''

Josh gave him a thumbs-up and another cocky grin.

Keith didn't look entirely convinced but seemed to realize this was the best he could do. "Okay, let's get going, then, before we have a riot on our hands."

"Go ahead," Shane said. "I've got to give Josh the book on Red Devil."

Dinah hesitated. "Should I stay or go, Shane?"

"You stay right where you are," he said. "I'm not even *close* to done with you yet."

"LADIES AND GENTLEMEN, if you'll just give me your attention up here in the announcer's booth—"

Shane's electronically reproduced voice echoed across the small rodeo arena and bounced off the hills behind the grandstand. Slowly the buzz of mostly unhappy voices dropped to a more manageable level. Heads began to turn, many with show-me expressions.

Dinah stood wedged into the corner of the small announcer's booth, up above the chutes at one end of the arena. There hadn't been a single minute for her to speak privately to Shane since he'd decided not to ride, but she'd live with whatever happened now. As long as he was safe, she would have to be satisfied.

Red Devil snorted and plunged in the chute below the open announcer's box. She said a silent prayer for Josh: please, Lord, let him come through this in one piece.

Shane pushed his hat onto the back of his head and leaned over the microphone. "My name is Shane Daniels and I'm supposed to be the main course here today. Now, I hear some of you wondering, what's he doing up there instead of in the chutes getting ready to ride? Well, the truth is, I'm a little banged up at the moment. It's kind of an occupational hazard, but Doc Kelly said if I even *thought* about climbing on a bull today he'd have me committed. You folks wouldn't want to see that happen to a local boy, now, would you?''

The "local boy" comment brought a smattering of applause.

Shane was just warming up. He spoke as if to old and dear friends. "I hope to be around for a while so you'll have plenty of chances to see me ride. But today we've got something real special for you. You're gonna see an up-and-coming young professional bull rider who's on a winning streak that's gonna take him all the way to the national finals rodeo in Las Vegas this year.

"His name is Josh Kilmer. Remember that, because you're gonna be proud someday to say you knew him when. Josh is down there now, climbing on board one of the biggest, baddest bulls ever to enter a rodeo arena. All together now, let's give him a great send-off. Josh Kilmer and Red Devil, roaring out of chute number—''

The gate swung open and bull and rider did indeed roar out. Dinah gasped; they seemed so close it was scary. The bull looked enormous and Josh looked dashing as he spurred and waved his free arm over his head.

Shane drew her forward to stand beside him at the front of the booth. His arm felt strong and sure around her waist and she let out her breath half in pleasure at his nearness, half in terror for Josh.

"He's okay," Shane murmured, pushing a button to turn off the microphone. "That is one rank bull. The longer he goes, the higher he jumps. But as long as Josh doesn't fall into the well—''

She knew what the well was—the hole surrounded by the bull when the animal spun in circles, all the world as if he were chasing his tail. She nodded but didn't think Shane noticed, he was so intensely focused on the ride.

"You're doin' great, Josh," he almost crooned. "No, don't let him pull you forward! Damn that bull! Tighten up, Josh! You're anticipating too much. You're almost home now...hang on! This is your day, dammit, your day!"

The buzzer sounded and the crowd went wild. But the fun wasn't over, for dismounting would be as dangerous as the ride. Even in that, it was Josh's day. He bailed off the plunging bull and hit the dirt running, the big red beast breathing down his neck with every step. In a smooth move, Josh flung his hat into the stands and himself against the fence as the bull turned away at the last possible moment. Clinging as if he were glued there, he waved to a crowd gone mad with appreciation.

The starch went out of Shane and Dinah glanced at him in alarm. He looked completely worn out, weak with relief that the ride was over.

"Are you all right?" She placed a hand against his chest.

He nodded. She'd never seen him look so used up, almost helpless.

Was this the chance she'd been waiting for? She could tell him about B.D. now and he couldn't get too worked up about it because he was already emotionally exhausted. Besides, they were in plain view of hundreds of people. In a minute he'd have to switch the microphone back on, say a few nice words about Josh, then turn the proceedings over to the mayor.

She took a deep, determined breath. "Shane, look at me." She tightened her grip on his shirt. "There's something I have to tell you, something really important."

He frowned. "You think this is the best time and place?"

"Yes, because if I don't, I'll lose my nerve. My God, I've been trying to tell you for days!" She licked her lips and said in a panicky whisper, "It's about B.D."

"Ah." It was almost a sigh. "Are you finally about to admit she's my daughter?"

"Yes, I have to tell you—" His words sank in belatedly and she gasped, "You know? But how...?"

"I finally put eight and nine and Danielle together. B.D.'s mine, and from this moment on, so is B.D.'s mother."

Dinah's head whirled. "I don't understand. What—"

Keith stuck his head into the booth, and he was grinning. "Hey, you two, can't you hear the crowd? You're gonna have to say something else to them, Shane."

"Glad to, Mayor." Shane poked one button, then another, finally identifying the correct one by a roar of static that quickly diminished. Into the mike, he said, "Did I steer you wrong, folks? Is that Josh Kilmer a comer or what?"

The crowd roared.

"Now I'd like to ask you all a question."

The noise level dropped only slightly, but nobody was looking anywhere except up at the announcer's booth.

Shane drew Dinah forward. "Most all of you know Dinah Hoyt Anderson of the Flying H, right?"

"Right!" they roared in response.

"I'm fixin' to try to talk her into dropping the Hoyt Anderson in favor of Daniels. How does Dinah Daniels work, folks?"

They were on their feet now, cheering. Shane took her chin in one hand and turned her face toward him. The whole thing was unfolding like a fairy tale.

"Dinah," he said, his words echoing back to her via the loudspeaker, "I love you. I was an idiot to leave—you don't *know* how much of an idiot I was. Will you marry me if I promise never to get close to another elk again?"

Her answer was entirely lost in the tumult, but he was close enough to read her lips before he kissed them: *Yes!*

THEY FOUGHT THEIR WAY through throngs of well-wishers, looking for B.D. and Georgia. Even in this crush, Dinah felt completely safe and cherished with Shane's arm around her. He hadn't run from *her* but from her father's wrath.

He leaned down, shouting to be heard. "I don't see them!"

"Georgia said they'd meet me at the Bushwhack chamber of commerce barbecue stand." She pointed. "It's in that direction."

He nodded and pushed forward.

People called out to them from all sides.

"Best wishes, Dinah."

"Congratulations, Shane."

"You got a great girl there."

"Thanks. I think so." Shane kept smiling, kept pressing forward.

At last they broke through the crowd. There was the barbecue stand, and beside it, the little girl and her grandmother. B.D. had a funny expression on her face, one even her mother didn't recognize.

Dinah glanced quickly at Georgia, who nodded.

"She heard." Georgia mouthed, more than said, the words. She glanced around at the people milling around. "You can't talk here. Why don't we go to my place?"

Dinah nodded, instantly seeing the wisdom of the suggestion. Georgia didn't live more than three blocks away.

"We'll meet you there," she agreed. "B.D., come with us, honey."

"Okay." The girl looked pointedly at Shane's arm around her mother's shoulder before turning away. She didn't seem hostile, exactly, maybe just...bewildered? Dinah prayed it was nothing more.

They found the pickup and climbed in, Shane behind the wheel. Instead of starting the engine, he looked at the girl wedged in the middle on the bench seat.

"B.D., did you hear what I said on the loudspeaker?"

B.D. nodded, her lower lip stubborn.

"Then you know I want to marry your mother."

After a slight hesitation, she nodded again, more slowly this time.

"So what's the matter?" he asked with barely concealed frustration. "I thought you liked me."

"I do," she said in a thin little voice.

"Then I don't get it."

B.D. drew a ragged breath. "Are you taking Mama away with you to the rodeo? Am I going to live with Grandma all the time? I love Grandma and all, but—"

"B.D.!" Dinah grabbed her daughter from behind, wrapping her arms around the slim figure. "I'd never leave you, never. You're the most important person in the world to me."

"More important than Shane?" The way she said it made the question sound completely reasonable.

Before Dinah could reply, Shane spoke. "More important than me, more important than anything. I love your mother, B.D., but I also love you, just like she does."

B.D. sighed. "But when you go to the rodeo—"

Shane seemed to hold his breath. "I...don't think I'll be doing all that much rodeoing from here on out."

"You won't?" Dinah's heart leaped.

He spoke slowly and thoughtfully. "I never thought I'd hear myself say this, but...I'm thinking maybe it's time for me to take a look at ranching instead of—"

"But what about me?" B.D. broke in. "What about *me?* My friend—" She was almost whimpering. "My friend's stepfather...he doesn't love her like her real daddy did. Maybe you don't love *me,* just Mama."

Dinah heard the fear in the little girl's voice and she tightened her arms protectively. Her gaze met Shane's; his asked a question and she nodded, praying that he'd find the right way to say it.

"B.D.," he said gently, "I *am* your real father."

"Oh, no, Shane." She shook her head vigorously. "My real daddy died."

"Honey, it was your stepfather who died, but you loved him so much and he loved you so much that it didn't matter." He stroked her cheek and his fingers trembled. "See, your mama and I..." He gave Dinah a quick glance. "We knew each other a long time ago."

She nodded. "You used to work for my grandpa. He died before I was born."

"That's right. I worked for your grandpa and I loved your mama, only I didn't know it and she wasn't your mama then. When I went away...well, I didn't know she was going to have a baby and that baby would be you."

"If you knew," B.D. said with the clear logic of a child, "would you have stayed?"

Dinah wanted to know the answer to that, too.

"I would have stayed," he said, "but then you'd only have had one daddy who loved you instead of two." He gave her a whimsical smile. "That's kind of feeble reasoning—" he shook his head as if he couldn't believe it himself "—but it's the best I can do at the moment. I...hope this is all right with you?"

"Two daddies, huh." B.D. scooted around in the seat so she could see her mother. She frowned. "I guess two daddies are all right," she said slowly, "if you only have one at a time. Shane—"

"Uh-uh. No more of that 'Shane' stuff. You didn't call your other daddy by his first name, did you?"

B.D. laughed and shook her head. "I called him *Daddy*."

"Do you think you can call me Daddy, too? I'd really like it if you could."

B.D. didn't hesitate. She threw her arms around his neck, screaming "Daddy!" at the top of her lungs.

Dinah could barely see them through her tears.

GEORGIA WAITED FOR THEM at the door of her two-story Tudor home. She looked anxious as she ushered them in.

"Is everything all right?" she asked.

"Couldn't be better." Without missing a beat, Shane added what he and Dinah had agreed upon. "B.D. and I are thirsty. Is it all right if we just help ourselves to a—"

"I'll get you something," Georgia said quickly. "Dinah?"

"Please, Mom." Dinah felt funny calling her that in light of what she must now reveal. "Let them go."

"All right." Georgia caught on instantly. "Why don't we go into the family room where we can talk."

Dinah followed the older woman into the comfortable room with its oversize couches and a fireplace cold now in July. She licked her lips. How was she going to make this come out right?

They sat together, facing each other on the couch. Georgia looked perfectly composed, although she had to know something was up.

Gently she said, "What is it, Dinah? You can tell me, dear."

"I know I can." Dinah licked her lips. "You truly have been a mother to me, you know? I'd never do anything to hurt you...if I could help it."

"Oh dear." Georgia laughed lightly. "This is beginning to sound ominous."

"Yes, well—" *Just plunge in, Dinah!* "I have to tell you something I hoped you'd never have to hear. Mike knew this long before we were married. He—" She bit her lip, realized she was talking in circles and said in a rush, "Mike wasn't B.D.'s real father. I was pregnant before we were married. I mean, I was pregnant with another man's baby when we were married. But I respected Mike so much, and eventually I came to love him with all my heart."

"I know, dear."

Dinah blinked. "Which part do you know?"

"I know all of it." Georgia took Dinah's hand and squeezed.

"That can't be." Dinah shook her head in disbelief. "Maybe you guessed a little—"

"Honey, Mike told me everything—not because he needed my approval, you understand. He was his own man and a son to be proud of."

"Amen," Dinah agreed faintly.

"He told me because he wanted me to give you special...I guess the proper word is *consideration*. He wanted me to know that you were having an even tougher time than was apparent. After that one conversation, he never spoke of it again. It didn't matter to him who B.D.'s real father was."

"Oh, Georgia." Dinah dropped her chin onto her chest, humbled by her husband's goodness—and his mother's, too. "Even knowing the truth, you've always been the most wonderful mother-in-law...the most wonderful grandmother...."

She couldn't hold back the tears an instant longer. Georgia opened her arms and Dinah fell into them, sobbing with gratitude and love.

"There, there." Georgia patted the younger woman's back and spoke in the soothing tones of grandmothers everywhere. "Mike said he knew my heart was big enough to love his stepchild just as much as if she were his own flesh and blood. It's also big enough to love Shane, not just because he's a nice guy, but because he's my granddaughter's real father."

"How'd you guess that?" Dinah croaked.

Georgia smiled. "I know because I've seen the two of you together. Now, it's time for you to tidy up so I can welcome the newest member to my family."

Dinah straightened, sniffling and reaching for the tissue Georgia offered. "Shane grew up in an orphanage, basically," she said, scrubbing at her wet eyes. "If your kindness hasn't already been stretched to the limit—" she managed a watery smile "—I think he could use a mother, too."

"Then," Georgia said, "he's got one."

SHANE COULD SEE DINAH had been crying the moment she and Georgia walked into the kitchen. But he could also see that the two women were on the best of terms, so he kept his mouth shut, although it wasn't easy.

B.D. looked up from her can of soda. "Are you mad, Grandma?"

Shane waited warily. Jeez, nothing like a kid to cut through the crap.

"What on earth would I have to be mad about, Blossom Danielle?"

B.D. giggled at hearing her full name. "You know, because I've got another daddy."

"Honey," Georgia said, "I couldn't be happier." She stopped beside Shane's chair. "Give me a hug, cowboy. Looks like we're in this together, and for the long haul at that."

Shane stood up awkwardly, his gaze seeking out Dinah. She smiled through tears and nodded encouragement, so he put his arms around short little Georgia. She was surprisingly strong for a grandma, he thought.

"Thanks, Mrs. Anderson," he said gruffly. "I didn't know how you'd take this. Did Dinah tell you...?"

"I already knew." Georgia tipped her head back so she could look at him but she didn't turn him loose. "Will you do me a favor, Shane?"

"Anything." He meant it, too.

"Would you never ever call me Mrs. Anderson again?"

He blinked. "Well, sure, but what should I call you?"

"You've got two choices." Her brown eyes sparkled. "You can call me Georgia...or you can call me Mom, like Dinah does. Whatever works."

His throat closed up on him entirely then, and he just hugged her until she gasped for mercy. With a flash of fierce pleasure, he realized that he'd just inherited the mother he'd always yearned for.

JOSH CAME BACK for the wedding in September.

Georgia had done all the planning as the adopted mother of both bride and bridegroom, not to mention grandmother of the flower girl. The event was set for Rustlers Park in order to accommodate all the Bushwhackers who were determined to see their very own rodeo star get married.

B.D. wanted her mother to wear a long white gown but Dinah drew the line at that. Instead she chose boots, a denim skirt and a lacy white western-cut shirt. Bandanas decorated her bouquet and the crown of her Stetson.

Shane, nervous as the proverbial cat, looked wonderful in his "rodeo star" garb, as did Josh. As flower girl, B.D. wore a frilly calico dress and boots, and so did her grandmother, the matron of honor. Not too surprisingly, their outfits matched, since this grandmother happened to be a whiz at the sewing machine.

Gathered behind the community building at the edge of the park, the wedding party waited for everyone to be seated on folding chairs so the ceremony could begin. Only B.D. seemed perfectly thrilled and not at all nervous about her part in the proceedings.

Dinah just wanted to get it over so she could be Mrs. Daniels for the rest of her natural life. She clung to Shane's hand, her anchor in the stormy sea of life.

"Oops," Josh said suddenly, turning to Georgia. "Ruben's waving at us, Mrs. Anderson. I think it's time to start."

"Okay," Georgia said, all business. "B.D., you go first. Just follow the path there and toss those rose petals along the way. Josh and I will follow you and then the bride and groom, but don't you two start until we're all out of the way."

Shane groaned. "Can we just get this show on the road? This is more nerve-racking than climbing up on a rank bull."

"The hell it is!" Josh laughed, white teeth flashing. He tucked Georgia's hand beneath the crook of his elbow and spoke in a confidential tone. "Gotta humor him, y'know. This really is Shane's last stand."

"Is it?" Dinah asked as they watched their loved ones walk away with measured steps.

"Is it what?" Shane growled, staring straight ahead.

"Shane's last stand, what else?"

"Honey," he said, flashing her a strained smile but a smile nonetheless, "If it is, I'm goin' out a winner. I've got everything in the world I ever wanted...with one little bitty exception...."

EPILOGUE

DINAH AND SHANE DANIELS, with daughter B.D., traveled to Lost Springs Ranch for Boys that Thanksgiving.

"I'm not sure I want a brother," B.D. had whined on the long trip in the new minivan required by an expanding family.

Shane just grinned. "You'll want this one," he predicted. "He's as full of the devil as you are, B.D., and that's sayin' something."

They spent the night at the Starlite Motel and drove out to the ranch early the next morning. Business completed, Shane stood there where he'd grown up with snow falling softly around him, breathing the cold, crisp air.

Dinah slipped an arm around his middle, made bulky by a heavy sheepskin-lined jacket. "Bring back memories?" she asked softly.

He nodded, not trusting his voice.

"Daddy," B.D. yelled, "Eli's gonna hit me with a snowball!"

Looking around, Shane saw his daughter cowering beneath an evergreen tree, covering her face with mittened hands. Unfortunately for her credibility, the hands slipped and he saw her laughing face. Eli stood nearby, splendid in his righteous indignation.

Shane could just imagine who'd thrown the first snowball.

"Okay," he called, "you kids come on over here on the double."

B.D. made a face at the little boy and skipped past him. Eli followed more slowly, his expression cautious. He was obviously still trying to get used to the change in his fortune.

The kids halted expectantly in front of their parents. Shane said to the boy, quickly and forcefully, "What's your name, kid?"

"Eli," the boy shot back. "Eli Dodge—" He stopped, his eyes growing wide with wonder in his thin face.

"Eli *Daniels!*" B.D. shouted. "Eli Daniels! And I'm B.D. Daniels, okay?"

An enormous smile lit up the boy's face like sunshine. "Right!"

She broke away and ran laughing through the snow, and Eli ran after her.

He was probably going to spend the rest of his life running after her, Shane thought.

Dinah, who'd watched the exchange with a smile of approval, looked up at Shane. "I think it's time to take our kids and go home, cowboy," she said softly.

The word *home* hit him hard. In this place where he'd grown up a maverick, wearing the world champion buckle Eli had shyly returned to him, he realized with a sense of shock that he actually did have a home to go to, people to love and to be loved by.

"Yeah," he agreed, trying to cover the depth of his feelings with gruffness. He wrapped a possessive arm around the waist of his wife. "Let's call our kids and go home."

HEART OF THE WEST

continues with

A BABY BY CHANCE

by

Cathy Gillen Thacker

Men of Chance Cartwright's caliber were hard to find,
and Madison Burnes needed, wanted, was determined to
have him as the spokesman for her ad campaign. Even if
it meant seducing him! She'd stop at nothing...but then,
she hadn't bargained on morning sickness or falling in
love with her prey!

Available in March

Here's a preview!

"JUST TELL ME what you want," Madison said. "I'll see you get it, I promise."

"I'll just bet you would," Chance drawled, wishing she didn't look so damn pretty standing there in jeans and a shirt, the blush of sun on her upturned face, the fire of her considerable ambition in her eyes.

Madison shrugged, unable to see the problem. "Then...?"

Chance took a deep breath, summoning the very last ounce of his patience, then spoke in labored tones she couldn't possibly fail to understand. "I don't want to make a deal with you."

Once again, to Chance's frustration, Madison refused to back down. "Why decide now?" she asked pleasantly, pushing all the harder for what she wanted. "You can take the whole weekend to make up your mind, Chance."

"I don't need the whole weekend to make up my mind. I'm not doing it. Not now. Not ever," he stated flatly. He wasn't climbing into bed with her or the people she represented—even if he couldn't seem to stop imagining how she'd feel beneath him, or if she'd kiss with as much gusto and aggression as she lived. As much as he hated to admit it, he was turned on by her confidence and drive, her take-no-prisoners personality. More damning yet, he wanted to see some of that fire turned on him behind closed doors.

Madison stared at him, incensed. "That's a lousy attitude to have. Particularly when you haven't even bothered to hear me—or my agency, or the people from the AMV Corporation—out.''

Maybe it was. Maybe it wasn't, Chance thought, but that's how it was going to be, and it was high time Madison realized it. He didn't have to be fair. He didn't owe her anything.

Figuring this was one city girl who had been designing events to suit herself long enough, he took her by the arms, backed her up. Ignoring her soft gasp of dismay, he closed the distance between them, aligning his body against hers, trapping her against the wall. ''Just how far would you go to close this deal, Madison?'' Chance taunted softly, watching her chin jut forward and her eyes turn a hot, fiery green.

She tried to shove him away.

Determined to ruffle her all-business facade, he caught her hands and held them on either side of her. ''Would you go this far?'' He ducked his head and touched his lips to hers, softly, evocatively.

He expected her to cry uncle immediately, of course. Realize she'd gone too far in her pursuit of him, promise to leave immediately and never darken his doorway or intrude upon the life he'd made for himself again. Instead, she kissed him.

HARLEQUIN®
Presents

**The world's bestselling romance series...
The series that brings you your favorite authors,
month after month:**

Helen Bianchin...Emma Darcy
Lynne Graham...Penny Jordan
Miranda Lee...Sandra Marton
Anne Mather...Carole Mortimer
Susan Napier...Michelle Reid

and many more uniquely talented authors!

Wealthy, powerful, gorgeous men...
Women who have feelings just like your own...
The stories you love, set in exotic, glamorous locations...

HARLEQUIN®
Presents

Seduction and Passion Guaranteed!

HPDIR104

Harlequin Historicals®
Historical Romantic Adventure!

From rugged lawmen and valiant knights to defiant heiresses and spirited frontierswomen, Harlequin Historicals will capture your imagination with their dramatic scope, passion and adventure.

Harlequin Historicals... they're too good to miss!

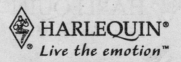

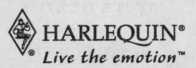

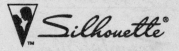

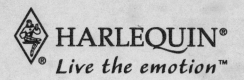
HARLEQUIN®
Live the emotion™

Upbeat,
All-American Romances

flipside Romantic Comedy

Harlequin Historicals®

Historical,
Romantic Adventure

INTRIGUE Romantic Suspense

HARLEQUIN®
HARLEQUIN ROMANCE®

The essence of
modern romance

HARLEQUIN®
Presents

Seduction and passion
guaranteed

Emotional,
Exciting, Unexpected

Temptation

Sassy, Sexy, Seductive!